I0563647

THE SECRET OF
THE REEF

THE SECRET OF THE REEF

HAROLD BINDLOSS

BINDLOSS PRESS

Published by Bindloss Press
An imprint of Wildside Press, LLC
www.wildsidebooks.com

CHAPTER I

DISMISSED

The big liner's smoke streamed straight astern, staining the soft blue of the sky, as, throbbing gently to her engines' stroke, she clove her way through the smooth heave of the North Pacific. Foam blazed with phosphorescent flame beneath her lofty bows and, streaking with green and gold scintillations the long line of hull that gleamed ivory-white in the light of a half moon, boiled up again in fiery splendor in the wake of the twin screws. Mastheads and tall yellow funnels raked across the sky with a measured swing, the long deck slanted gently, its spotless whiteness darkened by the dew, and the draught the boat made struck faint harmonies like the tinkle of elfin harps from wire shroud and guy. Now they rose clearly; now they were lost in the roar of the parted swell.

A glow of electric light streamed out from the saloon-companion and the smoking-room; the skylights of the saloon were open, and when the notes of a piano drifted aft with a girl's voice, Jimmy Farquhar, second mate, standing dressed in trim white uniform beneath a swung-up boat, smiled at the refrain of the old love song. He was in an unusually impressionable mood; and he felt that there was some danger of his losing his head as his eyes rested admiringly on his companion, for there was a seductive glamour in the blue and silver splendor of the night.

Ruth Osborne leaned on the steamer's rail, looking forward, with the moonlight on her face. She was young and delicately pretty, with a slender figure, and the warm coloring that often indicates an enthusiastic temperament. In the daylight her hair had ruddy gleams in its warm brown, and her eyes a curious golden scintillation; but now it arched in a dusky mass above the pallid oval of her face, and her look was thoughtful.

She had fallen into the habit of meeting Jimmy when he was not on watch; and the mate felt flattered by her frank preference for his society, for he suspected that several of the passengers envied him, and that Miss Osborne was a lady of importance at home. It was understood that she was the only daughter of the American merchant who had taken the two best deck rooms, which perhaps accounted for the somewhat imperious way she had. Miss Osborne did what she liked, and made it seem right; and it was obvious that she liked to talk to Jimmy.

"It has been a delightful trip," she said.

"Yes," agreed Jimmy; "the finest I recollect. I wanted you to have a smooth-water voyage, and I am glad you enjoyed it."

"That was nice of you," she smiled. "I could hardly help enjoying it. She's a comfortable boat, and everybody has been pleasant. I suppose we'll see Vancouver Island late tomorrow?"

"It will be dark when we pick up the lights, but we'll be in Victoria early the next morning. I think you leave us there?"

The girl was silent for a few moments, and in her expression there was a hint of regret that stirred Jimmy's blood. They had seen a good deal of each other during the voyage; and it was painful to the man to realize that in all probability their acquaintance must soon come to an end; but he ventured to think that his companion shared his feelings to some extent.

"In a way, I'm sorry we're so nearly home," Ruth said frankly; and added, smiling, "I'm beginning to find out that I love the sea."

Jimmy noted the explanation. He was a handsome young Englishman of unassuming disposition, and by no means a fortune-hunter, but he had been bantered by the other mates, and he knew that it was not an altogether unusual thing for a wealthy young lady to fall in love with a steamboat officer during a long, fine-weather run. Miss Osborne, however, had shown only a friendly liking for him; and, as he would see no more of her after the next day, he must not make a fool of himself at the last moment.

"The sea's not always like this," he replied. "It can be very cruel; and all ships aren't mailboats."

"I suppose not. You mean that life is harder in the others?"

Jimmy laughed. He had been a Conway boy, but soon after he finished his schooling on the famous old vessel the death of a guardian deprived him of the help and influence he had been brought up to expect. As a result of this, he had been apprenticed to a firm of parsimonious owners, and began his career in a badly found and undermanned iron sailing ship. On board her he had borne hunger and wet and cold, and was often worked to the point of exhaustion. Pride kept him from deserting, and he had come out of the four years' struggle very hard and lean, to begin almost as stern a fight in steam cargo-tramps. Then, by a stroke of unexpected luck, he met an invalid merchant on one of the vessels, and the man recommended him to the directors of a mail company. After this, things became easier for Jimmy. He made progress, and, after what he had borne, he found his present circumstances almost luxuriously easy.

"Steam is improving matters," he said; "but there are still trades in which mates and seamen are called upon to stand all that flesh and blood can endure."

"And you have known something of this?"

"All I want to know."

"Do tell me about it," Ruth urged. "I am curious."

Jimmy laughed.

"Well, on my first trip round Cape Horn we left the Mersey undermanned and lost three of our crew before we were abreast of the Falkland Isles; two of them were hurled from the royal yard through the breaking of rotten gear. That made a big difference, and we had vile weather: gales dead ahead, snow, and bitter cold. The galley fire was washed out half the time, the deckhouse we lived in was flooded continually; for weeks we hadn't a rag of dry clothes, and very seldom a plateful of warm food. It was a merciful relief when the gale freshened, and she lay hove to, with the icy seas bursting over her weather bow while we slept like logs in our soaking bunks; but that wasn't often. With each shift or fall of wind we crawled out on the yards, wet and frozen to the bone, to shake the hard canvas loose, and, as it generally happened, were sent aloft in an hour to furl it tight again. Each time it was a short-handed fight for life to master the thrashing sail. Our hands cracked open, and the cuts would not heal; stores were spoiled by the water that washed over everything, and some days we starved on a wet biscuit or two; but the demand for brutal effort never slackened. We were worn very thin when we squared away for the north with the first fair wind."

"Ah!" exclaimed Ruth. "It must have been a grim experience. Didn't it daunt you, and make you hate the sea?"

"I hated the ship, her skipper, and her owners, and most of all the smart managing clerk who had worked out to the last penny how cheaply she could be run; but that was a different thing. The sea has a spell that grips you, and never lets go again."

"Yes," said Ruth; "I have felt that, though I have seen it only in fine weather and from a liner's saloon deck." She mused for a few moments before she went on. "It will be a long time before I forget this voyage, steaming home over the sunlit water, with the wind behind us and the smoke going straight up, the decks warm, everything bright and glittering, and the glimmer of the moon and the sea-fire about the hull at night."

There was an opening here for an assurance that the voyage would live even longer in his memory; but Jimmy let it pass. He feared that he might say too much if he gave the rein to sentiment.

"Were you not charmed with Japan?" he asked.

Ruth acquiesced in the change of topic, and her eyes sparkled enthusiastically.

"Oh, yes! It was the time of the cherry-blossom, and the country seemed a fairyland, quainter, stranger, and prettier than anything I had ever dreamed of!"

"Still, you must have seen many interesting places."

"No," she said with a trace of graveness. "I don't even know very much about my own country."

"All the Americans I have met seemed fond of traveling."

"The richer ones are," she answered frankly. "But until quite lately I think we were poor. It was during the Klondyke rush that my father first became prosperous, and for a number of years I never saw him. When my mother died I was sent to a small, old-fashioned, New England town, where some elderly relatives took care of me. They were good people, but very narrow, and all I heard and saw was commonplace and provincial. Then I went to a very strict and exclusive school and stayed there much longer than other girls." Ruth paused and smiled. "When at last I joined my father I felt as if I had suddenly awakened in a different world. I had the same feeling when I saw Japan."

"After all, you will be glad to get home."

"Yes," she said slowly; "but there's a regret. We have been very happy since we left; my father has been light-hearted, and I have had him to myself. At home he often has an anxious look, and is always occupied. I have some friends and many acquaintances, but now and then I feel lonely."

Jimmy pondered, watching her with appreciative eyes. She was frank, but not with foolish simplicity; quite unspoiled by good fortune; and had nothing of the coquette about her. Indeed, he wondered whether she realized her attractiveness, or if the indifference she had shown to admiration were due to pride. He did not know much about young women, but he thought that she was proud and of strong character.

"You must come to see us if you are ever near Tacoma," Ruth said cordially.

Jimmy thanked her, and soon afterward left her, to keep his watch on the bridge. As they were still out of sight of land he had no companion except the quartermaster at the wheel in the glass-fronted pilot-house. There was no sail or smoke trail in all the wide expanse his high view point commanded. Rolling lazily to port and starboard, the big boat cleft a lonely sea that was steeped in dusky blue save where a broad belt of moonlight touched it with glittering silver. The voices and laughter gradually died away from the decks below, the glow of light was lessening, and the throb of the screws and the roar of flung-off water grew louder. A faint breeze had sprung up, and the smoke stretched out, undeviating, in a broad black smear over the starboard quarter; Jimmy noticed this while he paced to and fro, turning now and then to sweep a different arc of horizon. The last time he did so he stopped abruptly, for the smoke had moved forward. For a moment he fancied that the wind had changed, but a glance at the white-streaked wake showed him that the vessel was swinging round. Then he sprang to the pilot-house, and, looking in through the open door, saw the quartermaster leaning slackly on the small brass wheel. His face showed livid in the moonlight, and his forehead was damp with sweat.

"What's this, Evans?" Jimmy cried.

Pulling himself together with an effort, the man glanced at the compass in alarm.

"Sorry, sir," he said thickly, spinning the wheel. "She's fallen off a bit. Something came over me; but I'm all right now."

"It may come over you once too often. This isn't the first time," Jimmy reminded him.

A shadow obscured the moonlight; and, turning abruptly, Jimmy saw the captain in the doorway. The skipper looked at the compass and studied the quartermaster's face; then he beckoned Jimmy outside. He had come up in soft slippers which made no noise, and Jimmy was keenly concerned to know how long he had been there. Jimmy had never got on well with his captain.

"Evans had his helm hard over; was she much off her course?" the captain asked with an ominous calm.

"About thirty degrees, sir."

"How long is it since you checked his steering?"

Jimmy told him.

"You consider that often enough?"

"I had my eye on the smoke, sir."

"The smoke? I suppose you know a light breeze is often variable?"

"Yes, sir," said Jimmy. "She couldn't swing off much without my noticing it."

"One wouldn't imagine so after what I discovered. But I gathered that Evans had been seized in this way during your watch before."

"Yes, sir," Jimmy repeated doggedly.

"Didn't it strike you that your duty was to report the matter? You knew that Evans has a weakness of the heart that may seize him unexpectedly at any time. If it did so when we were entering a crowded harbor or crossing another vessel's course, the consequences might prove disastrous. In not reporting it you took upon yourself a responsibility I can't allow my officers. Have you anything to say?" Jimmy knew he could make no answer that would excuse him. When, as is now usual, a fast vessel's course is laid off in degrees, accurate steering is important, and he had been actuated by somewhat injudicious pity. Evans was a steady man, with a family in England to provide for, and he had once by prompt action prevented the second mate's being injured by a heavy cargo-sling.

"Perhaps the best way of meeting the situation," the captain said curtly, "would be for you to voluntarily leave the ship at Vancouver. You can let me know what you decide when you come off watch."

Jimmy moodily returned to his duty. He thought his fault was small, but there was no appeal. He would have no further opportunity for serving his present employers; and mailboat berths are not readily picked up. He kept his watch, and afterward went to sleep with a heavy heart.

The next evening he was idling disconsolately on the saloon deck when he saw Miss Osborne coming toward him. He was standing in the shadow of a boat and stayed there, feeling in no mood to force a cheerfulness he was far from feeling. Besides, he had now and then, when the girl was gracious to him, found it needful to practise some restraint, and now he felt unequal to the strain.

"I have been looking for you," she said. "As I suppose everybody will be busy tomorrow morning, I may not see you then. But you seem downcast!"

Jimmy shrank from telling her that he had been dismissed; and, after all, that was a comparatively small part of his trouble. The girl's tone was gentle, and there was in her eyes a sympathy that set his heart beating. He wished he were a rich man, or, indeed, almost anything except a steamboat officer who would soon be turned out of his ship.

"Well," he said, "for one thing, the end of a voyage is often a melancholy time. After spending some weeks with pleasant people, it's not nice to know they must all scatter and that you have to part from friends you have made and like."

A faint tinge of color crept into Ruth's face; but she smiled.

"It doesn't follow that they're forgotten," she replied; "and there's always a possibility of their meeting again. We may see you at Tacoma; it isn't very far from Vancouver."

Jimmy was not a presumptuous man, but he saw that she had given him a lead and he bitterly regretted that he could not follow it. Though of hopeful temperament, stern experience had taught him sense, and he recognized that circumstances did not permit of his dallying with romance. There was nothing to be gained and something to be lost by cultivating the girl's acquaintance.

"I may have to sail on a different run before long," he said.

She gave him a glance of swift but careful scrutiny. The moonlight was clear, and he looked well in his white uniform, which showed his solid but finely molded figure and emphasized the clean brownness of his skin. He had light hair and steady, dark blue eyes, which had just then a hint of trouble.

"Well," she responded, "you know best; but, whether you come or not, my father and I are in your debt. You have done much to make this a very pleasant voyage." She gave him her hand, which he held a moment. "And, now, since you wish it, good-by!"

When she turned away, Jimmy leaned on the rail, watching her move quietly up the long deck. He was troubled with confused and futile regrets. Still, he had acted sensibly: it was unwise for a dismissed steamboat officer to harbor the alluring fancies he had sternly driven from his mind.

CHAPTER II

A NEW VENTURE

The sun had dipped behind a high black ridge crested with ragged pines, when Jimmy, dressed in brown overalls and a seaman's jersey, sat cooking supper on a stony beach of Vancouver Island. In front of him the landlocked sea ran back, glimmering with a steely luster, into the east; behind, where the inlet reached the hillfoot, stood the City of the Springs, which then consisted of a shut-down sawmill, a row of dilapidated wooden houses, and two second-rate hotels. Shadowed by climbing pinewoods, sheltered by the rocks, the site was perhaps as beautiful as any in the romantic province of British Columbia, though man's crude handiwork defaced its sylvan charm with rusty iron chimney-stacks, rows of blackened fir-stumps, and unsightly sawdust heaps. For all that, giant, primeval forest rolled close up to it, and in front lay the untainted sea. The air had in it a curious exhilarating quality; the balsamic scent of the firs mingled with the sharp odors of drying weed, tar, and cedar shavings that lay about the camp; and Jimmy, stooping over his frying-pan, sniffed the air with satisfaction. These were odors that belonged to the sea and the wilds; and he had lately renounced the comforts of civilization and embarked upon an adventure that appealed to him.

Near him, a man with a rugged, weatherbeaten face was engaged in fitting a plank into the bilge of a hauled-up sloop. She was a small but shapely vessel of about forty feet in length, and had been built after a design adopted by a famous yacht club on the Atlantic coast. Jimmy could see that she was fast; but she had been put to base uses, and had suffered from neglect. As a matter of fact, he never learned her history, and had always some doubt as to whether the man from whom he and his companion bought her had an indisputable right to sell her.

Moran had been a Nova Scotian lobster catcher before he came to British Columbia to engage in the new halibut fishery, which had proved disappointing. Bethune, who lay upon the shingle in garments much the worse for wear, was a "remittance man," with a cheerful expression and a stock of unvarying good humor. It was some time since he had engaged in any exacting occupation, and now, after using the saw all day, he was resting from his unaccustomed exertions and bantering Moran.

Jimmy had met them both in a second-rate Vancouver boarding-house, to which he had resorted after failing to find a ship, and working on the wharf. He might have sailed before the mast, but he knew that when he next applied for a berth on board a liner he must account for his voyagings, and the fact that he had served as able seaman would not recommend him. When there was no cargo to be handled, he worked in the great Hastings mill; but he promptly discovered that he would never grow rich by this means; and the unrelaxing physical effort, demanded by foremen who knew how to drive hard, began to pall on him. He could have stood it had he come fresh from the sailing ships, but he frankly admitted that it was trying to a mailboat officer. He had, however, some small savings, and when Bethune proposed a venture, in which Moran joined, Jimmy agreed.

"Hank," Bethune drawled, after watching Moran for several minutes, "you Maritime Provinces people are a hard and obstinate lot, but you won't get the plank in that way if you stick at it until tomorrow."

Moran looked up with the sweat dripping from his brow.

"I surely hate to be beat," he admitted. "I can spring her plumb up lengthways, but her edges won't bend into the frames."

"Exactly. This isn't a cod-fishing dory or a lobster punt. Take your plane and hollow the plank up the middle."

After doing as he was instructed, Moran had not much trouble in fitting it into place.

"Why didn't you tell me that before?" he asked.

"I've known you some time," Bethune answered with a grin. "There are people to whom you can't show the easiest way until they've tried the hardest one and found it won't do. It's not their fault; I hold you can't make a man responsible for his temperament—and it's a point on which I speak feelingly, because my temperament has been my bane."

"How d'you know these things, anyway? I mean about bending planks. You never allowed you'd been a boatbuilder."

"Do you expect a man to exhibit all his talents? Here's another tip. Don't nail that plank home now. Leave it shored up until morning, and you'll get it dead close then with a wedge or two. And now, if Jimmy hasn't burned the grub, I think we'll have supper."

The meal might have been better, but Moran admitted that he had often eaten worse, and afterward they lay about on the shingle and lighted their pipes. Bethune, as usual, was the first to speak.

"The lumber, and the canvas Jimmy gets to work upon tomorrow, have emptied the treasury," he remarked. "If we incur any further liabilities, there's a strong probability of their not being met; but that gives the job an interest. Prudence is a cold-blooded quality, which no man of spirit has much use for. To help yourself may be good, but doing so consistently often makes it harder to help the other fellow."

"When you have finished moralizing we'll get to business," Jimmy rejoined. "Though I'm a partner in the scheme, I know very little yet about the wreck you're taking us up to look for. Try to be practical."

"Moran is practical enough for all three of us. I'll let him tell the tale; but I'll premise by saying that when he found the halibut fishing much less remunerative than it was cracked up to be, he sailed up the northwest coast with another fellow to trade with the Indians for furs. It was then he found the vessel."

"The reef," said Moran, "lies open to the south-west, and I got seven fathoms close alongside it at low water. A mile off, and near a low island, a bank runs out into the stream, and the after-half of the wreck lies on the edge of it, worked well down in the sand. At low ebb you can see the end of one or two timbers sticking up out of the broken water."

"Is it always broken water?" Jimmy interrupted.

"Pretty near, I guess. Though there's a rise and fall on the island beach, the stream ran steady to the northeast at about two miles an hour, the whole week we lay sheltering in the bight, and the swell it brings in makes a curling sea on the edge of the shoals."

"Doesn't seem a nice place for a diving job. How did you get down to her?"

"Stripped and swam down. One day when it fell a flat calm for a few hours and Jake was busy patching the sail, I pulled the dory across. I wanted to find out what those timbers belonged to, and I knew I had to do it then, because the ice was coming in, and we must clear with the first fair wind. Well, I got a turn of the dory's painter round a timber, and went down twice, seeing bottom at about three fathoms with the water pretty clear. The sand was well up her bilge, but she was holding together, and when I swam round to the open end of her there didn't seem much in the way except the orlop beams. I could have walked right aft under decks if I'd had a diving dress; but I'd been in the water long enough, and a sea fog was creeping up."

Moran apparently thought little of his exploit; but Jimmy could appreciate the hardihood he had shown. The wreck lay far up on the northern coast, where the sea was chilled by currents from the Pole, and Moran had gone down to her when the ice was working in. Jimmy could imagine the tiny dory lurching over the broken swell, and the half-frozen man painfully crawling on board her with many precautions to avoid a capsize, while the fog that might prevent his return to his vessel crept across the water. It was an adventure that required unusual strength and courage.

"Why didn't you take your partner out with you?" he asked.

"I'd seen Jake play some low-down tricks when we traded for the few furs we got, and I suspicioned he wasn't acting square with me. Anyhow, he allowed he didn't take much count of abandoned wrecks, and when he saw I'd brought nothing back, he never asked me about her."

"But if she was lost on the reef, how did she reach the bank a mile away?"

"I can't tell you that, but I guess she shook her engines out after she broke her back, and then slipped off into deeper water. The stream and surge of sea may have worked her along the bottom."

"It came out that she had only a little rock ballast in her," Bethune explained. "There may not have been enough to pin her down; but the important point is that the strong-room was aft, and Hank says that part is sound."

Jimmy nodded.

"Suppose you tell me all you know about the matter," he said.

It was characteristic of both of them that when they first discussed the venture the one had been content with sketchily outlining his plans, and the other had not demanded many details. The project appealed to their imagination, and once they had decided upon it the necessary preparations had occupied all their attention.

Leaning back against a boulder, Bethune refilled and lighted his pipe. His clothes were far from new, and were freely stained with tar, but he spoke clean English, and his face suggested intelligence and refinement.

"Very well," he said. "When Hank mentioned his discovery I thought I saw an opportunity of the kind I'd been waiting for; and I took some trouble to find out what I could about the vessel. She was an old wooden propeller that came round Cape Horn a good many years ago. When she couldn't compete with modern steamboats, they strengthened her for a whaler, and she knocked about the Polar Sea; but she burned too much coal for that business, and wouldn't work well under sail. It looked as if there wasn't a trade in which she could make a living; but the Klondyke rush began, and somebody bought her cheap, and ran her up to Juneau, in Alaska, and afterward to Nome. There were better boats, but they were packed full, fore and aft, and the crowd going north was not fastidious: all it wanted was to get on the goldfields as soon as possible. Well, she made a number of trips all right, though I believe her owners had trouble when the pressure eased and the United States passenger-carrying regulations began to be properly applied. It was probably because no other boat was available that a small mining syndicate, which seems to have done pretty well, shipped a quantity of gold down from the north in her. Besides this, she brought out a number of miners, who had been more or less successful. Something went wrong with the engines when she had been a day or two at sea; but they got sail on her, and she drove south before a fresh gale until she struck the reef on a hazy night. It broke her back, and the after hold was flooded a few minutes after she struck. The strong-room was under water, there was no time to cut down to it; but they got the boats away, and after the crew and passengers were picked up, a San Francisco salvage company thought it worth while to attempt the recovery of the gold. It was late in the season when their tug reached the spot, and the ice drove her off the reef; the sea was generally heavy, and after a week or two they threw up the contract. The underwriters paid all losses, and that was the end of the matter. It is only the drifting of the stern half into shoal water that gives us our chance. Now I think you know as much as I do."

Jimmy sat thoughtfully silent for a few minutes, realizing that it was a reckless venture he had undertaken. The wreck lay in unfre-quented waters which were swept by angry currents that brought in the ice, vexed by sudden gales, and often wrapped in fog. The appliances the party had been able to procure were of the cheapest description, and there was a risk in making the long voyage in so small a vessel as the sloop. Still, Jimmy's fortunes needed a desperate remedy, and he was not much daunted by the difficulties he must face.

"Well," he said, "I suppose we have some chance; but I don't quite see what made you so keen on taking up the thing."

"It's explainable," Bethune drawled, picking up a pebble and lazily flipping it out over the water. "Victoria's a handsome city, and the views from it are good. For all that, when you can find no occupation, and have spent some years lounging about the waterfront and the bars of cheap hotels, the place, to put it mildly, loses its charm."

"You could leave it. As a matter of fact, I met you at Vancouver."

"Oh, yes. I could leave it for a maximum period of thirty days, because, with the exception of Sundays and one or two holidays, I was required to present myself at a lawyer's office on the first of every month. Then I was paid enough to keep me, with rigid economy, for the next four weeks; but on the first occasion I failed to come up to time the allowance was to stop for good. It's a system that has some advantages for the people who provide the funds in the old country, since it assures the payee's stopping where he is—but it has its drawbacks for the latter. How can a man get a job and hold it anywhere outside the town if he must return at a fixed hour every month? When I was in Vancouver it cost me a large share of the allowance to collect it."

"And now, by going north, you throw it up?"

"Exactly," said Bethune. "It should have been done before, but, as I had never been taught to work or go without my dinner, the course I am at last taking needed some moral courage. It's sink or swim now."

Jimmy made a sign of agreement. All the money he possessed had been sunk in the undertaking; and now, in order to get it back, he must succeed where a well-equipped salvage expedition had failed. Though the wreck had since changed her position, the prospects were not very encouraging.

"Well," he said, "we must do the best we can; but I wish our funds had run to a better supply of stores."

"Hank can fish," grinned Bethune. "In fact, he'll have to whenever there's anything to catch. Fortunately, fish is wholesome and sustaining. However, as this job must be finished tomorrow, we had better get to sleep early."

Jimmy sat smoking for a few minutes after the others went on board the sloop. It was getting dark, but a band of pure green light still glimmered along the crest of the black ridge to the west. The air was cold and very still, and gray wood smoke hung in gauzy wreaths above the roofs of the town. The tall pines were growing blurred, but their keen, sweet fragrance hung about the beach, and the smooth swell lapped with a drowsy murmur upon the shingle.

Jimmy loved the sea; and now he was to go afloat again, in his own vessel, bound by no restrictions except the necessity for making the voyage pay. This would not be easy; but there was a romance about the undertaking that gave it a zest.

CHAPTER III

THE FURY OF THE SEA

In the evening of the day on which they saw the last of Vancouver Island, Jimmy sat in the Cetacea's cockpit with a chart of the North Pacific spread out before him on the cabin hatch. It showed the tortuous straits, thickly sprinkled with islands of all sizes, through which they had somehow threaded their way during the last week, in spite of baffling head winds and racing tides, and though Jimmy was a navigator he felt some surprise at their having accomplished the feat without touching bottom. Now he had their course to the north plotted out along the deeply fretted coast of British Columbia, and rolling up the chart he rose to look about.

It was nine o'clock, but the light was clear, and a long, slate-green swell slightly crisped with ripples rolled up out of the south; to the northwest a broad stripe of angry saffron, against which the sea-tops cut, glowed along the horizon; but the east was dim, and steeped in a hard, cold blue. Shadowy mountains were faintly visible high up against the sky; and, below, a few rocky islets rose, blurred by blue haze, out of the heaving sea.

The sloop rolled lazily, her boom groaning and the tall, white mainsail alternately swelling out and emptying with a harsh slapping of canvas and a clatter of shaken blocks. Above it the topsail raked in a wide arc across the sky. Silky lines of water ran back from the stern, there was a soft gurgle at the bows; Jimmy computed that she was slipping along at about three miles an hour.

"What do you think of the weather?" Bethune asked, as he lounged at the steering wheel.

"It doesn't look promising," Jimmy answered. "If time wasn't an object, I'd like the topsail down. We'll have wind before morning."

"That's my opinion; but time is an object. When the cost of every day out is an item to be considered, we must drive her. Have you reckoned up what we're paying every week to the ship-chandler fellow who found us the cables and diving gear?"

"I haven't; his terms were daunting enough as a whole without analyzing them. Have you?"

Bethune chuckled.

"I have the cost of everything down in my notebook; although I will confess that I was mildly surprised at myself for taking the trouble. If I'd occasionally made a few simple calculations at home and acted on them, the chances are that I shouldn't be here now." Bethune made a gesture of disgust. "Halibut boiled and halibut fried begins to pall on one; but this is far better than our quarters in Vancouver, and they were a big improvement on those I had in Victoria. I daresay it was natural I should stick to the few monthly dollars as long as possible, but it will be some time before I forget that hotel. I never quite got used to the two wet public towels beside the row of sloppy wash-basins, and the gramophone going full blast in the dirty dining-room; and the long evening to be dawdled through in the lounge was worst of all. You have, perhaps, seen the hard-faced toughs lolling back with their feet on the radiator pipes before the windows, the heaps of dead flies that are seldom swept up, the dreary, comfortless squalor. Imagine three or four hours of it every night, with only a last-week's Colonist to while away the time!"

"I should imagine things would be better in a railroad or logging camp."

"Very much so, though they're not hotbeds of luxury. The trouble was that I couldn't come down to Victoria and hold my job. Once or twice when the pay days approximated, I ran it pretty fine; and I've a vivid memory of walking seventy miles in two days over a newly made wagon trail. The softer parts had been graded with ragged stones from the hillside, the drier bits were rutted soil—it needed a surgical operation to get my stockings off."

"It might have paid you better to forfeit your allowance," Jimmy suggested.

"That's true," said Bethune. "I can see it now, but I had a daunting experience of clearing land and laying railroad track. Dragging forty-foot rails about through melting snow, with the fumes of giant-powder hanging among the rocks and nauseating you, is exhausting work, and handspiking giant logs up skids in rain that never stops is worse. The logs have a way of slipping back and smashing the tenderfoot's ribs. I suppose this made me a coward; and, in a sense, the allowance was less of a favor than a right. The money that provided it has been a long time in the family; I am the oldest son; and while I can't claim to have been a model, I had no serious vices and had committed no crime. If my relatives chose to banish me, there seemed no reason why they shouldn't pay for the privilege."

Jimmy agreed that something might be said for his comrade's point of view.

"Now I stand on my own feet," Bethune went on, with a carefree laugh; "and while it's hard to predict the end of this adventure, the present state of things is good enough for me. Is anything better than being afloat in a staunch craft that's entirely at your command?"

Jimmy acquiesced heartily as he glanced about. Sitting to windward, he could see the gently rounded deck run forward to the curve of the lifted bows, and, above them, the tall, hollowed triangle of the jib. The arched cabin-top led forward in flowing lines, and though there were patches on plank and canvas, all his eye rested on was of harmonious outline. The Cetacea was small and low in the water, but she was fast and safe, and Jimmy had already come to feel a certain love for her. Their success depended upon her seaworthiness, and he thought she would not fail them.

"I like the boat; but I've been mending gear all day, and it's my turn below," he said.

The narrow cabin that ran from the cockpit bulkhead to the stem was cumbered with dismantled diving pumps and gear, but there was a locker on each side on which one could sleep. It was, moreover, permeated with the smell of stale tobacco smoke, tarred hemp, and fish, but Jimmy had put up with worse odors in the Mercantile Marine. Lying down, fully dressed, on a locker, he saw Moran's shadowy form, wrapped in old oilskins, on the opposite locker, rise above his level and sink as the Cetacea rocked them with a rhythmic swing. The water lapped noisily against the planks, and now and then there was a groaning of timber and a sharp clatter of blocks; but Jimmy soon grew drowsy and noticed nothing.

He was awakened rudely by a heavy blow, and found he had fallen off the locker and struck one of the pump castings. Half dazed and badly shaken, as he was, it was a few moments before he got upon his knees—one could not stand upright under the low cabin-top. It was very dark, Jimmy could not see the hatch, and the Cetacea appeared to have fallen over on her beam-ends. A confused uproar was going on above: the thud of heavy water striking the deck, a furious thrashing of loose canvas, and the savage scream of wind. Bethune's voice came faintly through the din, and he seemed to be calling for help.

Realizing that it was time for action, Jimmy pulled himself together and with difficulty made his way to the cockpit, where he found it hard to see anything for the first minute. The spray that drove across the boat beat into his face and blinded him; but he made out that she was pressed down with most of her lee deck in the water, while white cascades that swept its uplifted windward side poured into the cockpit. The tall mainsail slanted up into thick darkness, but it was no longer thrashing, and Jimmy was given an impression of furious speed by the way the half visible seas raced past.

"Shake her! Let her come up!" he shouted to the dark figure bent over the wheel.

He understood Bethune to say that this would involve the loss of the mast unless the others were ready to shorten canvas quickly.

Jimmy scrambled forward through the water and loosed the peak-halyard. The head of the sail swung down and blew out to leeward, banging threateningly, and he saw that the half-lowered topsail hung beneath it. This promised to complicate matters; but Moran was already endeavoring to change the jib for a smaller one, and Jimmy sprang to his assistance. Though the sail was not linked to a masthead stay, it would not run in; and when Bethune luffed the boat into the wind, the loose canvas swept across the bows, swelling like a balloon and emptying with a shock that threatened to snap the straining mast. It was obvious to the men who knelt in the water dragging frantically at a rope that something drastic must be done; but both were drenched and half blinded and had been suddenly roused from sleep. The boat was large enough to make her gear heavy to handle, and yet not so large as to obviate the need for urgent haste when struck with all her canvas set by a savage squall. Though they recognized this, Jimmy and his comrade paused a few moments to gather breath. The jib, however, must be hauled down; and with a hoarse shout to Moran, Jimmy lowered himself from the bowsprit until he felt the wire bobstay under his feet.

The Cetacea plunged into the seas, burying him to the waist, but he made his way out-board with the canvas buffeting his head until he seized an iron ring. It cost him a determined effort to wrench it loose so it could run in, and when, at last, the sail swept behind him he felt the blood warm on his lacerated hand. Then he crawled on board, and when he and Moran had set a smaller jib it was high time to reef the mainsail; but they spent a few moments in gathering strength for the task.

She was down on her beam-ends, with the sea breaking over her. Jimmy could not imagine what Bethune was doing at the wheel. The foam that swirled past close under the boom on her depressed side lapped to the cabin top; it looked as if she were rolling over. They felt helpless and shaken, impotent to master the canvas that was drowning her. But the fight must be made; and, rousing themselves for the effort, they groped for the halyards. The head of the sail sank lower; gasping, and straining every muscle, they hauled its foot down, and then Jimmy, leaning out, buried to the knees in rushing foam, with his breast on the boom, knotted the reef-points in. It was done at last. Rising more upright, she shook off some of the water.

Moran turned to Bethune, who was leaning as if exhausted on his helm, and demanded why he had not luffed the craft, which would have eased their work. Then the dripping man showed them that the boat they carried on deck had been washed against the wheel so that he could not pull the spokes round. They moved her, and when Bethune regained control of the sloop, he told them what had happened, in disjointed gasps.

"Wind freshened—but I—held her at it. Then there was a—burst of rain and I—let the topsail go—thinking the breeze would lighten again. Instead of that—it whipped round ahead—screaming—and I called for you."

Conversation was difficult amid the roar of the sea, with the spray lashing them and their words blowing away, but Jimmy made himself heard.

"Where's the compass?"

"In the cockpit, or overboard—the dory broke it off."

Moran felt in the water that washed about their feet and, picking something up, crept into the cabin, where a pale glow broke out. It disappeared in a minute or two and he came back.

"Binnacle lamp's busted," he reported. "She's pointing about east."

"Inshore," said Jimmy. "When you're ready, we'll have her round."

She would not come. Overpowered by wind and sea, she hung up for a few moments, and then fell off on her previous course. They tried it twice, not daring to wear her round the opposite way; and afterward they sat in the slight shelter of the coaming, conscious that there was nothing more they could do.

"She may keep off the beach until daylight," Jimmy observed

hopefully; "then we'll see where we are."

The glance he cast forward did not show him much. The long swell had rapidly changed into tumbling combers that rolled down upon the laboring sloop out of the dark. As she lurched over them, the small patch of storm-jib swept up, showing the sharply slanted strip of mainsail; but the rest of her was hidden by spray and rushing foam. She was sailing very fast, close-hauled, and was rushing toward the beach. Jimmy could feel her tremble as she pitched into the seas.

Morning seemed a very long time in coming; but at last the darkness grew less thick. The foam got whiter and the gray bulk of the rollers more solid and black, as they leaped, huge and threatening, out of the obscurity. Then the sky began to whiten in the east, and the weary men anxiously turned their eyes shoreward as they shivered in the biting cold of dawn. After a time, during which the horizon steadily receded, a gray and misty blur appeared on the starboard hand, and, now that they could see the combers, they got the Cetacea round. As she headed offshore a red flush spread across the sky, and rocks and pines grew into shape to the east. Then a break in the coast-line where they could see shining water instead of foam indicated an island; and, getting her round again, they stood in cautiously, because she could make nothing to windward through the steep, white seas outshore. Reeling before them, with lee deck in the water as she bore away, she opened up the sound, and presently her crew watched the rollers crumble on a boulder-sprinkled point. Moving shoreward majestically in ordered ranks, the waves hove themselves up when they met the shoal and dissolved into frothy cataracts. It was an impressive spectacle, and the sloop looked by contrast extremely small. Still, she drove on, and Jimmy, standing at the wheel, gazed steadily ahead.

"We'll have to chance finding water, because the lead's no guide," he said. "If there's anything in the sound, it will be a steep-to rock."

She lurched in past the point, rolling, spray-swept, with two rags of drenched canvas set. As Jimmy luffed her into the lee of the island there was a sudden change. The water, smoothing to a measured heave, glittered with tiny ripples; the slanted mast rose upright; and the sloop forged on toward a shelving beach, through variable flaws. Then, as she slowed and the canvas flapped, the anchor was flung over, and the rattle of running chain sent a cloud of birds circling above the rocks.

Half an hour later the men were busy cooking breakfast, and soon afterward they were fast asleep; but the night's breeze had made a change in their relations. Their mettle had been rudely tested and had not failed. Henceforward it was not to be mere mutual interest that held them together, but a stronger though more elusive bond. They were comrades by virtue of a mutual respect and trust.

CHAPTER IV

THE ISLAND

On a gray afternoon, with a fog hovering over the leaden water, they sighted the island where the wreck lay. What wind there was blew astern, but it had scarcely strength enough to wrinkle the long heave that followed the sloop; the tide, Jimmy computed, was at half flood. This was borne out by the way a blur on their port hand grew into a tongue of reef on which the sea broke in snowy turmoil, and by the quickness with which the long, gray ridge behind it emerged from the fog. Sweeping it with the glasses, Jimmy could distinguish a few dark patches that looked like scrub-pines or willows. Then, as she opened up the coastline, he noticed the strip of sloppy beach sprinkled with weedy boulders, and the bare slopes of sand and stones beyond. The spot was unlike the islands at which they had called on their way up; for they were thickly covered with ragged firs and an undergrowth of brush and wild-fruit vines; this had a desolate, forbidding look, as if only the hardiest vegetation could withstand the chill and savage winds that swept it.

The men were all somewhat worn by the voyage, which had been long and difficult. Their clothes were stiff with salt from many soakings, and two of them suffered from raw sores on wrists and elbows caused by the rasp of the hard garments. Their food had been neither plentiful nor varied, and all had grown to loathe the sight of fish.

"I've seen more cheerful places," Bethune declared, when Jimmy had handed him the glasses. "I suppose we bring up under its eastern end?"

Moran nodded.

"Pretty good shelter in the bight in about two fathoms. Watch out to starboard and the reef will show you where she is."

Jimmy turned his eyes in that direction, but saw nothing for a minute. Then the swell, which ran after them in long undulations nearly as smooth as oil, suddenly boiled in a white upheaval, and a cloud of fine spray was thrown up as by a geyser.

"One can understand the old steamboat's breaking her back," he said. "Where's she lying?"

"Not far ahead; but by the height of the water on the beach, there'll be nothing to be seen of her for the next nine hours."

"And it will be dark then!" Bethune said gloomily. Jimmy shared his comrade's disappointment. After first sighting land they had felt keen suspense. There was a possibility that the wreck had broken up or sunk into the sand since Moran had visited her; and, after facing many hardships and risks to reach her, they must go back bankrupt if she had disappeared. The important question could not be answered until the next day.

"Couldn't we bring up here and look for her in the dory when the tide falls?" Jimmy suggested.

"It sure wouldn't be wise. When you get your anchor down in the bight you're pretty safe; but two cables wouldn't hold her outside when the sea gets up—and I don't know a place where it blows oftener."

"Then you had better take her in. I can't say that we've had much luck this trip; and we've been a fortnight longer on the way than I calculated. It will be something to feel the beach beneath our feet."

They ran into a basin with gray rocks and stones on its landward side, and a shoal on which the surf broke to seaward; and, soon after dropping anchor, they rowed ashore.

The island appeared to be two miles long, and nothing grew on it except a few patches of scrub in the hollows of its central ridge; but it had, as Moran pointed out, two springs of good water. Birds screamed above the surf and waded along the sand, and a seal lolled upon a stony beach; but these were the only signs of life, and the raw air rang with the dreary sound of the sea.

When dusk crept in they went back on board, and with the lamp lighted the narrow cabin looked very cozy after the desolate land; but conversation languished, for the men were anxious and somewhat depressed. Daylight would show them whether or not their work had been thrown away. With so much at stake it was hard to wait.

"As soon as we've found if she's still on the bank," Moran said, as they were arranging their blankets on the lockers, "we'll get out the net and all the lines we brought; then I guess we had better keep the diving pump in a hole on the beach."

"I suppose we must fish and save our stores," Jimmy agreed; "though the worst beef they ever packed in Chicago would be a luxurious change. But what's your reason for putting the pump ashore?"

Moran was not a humorous man, but he smiled.

"Well," he said, "we certainly haven't a lien on the wreck, and if it was known where she's now lying, we'd soon have a steamboat up from Portland or Vancouver with proper salvage truck. This island's off the track to the Alaska ports; but, so far's my experience goes, it's when you least want folks around that they turn up."

"He's right," Bethune declared. "There's no reason why we should make our object plain to anybody who may come along. I don't know much about the salvage laws, but my opinion is that the underwriters would treat us fairly if we brought back the gold; and if we couldn't come to terms with them, the courts would make us an award. Still, there's need for caution; we have nobody's authority, and might be asked why we didn't report the find instead of going off to get what we could on the quiet."

They went to sleep soon after this, and awakening in a few hours, found dawn breaking; for when the lonely waters are free from ice there is very little night in the North. A thin fog hid the land, leaving visible only a strip of wet beach, and there was still no wind, which Moran seemed to consider somewhat remarkable. As the tide was falling, Jimmy suggested that they should launch the dory and row off at once to look for the wreck; but Moran objected.

"It's a long pull, and we don't want to lose time," he said. "S'pose we find her? We couldn't work the pump from the boat, and we'd have to come back for the sloop. You don't often strike it calm here, and we have to get ahead while we can."

The others agreed; and after a hurried breakfast they hove the anchor and made a start, Moran sculling the Cetacea, Jimmy and Bethune towing her in the dory. They found the towing hard work, for stream and swell set against them and the light boat was jerked backward by the tightening line as she lurched over the steep undulations. Then, in spite of their care, the line would range forward along her side as she sheered, and there was danger of its drawing her under. Though the air was raw, they were bathed in perspiration before they had made half a mile; and Bethune paused a moment to cool his blistering hands in the water.

"This kind of thing is rather strenuous when you're not used to it," he grumbled.

Jimmy was glad of a moment's rest; but immediately there came a cry from Moran. "Watch out! Where you going to?"

Looking round, they saw the Cetacea's bowsprit close above their heads as she lurched toward them on the back of a smooth sea. Pulling hard, with the hampering rope across her, they got the dory round, and afterward rowed steadily, while their breath came short and the sweat dripped from them. It was exhausting work; but

Bethune pointed out the fact that they had not embarked on a pleasure excursion.

At last Moran dropped anchor; and, boarding the sloop, the men spent an hour of keen suspense watching the sea. The island had faded to a faint, dark blur, and all round the rest of the circle an unbroken wall of mist rested on the smoothly lifting swell. None of them had anything to say; they smoked in anxious silence, their eyes fixed on the glassy water which gave no sign of hiding anything below.

Bethune impatiently jumped up.

"This is too tedious for me!" he exclaimed. "Can't we sweep for the wreck from the dory with the bight of a line?"

"You want to keep fresh," Moran warned him. "If she's there, she'll show up before long."

They waited, Jimmy quietly glancing at his watch now and then; and at last Moran stretched out a pointing hand.

"What's that, to starboard?" he asked.

For a few moments, during which the tension set their nerves on edge, the others saw nothing; and then a faint ripple broke the glassy surface of the swell. It smoothed out and the long heave swung undisturbed across the spot for a time; but the ripple appeared again, with a dark streak in the midst of it.

"Weed!" cried Bethune. "It must grow on something!"

"I guess so," said Moran. "It's fast to a ship's timber."

Five minutes later the head of the timber was visible, and in keen but silent excitement they took out a line to it and hove the sloop close up. The diving pumps were already rigged, and when they had lowered and lashed a ladder, Moran coolly put on the heavy canvas dress. He said that, as the show was his, he would go down first. It was with grave misgivings that his companions screwed on the copper helmet and hung the lead weights about him, for neither of them knew anything about the work except what they had learned from a pamphlet issued by a maker of diving apparatus. This they had diligently studied and argued over on the voyage up, but there was the unpleasant possibility that it might not contain all the information needful, and a small oversight might have disastrous consequences.

When the copper helmet sank below the surface and a train of bubbles rushed up, Jimmy felt his heart beat and his hand grow damp with perspiration. He held the signal line and knew the code, as well as the number of strokes to the minute that should give air enough;

but he had not much confidence in the pumps. Though he had had to pay a heavy deposit on them, and their hire was costly, they were far from new. The bubbles moved, however, drawing nearer the weed-crusted wood.

Suddenly the line jerked, and Bethune looked at Jimmy sharply.

"More air!" he cried. "Give her a few more revolutions—he's all right so far."

It was a relief to both when the bubbles moved back toward the ladder, and when the diver crawled on board they eagerly unscrewed the helmet. Moran gasped once or twice and wiped his face before he turned to them.

"It's not too bad after the first minute or two," he said, and this was the only allusion he made to his sensations. "Now, so far as I can make out, there's no getting into her from the deck. Poop's badly smashed, and you'd certainly foul the pipe or line among the broken beams; but it looks pretty clear in the hold. Guess we'll have to break through the after bulkhead; but it's sanded up and there's a pile of stuff to move. You're sure about the strong-room, Bethune?"

"I took some trouble to find out, and was told it was under the poop cabin. I couldn't get a plan of her."

"We'll try the bulkhead." Moran turned to Jimmy. "If you're going next, take the shovel and see if you can shift some of the sand."

Jimmy was not a timid man, but he felt far from happy as his comrades encased him in the dress and helmet. He found them an intolerable weight as he moved toward the ladder and went down it, clinging tightly to the rungs, and then, as a green mist crept across the glasses, he was conscious of an unnerving fear. Struggling with it, he descended, and was next troubled by a pain in his head and an unpleasant feeling of pressure. Something throbbed in his ears, his breathing did not seem normal, and he stopped, irresolute, at the foot of the ladder. He could see a short distance, but it was like looking through dirty, greenish glass, and the wavering light had puzzling reflections in it. He watched the air globules rush to the surface and the shadow of the sloop's bottom move to and fro; and then he fixed his eyes on a badly defined dark object which he supposed was the wreck.

As he reluctantly let go the ladder he was surprised by another change. Instead of carrying a crushing weight, he felt absurdly light and, in spite of his weighted boots, it was difficult to keep his balance.

His feet did not fall where he intended, and when he moved the shovel he carried, the motion of his arm was not perfectly controllable. It seemed to him that if the stream were strong, he must hopelessly float away; but he resolutely pulled himself together. He had not spent all his money and made a daring voyage to be daunted by a few unusual sensations. It was his business to break into the wreck; and he made his way cautiously toward her. Stopping at the place where her after-half had broken off, he saw in front of him a dark cavern, edged with ragged planking and parted timbers and garlanded with long streamers of weed. They uncoiled and wavered as the sea washed in and out, and Jimmy felt a strong reluctance to enter. The darkness might hide strange and dangerous creatures; for a few moments he allowed his imagination to run riot like that of a frightened child.

This, however, must be stopped. Jimmy remembered that he was supplied with an electric lamp. He fumbled clumsily with the switch, and, as a wavering beam of light ran through the water, he cautiously entered the hold. Sand had filled up the hollows among the stone ballast, and there was only a broken orlop beam in his way. He began to feel easier, reflecting that he was, after all, only a short distance beneath the surface; though he would have preferred more experienced assistants at the pumps. Making his way aft beside the shaft tunnel, he presently reached a bank of sand which ran up to the splintered deck. The bulkhead shutting off the lazaret was obviously behind it, and Jimmy began to use the shovel.

It proved difficult work. A vigorous movement upset his unstable equilibrium, and he wondered whether the weight he carried and the pressure applied were adapted to the depth. This could be ascertained only by experiment; and Jimmy feared to make it. Gripping himself, however, he removed a few shovelfuls of sand; and then the pain in his head got worse, and, driving in the shovel deeper than before, he fell forward with the effort. Instead of coming to the ground, he made some ridiculous gyrations before he recovered his footing; and then the signal line, which he felt at to reassure himself, seemed tauter than it should be.

Grabbing up the shovel, Jimmy commenced his retreat. The line might be foul of something, and if so there was a danger of the air pipe's entanglement. It was disconcerting to contemplate the result of that. When he left the hull he felt a strong inclination to kick off his leaded shoes and try to swim to the surface instead of slowly mounting the ladder; but he conquered it and climbed up.

When at last the glasses were unscrewed and the air flowed in on his face, Jimmy was conscious of intense relief. For a minute he sat limply on the cabin top.

"I dare say we'll get accustomed to the thing," he said slowly to Bethune; "but you'll find out that one mustn't expect to do much at first."

Bethune went down, and when he came up Moran asked him dryly:

"How much of that sand did you shift?"

"Three good bucketfuls, which I imagine is more than Jimmy did," Bethune answered with a grin. Then his face grew serious. "As there seems to be forty or fifty tons of it, we'll have to do better."

"That," agreed Moran, "is a sure thing."

They were silent after this, and Jimmy lighted his pipe. Though the day was chilly, it was pleasant to lie on the open deck and breathe air at normal pressure. The stream was not strong, the sea was as smooth as he thought it likely to be, and all the conditions were favorable to the work; but he shrank from going down again, and he imagined that his companions shared his unwillingness. Though he censured himself for feeling so, he was glad when the mist, which had grown thinner, suddenly streamed away and revealed a dark line advancing toward them across the heaving water.

"A breeze!" he exclaimed. "Perhaps we'd better get back while we can. There won't be much water up the channel at lowest ebb."

Bethune nodded agreement as a puff of cold air struck his face, and while they shortened in the cable small white ripples splashed against the bows. These grew larger and angrier as they ran the mainsail up; and, getting the anchor, they bore away for the bight with the swell crisping and frothing astern. Before they ran in behind the sheltering sands it was blowing hard, and they spent the rest of the day lounging on the cabin lockers, while the sloop strained at her cable and the halyards beat upon the mast.

CHAPTER V

AN INTERRUPTION

For three days a bitter gale raged about the island, blowing clouds of sand and fine shingle along the beach and piling the big Pacific combers upon the shoals. The air was filled with the saltness of the spray, and even below deck the men's ears rang with the clamor of the sea. Then the wind fell, and when the swell went down they set to work again and found their task grow less troublesome. They learned the pressure best suited to the very moderate depth, their lungs got accustomed to the extra labor, and none of them now hesitated about entering the gloomy hold. Though they were interrupted now and then by the rising sea, they steadily removed the sand. Their greatest difficulty was the shortness of the time one could remain below. There was no sign of the bulkhead yet, and a gale from the eastward might wash back the sediment they had laboriously dug out. If this happened, they must try to break an opening through the side of the hull; and none of them was anxious to do that, because the timbers of a wooden ship are closely spaced and thick.

For a while nothing but the weather disturbed them; and then, one calm day when trails of mist moved slowly across the water, Jimmy saw a streak of smoke on a patch of clear horizon.

"Somebody farther to the east than he ought to be," he said, leaning on the pump-crank; and then he fixed his eyes on the spot where the bubbles broke the surface. Though he had grown used to the work, the bubbles had still a curious fascination. It was difficult to turn his glance from them as they traced a milky line across the green water or stopped and widened into a frothy patch. So long as they did either, all was well with the man below.

An hour later, when the mist closed in again, Jimmy lay smoking on the deck. He had gone down and stayed longer than usual, and he felt tired and somewhat moody. Of late he had been troubled by a bad headache, which he supposed was the result of diving, and during the last few days he had found the sand unusually hard. The lower layers had been consolidated into a cement-like mass by the action of wave and tide. Moreover, the work was arduous even when they were not down at the wreck. It was no light task to tow the sloop out against the swell in the calms; and when the sea rose suddenly, as it often did, they were forced, if the tide was low, to thrash her out for an offing and face the gale until there was water enough to take them up the channel. Indeed, at times they dare not attempt the entrance, and lay to under storm canvas to wait for better weather. Then they sat at the wheel in turn while the hard-pressed craft labored among the frothing combers, and afterward lay, wedged into place with wet sails and gear, on the cabin lockers, while the erratic motion rendered sleep or any occupation impossible. The Cetacea was small enough to drift to leeward fast, and it sometimes took them hours to drive her back to the island against the still heavy sea when the wind began to lighten. It was a wearing life, and Jimmy felt his nerves getting raw.

Bethune had gone below and Jimmy was turning the crank of the pump when a dull, throbbing sound came out of the mist. Moran looked up sharply.

"That blame steamboat is coming here!" he cried, diving into the cabin to get their glasses.

The measured thud of engines was plainly distinguishable with the roar of water flung off the bows. Jimmy supposed the clank of the pump had prevented their hearing it before.

"She's pretty close! Keep turning, but bring him up; you have the line!" Moran exclaimed.

Bethune answered the signal; but as the bubbles drew near the sloop, the steamer appeared in an opening in the mist. Her white hull and small, cream funnel proclaimed her an auxiliary yacht.

"There's wind enough to move us, and we have to light out of this as quick as we can," Moran said, signaling again to Bethune.

When the copper helmet came into sight, they dragged Bethune on deck and then set to work to shorten cable. The yacht was now plainly visible about a mile off, and seemed to be moving slowly, which suggested that soundings were being taken preparatory to anchoring; but the sloop would not readily be seen against the land. There was, however, a quantity of heavy chain to get in before they hoisted sail, and Jimmy in haste slipped the breast rope that held them to the wreck. For convenience in picking it up, they had attached its outer end to a big keg buoy.

Getting under way, they headed for the bight, and presently saw a white gig following them.

"They won't stay long," said Bethune. "Want fresh water, or, perhaps, a walk ashore; but it's a pity we have no time to land and hide the pumps. The best thing we can do is to meet the party at the water's edge. It's lucky the big net is lying there."

Pulling ashore in the dory, they waited for the yacht's boat, which carried two uniformed seamen and a young man smartly dressed in blue serge with bronze buttons, and pipeclayed shoes. He had a good-humored look, and greeted them affably, glancing at the net.

"Glad to find somebody here; you're fishing, I suppose?" he said. "You'll know where there's water, and ours is getting short. The engineer has had some trouble with salting boilers and won't give us any. I'll take some fish, if you can spare it."

Bethune laughed.

"You can have all we've got," he said. "Any we keep we'll have to eat, and we're getting pretty tired of the diet. There's a good spring behind the ridge; we'll show you where it is."

The man beckoned the seamen, who shouldered two brass-hooped breakers, and the party set off up the beach. When they reached the spring the seamen returned with the breakers to empty them into the boat, using her as a tank to carry the water off, and Jimmy took the yachtsman into a hut they had roughly built of stones between two big rocks. Here they sometimes lived when wind or fog stopped their work. He gave them some cigars and told them that the yacht was returning from a trip to the North, where they had explored several of the glaciers. He was a bit of a naturalist and interested in birds, and that was why he had come ashore; but the desolate appearance of the island had deterred his friends, who were playing cards.

"Have you noticed any of the rarer sea-birds here?" he asked.

"There are a number of nests some distance off," Bethune answered. "I don't know what kind they are, but after making two or three attempts to eat them, I can't recommend the eggs."

The yachtsman laughed.

"You may have made omelettes of specimens collectors would give a good deal for. Anyway, I'd be glad if you would show me the place. As we must take off as much water as she'll carry, the boys will be busy for some time."

"I'll go with you in a minute," Bethune said, giving Jimmy a warning look. "Have you the ball of fine seizing?" he asked his comrade. "There are some hooks to be whipped on to the new line."

Jimmy, understanding that Bethune wanted a word with him in

private, went out, and Bethune followed.

"Well?" Jimmy queried.

"What do you think of the weather?"

Jimmy looked round carefully. The sky was clear overhead except for thin, streaky clouds, and the mist was moving, sliding in filmy trails along the shore.

"It won't be so thick presently, and we may have a breeze."

"That's my opinion. Has it struck you that it will be after half-ebb when our yachting friend leaves? Besides, it would look inhospitable and perhaps suspicious if we didn't take him off to supper."

"Ah!" exclaimed Jimmy. "The wreck will be showing, the pumps are on board, and it's unfortunate we forgot to move our buoy."

"Sure! There's no reason for supposing the man's a fool, and I've no doubt he'll draw conclusions if he sees the diving truck and the buoy. It's certain that somebody on board the steamer has heard about the wreck; and any mention of our doings in the southern ports would lead to the sending up of a proper salvage gang. We might finish before they arrived; but I'm doubtful."

"You're right," said Jimmy. "What's to be done?"

"The best plan would be for you and Hank to get the pumps ashore while there's fog enough to hide you. Then you can slip the buoy and leave it among the boulders abreast of the wreck. I'll keep our friend away from the water; but the high ground where the nests are looks down on the beach and you'll have the steamer not far outshore of you."

Turning at a footstep, Jimmy saw the stranger leave the hut.

"My partner will take you to the nests," he said. "I have something to do on board."

Beckoning Moran, Jimmy turned away, and as the two went down to the beach he explained his object to the fisherman. Moran agreed that if news of their doings leaked out, they might as well give up the search. They must, however, be careful, because there was a chance of their being seen by anybody with good glasses on board the yacht, which had moved close in to shorten the journey for the boat. Now and then they could see her white hull plainly, but it grew dim and faded into the mist again.

Boarding the sloop, they dismantled the pumps, and then found that with these, the lead weights, and the diving helmet, the small dory had a heavy load. The tide was, however, falling, and for some distance it carried them down a smooth channel between banks of uncovered sand. They had no trouble here, but when they reached open water they found a confused swell running against them. The fog had again thickened and they could see only the gray slopes of water that moved out of the haze. It was hard work rowing, and care was needed when an undulation curled and broke into a ridge of foam. If that happened before they could avoid it, the dory might be overturned; and the water was icy cold. They toiled across a broad shallow, sounding with the oars, until they lost touch of the bottom and pulled by guess for a spot where landing was safe.

Soon it seemed that they had gone astray, for they could see nothing of the beach and a harsh rattle broke out close ahead. Moran stopped rowing.

"Tide has run us well offshore," he said. "The yacht skipper's shortening cable or going to break out his anchor. Guess he's swung into shoaler water than he figured on."

While they waited and the tide carried them along, the rattle of the windlass grew louder; and when it stopped, a dim, white shape crept out of the fog. It increased in size and distinctness; they could see the sweeping curve of bow, the trickle of the stream along the waterline, and the low deckhouse above the rail. There was no avoiding the yacht by rowing away without being seen, but the dory was very small and low in the water.

"They've hove her short and found another fathom, and I expect they're satisfied," Jimmy said; "but they'll keep good anchor watch. The best thing we can do is to lie down in the bottom."

They got down on the wet floorings, and Jimmy looked over the gunwale. They were close to the yacht, and he could make out a figure or two in front of the house. As they drifted on, the figures grew plainer, and it seemed impossible that they could escape being seen. For all that, nobody hailed them, though they were near enough to hear voices and the notes of a piano. The vessel's tall, white side seemed right above them, but they were abreast of the funnel now, and the ash hoist began to clatter; Jimmy saw the dust and steam rise as the furnace clinkers struck the sea. Still, they were drifting aft, a gray blotch on the water, and were almost level with her stern when Jimmy saw a man leaning on the rail. By the way his head was turned he was looking toward the dory, and for several anxious moments Jimmy expected his hail. It did not come; the graceful incurving of the white hull ended in the sweep of counter above the tip of a propeller blade, and the dory drifted on into the mist astern.

"Now we'll have her round!" Moran exclaimed, with relief in his voice. "I guess you've got to pull."

It was difficult to prevent her heavy load from swamping her as they approached the beach; but they ran her in safely, and, after carrying up their cargo, set off for the wreck. Their buoy was visible some distance off, for the mist was now moving out to sea; and their chief trouble was to get the awkward iron keg ashore. They had hardly done so when the steamer showed up plainly through a rift in the fog and a draught of cold air struck Jimmy's face.

"It's coming!" he cried. "We've no time to lose in getting back!"

The tide was beginning to ripple as they pulled off the beach, and the yacht was plainly disclosed, shining like ivory on the clear, green water. It did not matter now that they could be seen; their one concern was to get home before the freshening wind raised the sea. In a short time the spray was flying about the dory and frothing ridges ran up astern of her. These got steeper as they reached the shoals, and the men had hard work to hold her straight with the oars as she surged forward, uplifted, on a rush of foam. They had no time to look about, but they heard the steamer whistle to recall her boat, and presently a gasoline launch raced by, rolling wildly, through deeper water.

As they entered the channel into the bight, they met the launch coming out more slowly with the boat in tow, and somebody on board her waved his hand. Then she disappeared beyond a projecting bank, and Jimmy and Moran rowed on to the sloop.

"They were only just in time," Bethune said as they got on board. "I suppose you saw our friend go; but if they don't tow her carefully, it won't be fresh water when it gets into their tank." He paused with a laugh and showed them some silver coins. "Anyhow, we have earned something this afternoon. The fellow insisted on paying for the fish, and I thought I'd better let him."

"It was wise," agreed Jimmy. "Moran and I have done our share, so it's up to you to get supper."

While they ate it, they heard the rattle of a windlass; and, looking out through the scuttle, they saw the yacht steam away to sea.

CHAPTER VI
BLOWN OFF

Though it was nearly eleven o'clock at night, the light had not quite gone and the sea glimmered about the sloop as she rose and fell at her moorings by the wreck. To the north the sky was barred with streaks of ragged cloud and the edge of the sea-plain was harshly clear; to the east the horizon was hidden by a cold, blue haze, and the tide was near the lowest of its ebb. An angry white surf broke along the uncovered shoals with a tremulous roar, and the swell, though smooth as oil on its surface, was high and steep. No breath of wind touched the water, but Jimmy agreed with Moran that there was plenty on the way.

A light burned in the low-roofed cabin where the men waited for the meal which Bethune was cooking. They felt languid as well as tired and hungry, for supper had been long deferred to enable them to continue diving, and they had been under water much oftener than was good for them during the day. The bulkhead they strove to clear of sand was still inaccessible, and, as bad weather had frequently hindered work, they felt compelled to make good use of every favorable minute. This was why they had held on to the wreck, instead of entering the bight before the falling tide rendered its approach dangerous. Moreover, their provisions were running low, and Bethune was experimenting with some damaged flour which had lain forgotten in a flooded locker for several days while they rode out a gale. The bannocks he turned in the frying-pan had a sour, unappetizing smell.

"They may taste better than they promise," he said encouragingly. "If the sky had looked as bad at half-tide as it does now, I'd have made you take her in. We won't get much done tomorrow."

Moran stretched himself out listlessly on the port locker.

"We ought to tie two reefs in the mainsail handy, but I feel played out, and the breeze may not come before morning. It strikes me the most important thing is the question of grub. We can't hang on much longer if that flour's too bad to eat. I can't see how it went so moldy in a day or two. You can leave a flour-bag in the water for quite a while and then find the stuff all right except for an inch on the outside."

"That's so," Jimmy put in. "My notion is that the flour was bad when we got it. The ship-chandler fellow had a greedy eye. But when you deal with the man who finds the money you can't be particular."

"He's pretty safe," grumbled Bethune. "With a bond on the boat for his loan and a big profit on everything he supplied, the only risk he runs is of our losing her—though I'll admit that nearly happened once or twice. However, you can try the flour."

Taking the frying-pan off the stove, he served out a thick, greasy bannock and a very small piece of pork to each of his companions. The food was too hot to eat, and Jimmy, breaking his with his knife, waited with some anxiety while it cooled. If they could use the flour, it would enable them to remain a week or two longer at the wreck; and he believed it would not take many days to reach the strong-room. Failing this, it looked as if he must return to his toil at the sawmill and the dreary life in the cheap hotels.

He believed that he had learned on board the sailing ships not to be dainty, but he sniffed at the food with repugnance and then resolutely cut off a piece. When he had eaten a bite of it he threw down his knife.

"It's rank!" he exclaimed.

Moran, reaching up through the scuttle, threw his bannock overboard.

"Very well!" said Bethune. "That shortens our stay. Perhaps we had better get the pumps down into the cockpit when you have finished the pork and tea."

They did so, grumbling, and then lay on the lockers, smoking and disinclined for sleep. There was a tension in the air, and something ominous in the roar of the surf, which seemed to grow louder and more insistent.

"Whether we'll find the gold or not is doubtful; the only thing certain is that we'll have an opportunity for doing a lot of work," Bethune observed after a while. "In a way, Hank's more to be pitied than either of us. He hadn't the option of taking things easily when he came out West."

"The big lobsters were most killed off; you couldn't make your grub with the traps," Moran explained. "Then I got some little books showing it was easy to get rich by fishing in British Columbia. Wish I had the liars who wrote them out in a half-swamped dory picking up a trawl."

"I don't see that I had much more option than he had," Jimmy objected.

"You could have stayed on board the liner, wearing smart uniforms and faring sumptuously, with a Chinese steward to look after you, if you'd exercised a little tact and shown a proper respect for authority. When the skipper disapproved of a man with heart trouble steering his ship, as he had every right to do, you should have agreed with him."

"I'm glad I didn't," Jimmy said stubbornly. "Anyhow, you're no better off, even if you practise what you preach."

"That would be too much to expect; but then I admit that I am a fool," Bethune laughed. "If I doubted it, the number of times it has been delicately pointed out would have convinced me. After all, it's easy to conform outwardly, which is all that is required, and you can do what you like in private. A concession to popular opinion here and there doesn't cost one much."

"If you mean I ought to have got the quartermaster sacked after he'd prevented a ton of cargo from dropping on my head, I'd rather starve."

"There's a risk of your doing so if you persist in your foolishness. If you had stopped to reason, you would have seen it was your duty to agree with your skipper. Misguided pity is a dangerous thing."

"Moralizing of this kind makes my headache worse!" said Jimmy disgustedly. "Drop it and light your pipe!"

"Let him alone; he has to talk," Moran interposed. "It doesn't matter so long as you don't worry about what he means."

"Well," drawled Bethune, "I'll conclude. Which of you is going to wash up?"

Moran picked up the dirty plates and thrust them into a locker.

"I'm played out and homesick! Wish I was back East, where I did my fishing in the natural way—on top of the water! But it's a sure thing none of us will be down at the wreck tomorrow."

There was silence except for the rumble of the surf and the occasional rap of a halyard against the mast. The sound became more frequent as Jimmy got drowsy, but he was used to the approach of bad weather. Stretched out comfortably on the locker, he soon fell asleep; and it was as dark as it ever is in the North in summer when he was rudely awakened by a terrific jar. The sloop seemed to be rearing upright, and Moran's hoarse shouts were all but drowned by the rattle of chain on deck.

Scrambling out quickly, Jimmy saw the fisherman stooping forward where the cable crossed the bits, and a narrow stretch of smoking sea ahead. Individual combers emerged from it, and the sloop alternately reeled over them with a white surge boiling at her bows and plunged into the hollows. Jimmy, however, wasted no time in looking about; they had hung on to their moorings longer than was prudent, and prompt action was needed.

With Bethune's assistance he close-reefed the mainsail and got the shortened canvas up; then all three were needed to break out the anchor, and Jimmy crouched in the water that swept the forward deck as he stowed it while his comrades hoisted a storm-jib. After that she drove away before the sea, and the men anxiously watched for the entrance to the channel. Though dawn had not broken, it was by no means dark, and they could see the streaky backs of the rollers that ran up the shoals, and beyond them a broad, white band of surf. Presently a break opened up, but it was narrow and crooked, and it seemed impossible that the sloop could get through. When they had run on for a minute or two longer, Moran stood up on deck to command a better view.

"We'd have about two feet under her at the bend, and if she didn't luff up handy she'd sure go ashore," he said. "Seems to me the chances are too blamed steep."

They might reach shelter by taking the risk, and to refuse it meant a struggle with the sea; but Jimmy reluctantly agreed with Moran.

"Yes," he said; "we had better stand off. Look out while I jibe her round."

She swung on before the sea as he put up his helm, followed close by a comber that reared its crest astern, her boom flung on end with the patch of wet mainsail swelling like a balloon. Moran and Bethune were desperately busy with the sheet, for safety depended on their speed. Jimmy moved his wheel another spoke, and sail and heavy spar swung over, while the Cetacea, coming round, buried her lee deck in the sea. With a wild plunge she shook off the water, and, while Bethune and his comrade flattened in the sheets, drove out to windward away from the dangerous shoal. Since they could not reach the bight, she would be safer in open water.

When dawn broke, ominously red, the Cetacea was hove to with a small trysail set, rising and falling with a drunken stagger, as the long, white seas rolled up on her weather bow. Though she shipped no heavy water, she was drifting fast to leeward: the island had faded to a gray streak on the horizon. It would be a day's work to beat back again, even if the wind abated, and it showed no sign of doing so. By noon the land was out of sight, and the sea had grown heavier. For an hour or two there was misty sunshine, and the oncoming walls of water glistened luminously blue beneath their incandescent crests. Some of them curled dangerously, and the trysail flapped, half empty, when the Cetacea sank into the trough. She lay there a few moments while her crew watched the comber that rose ahead. With slanted mast and rag of drenched sail she looked uncomfortably small; but somehow she staggered up the slope before the roller broke. Jimmy could not tell how far he helped her with the helm, but the sweat of nervous strain dripped from his face as he turned his wheel. Now and then she was a few seconds slow in responding to it, and when her bows swung clear her after-half was buried in a rush of spouting foam. It sluiced off, however, and the sharp swoop into the trough was repeated as comber after comber swept upon them.

When Moran relieved him, Jimmy felt worn out. He had had only an hour or two's sleep after a day of exhausting work; his breakfast had consisted of a morsel of stale, cold fish, hurriedly torn with his fingers from the lump in the pan; and they had had no opportunity for cooking dinner.

"I'll try to make some coffee," he said, as he went below.

It was difficult to light the stove. The cabin trickled with moisture like a dripping-well. Grate and wood were wet; and when at last the fire began to crackle, Jimmy had to kneel on a locker as he held the kettle on, in order to keep his feet out of the water which washed up from the bilge. There seemed to be a good deal of it.

"Can't you start the pump?" he called to Bethune.

"I might. I don't know that it would do much good. The suction's uncovered, and the delivery under water half the time."

"Then come in and cook, while I get at it!"

"Oh, I'll try!" Bethune answered morosely; and Jimmy resumed his watch on the kettle and left his companion alone.

He knew the curious slackness which sometimes seizes men exposed to the fury of the sea. It differs from fatigue in being moral rather than physical, and it is distinct from fear; its victim is overwhelmed by a sense of the futility of anything that he can do.

Determined effort is its best cure, and Jimmy smiled as he heard the clatter of the pump. He thought Bethune would feel better presently.

He made the coffee, found a few of the tough cakes Moran called biscuits, and recklessly opened a can of meat. After the meal, which they all found a luxurious change from fish, Jimmy lay down, wet through as he was, on a locker, and, wedging himself fast with parts of the dismantled diving pump, sank into broken sleep.

It was midnight when he went up again to take the helm. There was no moon, and gray scud obscured the sea. Foam-tipped ridges came rolling out of it, and the Cetacea labored heavily. Jimmy watched Moran pump a while before he went below, and then he pulled himself together to keep his dreary watch. The slow whitening of the east brought no change. Dawn came, and throughout another wearing day they still lay hove to. The sloop did not give them much trouble, and they could easily pump out all the water she shipped; but toward evening they began to feel anxious. The gale had increased. They must already have made a good deal of leeway and they might be drifting near the land; if so, she would not carry enough sail to drive her clear, and there would soon be an end of her if she were blown ashore.

Jimmy was on deck at dawn the next morning, but saw nothing except a narrow circle of foaming sea and the flying scud that dimmed the horizon. Toward noon, however, it began to clear, and, getting out the glasses, he waited eagerly during an hour or two of fitful sunshine. The wind seemed to be falling, and the haze had thinned. Slowly it blew away, and a high, gray mass rose into view, four or five miles off. Moran called out as he saw it, but Jimmy quietly studied the land through his glasses.

"The head, sure enough!" he said. "If it had kept thick, we'd have been ashore and breaking up long before dark. Now we have to decide what it's best to do. She might stand a three-reefed mainsail."

"It would take us a week to beat back to the island, and we wouldn't have many provisions left when we got there," Bethune pointed out. "I don't feel keen on facing the long thrash to windward."

"She wouldn't be long making Comox with this breeze over her quarter," Moran suggested. "We might get somebody to grubstake us at one of the stores."

"Considering that there's a bond on her, it isn't likely," Jimmy replied.

They let her drift while they looked gloomily to windward, where the island lay. It would need a stern effort to reach it unless the wind should change; a long stretch of foaming sea which the sloop must be driven across close-hauled divided the men from the wreck. They were all worn out and depressed; and neither of Moran's comrades protested when he got up abruptly and slacked off the mainsheet.

"I guess we'll go where there's something to eat," he said. "You can square off for the straits while I loose the mainsail."

Jimmy put up his helm with a keen sense of relief, and the Cetacea swung away swiftly for the south with the sea behind her. It was nervous work steering, and Jimmy advised Moran to leave the mainsail furled; but the worst of the strain had passed, and rest and shelter lay ahead.

CHAPTER VII

GRUBSTAKED

A light wind faintly ruffled the landlocked water when the Cetacea crept up to her anchorage off a small lumber port on the eastern coast of Vancouver Island. A great boom of logs was moored near the wharf, and stacks of freshly cut lumber and ugly sawdust heaps rose along the beach. Behind these were tall iron chimney-stacks, clusters of wooden houses, and rows of fire-blackened stumps; then steep, pine-clad hillsides shut the hollow in. Though there were one or two steamers at anchor, and signs of activity in the streets, the place had a raw, unfinished look; but the Cetacea's crew were glad to reach it. Cramped by their narrow quarters on board, it was a relief to roam at large; and the resinous smell that hung about the port was pleasant after the stinging saltness of the spray.

But they had come there on business, and Bethune presently stopped a man they met.

"Which is the best and biggest general store in the town?" he asked.

"Jefferson's; three blocks farther on. He's been here since the mills were started."

"Is it necessary to go to the best store?" Jimmy inquired as they went on.

Bethune laughed.

"Oh, no! Now that we've found out which it is, we can try somewhere else. I've a suspicion that our business won't have much attraction for a prosperous dealer who can choose his customers. It's the struggling man who's readiest to take a risk."

"We'll leave it to you," Jimmy said confidently. Bethune had arranged their commercial transactions with tact and shrewdness, and they had discovered that it was far from easy to obtain supplies without paying cash for them.

After strolling through the town, they entered a small, wooden store, which had an inscription, "T. Jaques: Shipping Supplied," and found its proprietor leaning idly on the counter. He was a young man with an alert manner, but, although he was smartly dressed, Bethune, studying him, imagined that he had not yet achieved prosperity.

Indeed, he thought he saw signs of care in the man's keen face.

Taking out his notebook, he enumerated the supplies they wanted, and examined samples. The provisions were good; the store was neatly kept and fairly well stocked; but Jimmy, leaning on the counter and looking about, thought the goods had been arranged with some skill to make the biggest show possible, which implied that the dealer had not much of a reserve. Then, while the man talked to Bethune, Jimmy noticed a woman approach the glass door at the back and stop a moment as if she were interested in the proceedings. All this suggested that his comrade had offered their custom at the right place. The provisions would not be a large item, but they needed ropes, chain, and marine supplies, which would cost a good deal more.

"I can send the small stores off whenever you want, but I can't give you the other truck until the Vancouver boat comes in, and that won't be for four days," Jaques said. He looked rather eager as he added: "I guess you can wait?"

"Oh, yes. I expect it will be a week before we get off."

"Then, I'll wire the order. You'll pay on delivery?"

"That," answered Bethune, smiling, "is a point we must talk about. I think I could give you ten dollars down."

The dealer's face fell and he looked thoughtful.

"Well," he said slowly, "I'd certainly like this order. What's your proposition?"

"I don't know that I have one ready. Perhaps I'd better tell you how we stand and leave you to suggest a way out of the difficulty."

"Come into the back store and take a smoke," invited Jaques; and they followed him into an apartment which seemed to serve as warehouse, general living room, and kitchen. A young woman was busy at the stove, and after looking up with a smile of welcome she went on with her cooking; but Jimmy felt that she had given him and his comrades a keen scrutiny.

Jaques brought them chairs and laid a few cigars on the table.

"Now," he said to Bethune, "you can go ahead."

"First of all, I want your promise to keep what I tell you to yourself." Bethune glanced quietly toward the woman.

"You have it, and you can trust Mrs. Jaques. Susie does all her talking at home; and there's a good deal of her own money in this store. That's why I brought you in. I allow she's sometimes a better judge than I am."

Bethune bowed to Mrs. Jaques; and then, to Jimmy's surprise, he began a frank account of their financial difficulties and their salvage plans. When it came to their doings at the wreck, he made a rather moving tale of it, and Mrs. Jaques listened with her eyes fixed on the speaker and a greasy fork poised in her hand. Jimmy wondered whether Bethune was acting quite judiciously in telling so much. The storekeeper leaned an elbow on the table, his brows knitted as if in thought; and Moran sat still with an expressionless brown face. Except for Bethune's voice it was very quiet in the small, rudely furnished room, and Jimmy surmised that the projected deal was of some importance to its occupants. It was certainly of consequence to his own party, for they could not continue operations without supplies.

"There's a bond on your boat already," Jaques objected, when Bethune paused.

"For about half her value. We could demand a public sale if she were seized, and the balance would clear your debt."

"It's hard to get full price for a vessel that's too small for a regular trade. You allowed you bought her cheap?"

"We did," Bethune carelessly answered. "Still, one has to take a risk."

They were interrupted by a knocking, and Jaques went into the store and did not return for some minutes.

"Nolan, the river-jack," he explained, as he came in. "Wanted gum-boots, and I thought I'd better let him have them; though he hasn't paid for the last pair yet."

"That," Bethune smiled, "bears out my argument."

Jaques looked at his wife, and she made a sign of assent, as if she understood him.

"Supper's nearly ready, and you had better stay," he said. "It's plain fare, but you won't find better biscuits and waffles than Susie's in the province. Besides, it will give us time to think the thing over."

They were glad to accept the invitation, and no more was said about business while they enjoyed the well cooked and daintily served meal. Jimmy was conscious of a growing admiration for his neat-handed hostess, with her bright, intelligent face, and her pretty but simple dress, and he tried to second Bethune in his amusing chatter. Jaques did not say much, but he looked pleased. As for Moran, he steadily worked his way through the good things set before him. His one remark was: "If we strike grub like this, ma'am, we'll want to stop right in your town."

"Then my husband will lose his order," Mrs. Jaques replied, and though she laughed, Jimmy thought her answer had some significance.

When she cleared the table Jaques lighted a cigar and smiled rather grimly when Jimmy inquired if trade was good.

"Well," he said, "it might be better—that's one reason why I'd like to make a deal with you. There's less money in keeping store than you might suppose. I've been two years in this town, and my customers are mostly of the kind the beginner gets—those who can't pay up in time, and those who don't mean to pay at all. The ones worth having go to the other man."

"Where were you before?" Jimmy asked.

"In Toronto. But the wages I was making in a department store were not enough to marry on. With a few dollars Susie had left her and with what I'd saved we thought we might make a start; but there's not much room for the small man now in the eastern cities, and we came out West. It's a pull all along; but we'd make some progress if the blame bush settlers would pay their bills."

Jimmy felt sympathetic. The man did not look as if he found the struggle easy.

"Have you got your business fixed?" Mrs. Jaques asked, coming in from an adjoining room.

"Not yet," Bethune answered. "I've a suspicion that your husband was waiting for you; and I couldn't object, because I ventured to believe you would say a word in our favor."

Mrs. Jaques studied him keenly. He was a handsome man, with graceful manners, and she thought him honest; and it was difficult to associate duplicity with Jimmy's open face.

"Well," she promised, "I'll go as far as I can."

"Then we'll get down to business." Jaques turned to his guests. "You feel pretty sure you'll find the gold when you get back?"

"No," said Jimmy frankly. "We hope so; but we can't even be sure we'll find the wreck. The gale may have broken her up and buried her in the sand."

"Then, if your plan falls through, I won't get paid."

"That's taking too much for granted. There'll be something left over if we have to sell the boat, and we're able to earn more than our keep on the wharf or in the mills. Your debt would have the first claim on us."

"It would take you a long time to wipe it off on what you'd save out of two dollars a day."

"Very true," Bethune admitted. "To clear the ground, I suppose you believe we'd try?"

"We'll take it that you mean to deal straight with me. Anyway, you believe you have a pretty good chance of getting at the gold?"

"I think it's a fair business risk. In proof of this, we're going back to do our best if you will give us the supplies we want. We wouldn't be willing to incur the liability unless we had some hope of success."

"Very well; you don't suggest my letting you have the truck and taking a partner's share on the strength of it?"

"No," Bethune answered decidedly; "not unless you press the point."

Mrs. Jaques nodded as if she had approved of the question and found the answer reassuring. It implied that the adventurers thought the scheme good enough to keep to themselves.

"I'd rather my husband stuck to his regular line," she said.

"Then," said Bethune, "this is my proposition: Give us the goods, and charge us ten per cent. interest until they're paid for. You'll get it as well as the principal, sooner or later."

Jaques looked at his wife; and she made a sign of assent.

"Well, it's a deal!"

A half-hour later, when they rose to go, Jimmy turned to his hostess.

"While your husband has treated us fairly," he said, "we have to thank you, and that makes it a point of honor to show you were not mistaken."

He noticed now that there were wrinkles which suggested anxious thought already forming about her eyes, and that her hands were work-hardened; but she smiled at him.

"One learns in keeping store that a customer's character is quite as important as his bank account."

"That's the nicest thing I've had said about me since I came to British Columbia!" Bethune declared gaily.

Mrs. Jaques smiled.

"If you find the evenings dull before you sail, come in and talk to us," she said.

When they went outside, Bethune made a confession.

"I felt strongly tempted to take our custom somewhere else. They're nice people, and it looks as if they found it hard enough to get along."

"Whatever happens, they must be paid," Jimmy declared.

"Yes," agreed Moran, who seldom expressed his opinion except on nautical matters; "that's a sure thing!"

"How would it do to ask them to a picnic on one of the islands?" Bethune suggested. "It would be an afternoon's outing, and it's generally smooth water here. I shouldn't imagine Mrs. Jaques gets many holidays."

The others thought it a good idea; and when the sloop was refitted and ready for sea, Bethune put his suggestion into practice. His guests were pleased to come, and with a moderate breeze rippling the blue water, they ran up the straits in brilliant sunshine. Jimmy laid a cushion for Mrs. Jaques near the wheel, and her rather pale face lighted up when he asked if she would steer. He saw that she knew how by the way she held the spokes.

"This is delightful!" she exclaimed, as they sped on swiftly. "I used to go sailing now and then at Toronto, but all the time we have lived here I've never been on the water."

She glanced in a half-wistful manner at the sparkling sea. A gentle surf made a snowy fringe along the shingle beach, and beyond that dark pinewoods rolled back among the rocks toward blue, distant peaks. Overhead, the tall, white topsail swayed with a measured swing across the cloudless sky. Silky threads of ripples streamed back from the bows, and along the Cetacea's side there was a drowsy gurgle and lapping of water.

"You're to be envied when you sail away," Mrs. Jaques said, with something that was almost a sigh. "Still, it isn't all sunshine and smooth water in the North."

"By no means," Jimmy assured her. "I can think of a number of occasions when I'd gladly have exchanged the sloop for your back room, or, for that matter, for a yard or two of dry ground."

"One can imagine it," she laughed. "Well, you have to face the gale and fog, while we try not to be beaten by Jefferson and to meet our bills. I don't know which is the harder."

Jimmy felt compassionate. She was young, but she had a careworn look, and he surmised that she found life difficult in the primitive wooden town. It seemed to be all work and anxious planning with her; there was something pathetic in the keen pleasure she took in her rare holiday.

Late in the afternoon they dropped anchor in a rock-walled cove with a beach of white shingle on which sparkling wavelets broke. Dark firs climbed the rugged heights above, and their scent drifted off across the clear, green water. Bethune, who had been busy cooking, brought up an unusually elaborate meal and laid it out on the cabin top with the best glass and crockery he had been able to borrow. His expression, however, was anxious as he served the first course to his guests.

"I've done my best. I used to think I wasn't a bad cook; but after the supper Mrs. Jaques gave us, I'm much less confident," he said. "It's easier to get proud of yourself when you have nothing to compare your work with, and your critics are indulgent. Jimmy's been very forbearing; and it's my opinion that Moran would eat anything that's fit for human food."

"I've had to," Moran retorted. "Anyway, I've seen you set up worse hash than this."

There were no complaints, and the appetite every one showed was flattering. They jested and talked with great good humor; until at last Moran indicated the lengthening shadow of the mast which had moved across the deck.

"It's mighty curious, but we've been an hour over supper, and there's something left. Guess I never spent more'n about ten minutes at my grub before."

Bethune took a bottle from a pail of ice in a locker and filled the borrowed glasses.

"To our happy next meeting!" he proposed. "Our guests, who have made the trip possible, will not be forgotten while we are away."

The glasses were drained and filled again, and Mrs. Jaques turned to her hosts with a cordial smile.

"May you win the success you deserve!" she responded; and a few minutes afterward Bethune, beckoning Moran, went forward to raise the anchor.

The light was fading when they hove the Cetacea to near the wharf and a boat came off. With many good wishes Jaques and his wife went ashore, and the sloop stood away for the lonely North.

CHAPTER VIII
PUZZLING QUESTIONS

Hot sunshine poured into the clearing on the shore of Puget Sound where Henry Osborne had his dwelling. The pretty, wooden house, with its wide veranda and scrollwork decoration, was finely situated in a belt of tall pine forest. The resinous scent of the conifers crept into its rooms; and in front a broad sweep of grass, checkered with glowing flower-beds, ran down to the shingle beach. Rocky islets, crested with somber firs, dotted the sparkling sound, and beyond them, climbing woods and hills, steeped in varying shades of blue, faded into the distance, with behind them all a faint, cold gleam of snow. The stillness of the afternoon was emphasized by the soft splash of ripples on the beach and the patter of the water which the automatic sprinklers flung in glistening showers across the thirsty grass.

Caroline Dexter, lately arrived from a small New England town, sat in the shade of a cedar. She was elderly and of austere character. The plain and badly cut gray dress displayed the gauntness of her form, and her face was of homely type; but her glance was direct, and those who knew her best had learned that her censorious harshness covered a warm heart. Now she was surveying her brother-in-law's house and garden with a disapproving expression. All she saw indicated prosperity and taste, and though she admitted that riches were not necessarily a snare, she hoped Henry Osborne had come by them honestly.

She had never been quite sure about him, and it was not with her goodwill that he had married her younger sister. She thought him lax and worldly; but after his wife's death, which was a heavy blow to Caroline, she had taken his child into her keeping and tenderly cared for her. Indeed, she ventured to believe that she had molded Ruth Osborne's character and won her affection. The girl might have fallen into worse hands, for, in spite of her narrow outlook, Caroline Dexter was unflinchingly upright.

Sitting stiffly erect in the garden chair, she turned to her niece, who reclined with negligent grace in a canvas lounge. This, Caroline thought, was typical of the luxurious indolence of the younger generation, but, for all that, Ruth had some of the sterner virtues. The girl was pretty, and though her aunt believed that beauty is a deceptive thing, it was less dangerous when purged of pride and vanity. Caroline hoped that the strictness with which she had brought up her niece had freed her of these failings.

"Well, dear," she said, "this is a pretty place; and your father's affairs have evidently improved. It's sad your dear mother didn't live to enjoy it."

Though her dress and appearance were provincial, the austere simplicity of her manner had in it something of distinction, and her accent was singularly clean.

Ruth looked up at her with an air of thoughtful regret.

"Yes; I often feel that, when I think of the hard struggle she must have had. Though I was very young then, I can remember the shabby boardinghouses we stayed in, and my mother's pale, anxious face when she and my father used to talk in the evenings. He seldom speaks about those days, but I know he does not forget."

"It is to his credit that he never married again," Miss Dexter remarked with a bluntness in which there was nothing coarse. "He loved your mother, and one can forgive him much for that."

"But have you much to forgive? And, after all, men do sometimes marry twice."

"And sometimes oftener! No doubt they're good enough for the women who take them; but the love of a true man or woman is stronger than death!"

There was a warmth in the voice of this apparently unsentimental aunt that surprised Ruth.

"You seem to speak with feeling," the girl said, half mockingly.

A shadow crept into Miss Dexter's eyes as she gazed, unseeingly, at a seabird poised over the water; but almost immediately she turned to her niece with her usual matter-of-fact calm.

"We were talking of your father's affairs," she said. "I notice a sinful extravagance here: servants you do not need, a gasoline launch, and two automobiles."

Ruth laughed.

"Father must get to town quickly, and cars sometimes break down; besides, I believe he can afford them all. I sometimes think you are rather hard on him."

"I'll admit that I have often wondered how he got his money. One cannot make a fortune quickly without meeting many temptations. I suppose you know your Uncle Charles had to lend him a thousand dollars soon after you were born, and it was not paid back until a few years ago? Does your father never tell you anything about his business?"

"I haven't thought of asking him," Ruth answered with some warmth. "He has always been very kind to me, and I know that whatever he does is right."

"A proper feeling," her aunt commented. "No doubt, he is no worse than the others; but men's ideas are very lax nowadays."

Ruth was more amused than resentful. Though she was her father's staunch partisan, she believed her aunt distrusted the makers of rapid fortunes as a class rather than her brother-in-law in particular, and that her frugal mind shrank with old-fashioned aversion from modern luxury. For all that, Caroline Dexter had roused the girl's curiosity as to her father's fortune and she determined to learn something about his years of struggle when opportunity offered.

A moving cloud of dust rose among the firs where the descending road crossed the hillside, and a big gray automobile flashed across an opening. Ruth knew the car, and there was only one man of her acquaintance who would bring it down the water-seamed dip at that reckless speed.

"It's Aynsley," she said, with a pleased expression. "I'll bring him here."

"And who is Aynsley?"

"I forgot you don't know. He's Aynsley Clay, the son of my father's old partner, and runs in and out of the house when he's at home."

Turning away, she hurried toward the house, and as she reached it a young man came out on the veranda. He was dressed in white flannel, with a straw hat and blue serge jacket, and his pleasant face was bronzed by the sea.

"I came right through," he said, holding out his hand. "It was particularly nice of you to leave your chair to meet me."

"I'm glad to see you back," Ruth responded. "Did you have a pleasant time? When did you get home?"

"Left the yacht at Portland yesterday, and came straight on. Found the old man out of town, and decided I'd stop at Martin's place. I'm due there this evening."

"But it's twenty miles off over the mountains, and this isn't the nearest way."

Clay laughed, with a touch of diffidence that became him.

"What's twenty miles, even on a hill road, when you're anxious to see your friends?"

He watched her as closely as he dared, for some hint of response, but he was puzzled by her manner.

"It isn't a road," she laughed. "Some day you'll come here in pieces."

"I wonder whether you'd be sorry?"

"You ought to know. But come along—I believe my aunt is curious about you."

When he was presented, Miss Dexter gave him a glance of candid scrutiny. Aynsley was marked by a certain elegance and careless good humor, which were not the qualities she most admired in young men, but she liked his face and the frankness of his gaze. If he were one of the idle rich, he was, she thought, a rather good specimen.

"What is your profession?" she asked him bluntly, when they had talked a few moments.

"It's rather difficult to state, because my talents and pursuits are varied. I'm a bit of a naturalist, and something of a yachtsman, while I really think I'm smart at handling a refractory automobile. When I was younger, it was my ambition to ride a raw cayuse, but now one grapples with the mysteries of valves and cams. The times change, though one can't be sure that they improve."

"Then you don't do anything?"

"I'm afraid you hold my father's utilitarian views, but there's room for a difference of opinion about what constitutes hard work. Today, for instance, I spent two hours lying on my back beneath the car and fitting awkward little bolts into holes; then I drove her fifty miles in three hours over a villainous road, graded with rocks and split fir-trees. As I've another twenty miles to go, my own opinion is that I'll have done enough for any ordinary man when I get through."

"And how much better off is the community for your labors?"

"It's some consolation that nobody's much the worse, but I've known the community suffer when it was slow in getting out of the way."

Though she shook her head disapprovingly, there was a gleam of amusement in Miss Dexter's eyes.

"I suppose you're a product of your age, and can't be blamed for the outlook your environment has forced upon you. After all, there are more harmful toys than cars and yachts; enjoy them strenuously while you can. It may fit you for something sterner when you lose your taste for them. And there's something in your look which makes me think that time may come."

A half-hour later Ruth and Aynsley were strolling together through a grove of pines by the water's edge.

"What did you think of my aunt?" she asked.

"I think Miss Dexter is a very fine lady. What's more, I begin to see where you got something I've noticed about you. I suppose you know that you and she are not unlike?"

Ruth smiled. Her aunt was hard-featured and very badly dressed; but she knew that these were not the points which had impressed him.

"The good impression seems to have been mutual," she said; "and to tell the truth, I was slightly surprised. She's generally severe to idlers."

"I knew she'd spot me by my clothes, and I played up to the part. It pleases people when you fall in with the ideas they form about you. But speaking of idlers reminds me that before I went away the old man was getting after me about wasting my talents; opined it was time I did something, and said he'd stand for the losses I'd no doubt make in the first two years if I'd run the Canadian mill he's lately bought. I pointed out that it might cost him more than the boats and cars, and he answered that he'd consider it as a fine for the way he brought me up. However, we won't talk about that. It's too fine a day."

This was characteristic of him and Ruth laughed. He was careless and inconsequent, but they had been friends for a long time and she liked him. It was perhaps curious that she had never troubled herself about his feeling for her, and had gone on taking his unexacting friendship for granted. It was seldom that he became sentimental, and then she had no trouble in checking him.

"Well," she said, "you have told me nothing about your voyage. You must have seen something of interest, and had a few adventures."

"It's a good rule to avoid adventures when you can, and we followed it. Perhaps the most interesting thing was my meeting with three men who were fishing on a lonely island far up to the north."

"Fishing? That doesn't sound very exciting."

They sat down where an opening in the pines gave them a view of climbing forests and sparkling sound, and Aynsley lighted a cigarette.

"That's what they seemed to be doing, but I've had my suspicions about it since. If they caught anything, it would be a long way from a market, and, though they were dirty and ragged enough, two of them hadn't the look of regular fishermen. One rather amusing fellow was very much of the kind you'd meet at a sporting club, and the other had the stamp of a navy or first-class mailboat man. He was English."

Ruth looked up quickly. Jimmy had often been in her thoughts since she had last seen him; although, as he had shown no anxiety to avail himself of her invitation, she had made no inquiries about him. Osborne, however, had visited Vancouver, and, seeing the vessel at the wharf, had inquired about Farquhar and learned that he had left the ship on her previous voyage. Ruth resented his silence, but she could not forget him.

"What was the man like?" she asked.

"Which of them?"

"The last one; the navy man." She found it slightly embarrassing to answer the question.

Aynsley gave her a keen glance.

"So far as I can recollect, he had light hair, and his eyes were a darker blue than you often see; about my age, I think, and unmistakably a sailor, but he had a smart look and the stamp of command. Do you know anybody like that?"

Ruth did not answer with her usual frankness; although she did not doubt that this was the second mate with whom she had spent many evenings on the big liner's saloon deck.

"Oh, of course, we met several steamboat officers, and they're much of a type," she answered in an indifferent tone.

Aynsley saw that she was on her guard. Girls, he understood, often had a partiality for mailboat officers who were generally men of prepossessing appearance and manners. However, he kept his thoughts to himself, for he was usually diffident with Ruth. Although he had long admired her, he knew that he would not gain anything by an attempt to press his suit.

"Anyway," he said, "they were pleasant fellows, and seemed to be having a hard time. Between the ice and gales and fog, it's by no means a charming neighborhood."

"Wasn't it on one of those islands that my father was wrecked, and lost the gold he was bringing down?"

"Somewhere about there. Islands are plentiful in the North." Aynsley paused and laughed. "Still, as my respected parent had some interest in the gold, I shouldn't imagine they lost much. Losing things is not a habit of his. I believe he had a share in the vessel, too."

"But she went down."

"That wouldn't matter. The underwriters would have an opportunity for paying up—probably rather more than she was worth. Considering my parentage, it's curious I have no business talent."

"Your father and mine have had dealings for a long time, haven't they?"

"They have stood by each other for a good many years. It looks as if you and I were destined to be friends; but I sometimes think you don't understand just what your friendship is to me."

"Of course, we are good friends," Ruth said carelessly; "but you have plenty others."

"I have a host of acquaintances; but you're different from the rest. That doesn't sound very original, but it's what I feel. There's an intangible something that's very fine about you; something rare and old-fashioned that belongs more to the quiet corners of the New England States than to our mushroom cities. It comes of long and careful cultivation, and isn't to be found in places that spring up in a night."

"Both my father's and my mother's people lived frugally in a very provincial Eastern town."

"It proves my point. I know the kind of place: a 'Sleepy Hollow,' where nothing happens that hasn't happened in the same way before, left as it was when the tide of American life poured West across the plains. One can imagine your mother's people being bound by old traditions and clinging to the customs of more serious days. That, I think, is how you got your gracious calm, your depth of character, and a sweetness I've found in no one else."

Ruth rose with a smiling rebuke, and firmly turned the conversation into another channel.

"Yes, I know," Aynsley said despondently. "I'm not to talk like that. When I play the good-natured idiot people applaud, but they put me down smartly when I speak the truth."

"You are never in the least idiotic," Ruth smiled. "But if you are to cross the hills before dark, it's time we gave you something to eat."

He turned to her, half resigned and half indignant.

"Oh, well! If the auto jumps a bushman's bridge or goes down into a gulch, you'll be sorry you snubbed me."

"We won't anticipate anything so direful," Ruth responded; then, with a sudden change of tone, she added: "Take that post in your father's mill, Aynsley; I think you ought."

He studied her a moment and then made a sign of assent.

"All right! I'll do it," he said.

An hour later she watched him start the car, and then sat down among the pines to think, for there were questions which required an answer. Aynsley was very likable. Beyond that she did not go. Her thoughts turned to Farquhar, and she wondered why she so resented his dropping out of sight. She knew little about him, but she could not forget the evenings when they leaned on the rails together as the great ship went steadily across the moonlit sea. Now, for she believed he was the man Aynsley had met, he was in the desolate North, and she wondered what he was doing there, and what perils he had to face. It cost her an effort to banish him from her mind; but there was another question which had aroused her curiosity. How had her father spent the years when she was in her aunt's care, before he had grown rich? He had told her nothing about his struggles, but she must ask. Sometimes he looked careworn and she could give him better sympathy if it were based on understanding. And how had his riches been gained, so quickly? Ruth had the utmost confidence in her father, which even her aunt's doubts could not shake; nevertheless, she resolved to question him.

CHAPTER IX

THE MINE AT SNOWY CREEK

Osborne was sitting on his veranda one hot evening while Ruth reclined in a basket-chair, glancing at him thoughtfully. Of late she had felt that she did not know her father as well as she ought: there was a reserve about him which she had failed to penetrate. He had treated her with indulgent kindness and had humored her every wish since she came to him; but before that there had been a long interval, during which he had sent her no word, and these years had obviously left their mark on him. She felt compassionate and somewhat guilty. So far, she had been content to be petted and made much of, taking all and giving nothing. It was time there should be a change.

Osborne was of medium height and spare figure, and slightly lame in one foot. On the whole, his appearance was pleasing; though he was not of the type his daughter associated with the successful business man. There was a hint of imaginative dreaminess in his expression, and his face was seamed with lines and wrinkles that spoke of troubles borne, Ruth had heard him described as headstrong and romantic in his younger days, but he was now philosophically acquiescent, and marked by somewhat ironical humor. She wondered what stern experiences had extinguished his youthful fire.

"Aynsley was talking to me a few days ago," she said. "I understand that he means to take charge of the Canadian mill."

"Then I suppose you applauded his decision. In fact, I wonder whether he arrived at it quite unassisted? The last time Clay mentioned the matter he told me the young fool didn't seem able to make up his mind."

Ruth grew somewhat uneasy beneath his amused glance. Her father was shrewd, and she was not prepared to acknowledge that she had influenced Aynsley.

"But don't you think Aynsley's right?" she asked.

"Oh, yes; in a sense. We admire industrial enterprise, and on the whole that's good; but I've sometimes thought that our bush ranchers and prospectors, who, while assisting in it, keep a little in advance of civilized progress, show sound judgment. It's no doubt proper to turn the beauty of our country into money and deface it with mining dumps and factory stacks; but our commercial system's responsible for a good deal of ugliness, moral and physical."

The girl was accustomed to his light irony, and was sometimes puzzled to determine how far he was serious.

"But you are a business man," she said.

"That's true. I've suffered for it; but it doesn't follow that our methods are much better because I've practised them."

"Where did you first meet Aynsley's father?" Ruth asked. She preferred personal to abstract topics.

Osborne smiled reminiscently.

"At a desolate settlement in Arizona a number of years ago. The Southern Pacific had lately reached the coast, and I was traveling West without a ticket. When it was unavoidable I walked; but railroad hands were more sympathetic in those days, and I came most of the way from Omaha inside and sometimes underneath the freight cars. Down under them was a dusty position in the dry belts."

Glancing round from the pretty wooden house, which had been furnished without thought of cost, across the wide stretch of lawn, where a smart gardener was guiding a gasoline mower, Ruth found it hard to imagine her father stealing a ride on a freight train. But another thought struck her.

"Where was I then?" she asked.

"With your aunt, or perhaps you had just gone to school. I can't fix the exact time," Osborne answered unguardedly; and the girl was filled with a confused sense of love and gratitude.

The school was expensive, and her mother's relatives were by no means rich, but she knew that her father had been the recipient of a small sum yearly under somebody's will. It looked as if he had turned it all over for her benefit while he faced stern poverty.

Ruth impulsively pulled her chair nearer to her father, and her cool little fingers closed over one of his big hands.

"I understand now," she said softly, "why there are lines on your forehead and you sometimes look worn. Your life must have been very hard."

"Oh, it had its brighter side," Osborne answered lightly. "Well, Clay was also engaged in beating his passage, and I found him enjoying a long drink from the locomotive tank. We were confronted with the problem how to cross about a hundred miles of arid desert on a joint capital of two dollars. Clay got over the first difficulty by making a water-bag out of some railroad rubber sheeting which he borrowed, while I went round the settlement in search of provisions. I got some, though prices were ruinously high, and at midnight we hid beside the track, waiting for a freight train to pull out. The brakemen had a trick of looking round the cars before they made a start. Though the days were blazing hot, the nights were cold, and we shivered as we lay behind a clump of cacti near the wheels. A man almost trod on us as he ran along the line, but just afterward the engine bell rang, and Clay sprang up to push back one of the big sliding doors while I held the food and water. The runners were stiff, the train began to move; when he opened the door a few inches I had to trot; and by the time he could crawl through, it was too late for me to get up. Then, with a hazy recollection that he had a long way to go, I threw the food and water into the car."

"That was just like you!" Ruth exclaimed with a flush of pride.

"I imagine it was largely due to absence of mind. I felt very sorry for myself when I stood between the ties and watched the train vanish into the dark. What made it worse, was that of the joint two dollars only fifty cents was his."

"When did you meet him again?"

"Several years afterward in San Francisco. He seemed to be prospering, and my luck had not been good. Through him, I entered the service of the Alaska Commercial Company. That, of course, was before the Klondyke rush, and the A.C.C. ruled the frozen North."

"It was in Alaska that you were first fortunate, wasn't it? You have never told me much about the mine you found."

Osborne looked as if the recollection was unpleasant, but he saw that she was interested, and he generally indulged her. Though she believed in and was inclined to idealize him, Ruth was forced to admit that there was nothing in his appearance to suggest the miner. His light summer clothes were chosen with excellent taste, and there was a certain fastidiousness in his appearance and manners which was hardly in keeping with his adventurous past.

"Well," he said, "it was an unlucky mine from the beginning— and I was not the first to find it. I had been some years in the company's service when I was sent as agent to one of their factories. It was situated on a surf-beaten coast, with a lonely stretch of barrens and muskegs rolling away behind, and the climate was severe. There were no trees large enough to break the savage winds, and for six months the ground was covered deep with snow. A small bark came up once or twice a year, and my business was to trade with the Indians and the Russian half-breeds for furs. In winter we had only an hour or two's daylight, but I got books from San Francisco, and read them by the red-hot stove while the blizzards shook the factory. Even in those days, it was suspected that there was gold in Alaska; but the A.C.C. did not encourage prospecting, and the roughness of the country made it almost impossible for a stranger to traverse. Still, a few prospectors somehow made their way into it, and probably died, for they were seldom seen after their first appearance. I can recollect two or three, hard-bitten men who stayed a day or two with us and then vanished into the wilds.

"It was late in the fall when one arrived with two Aleut Indians in a skin canoe. I never learned where he came from nor how he got so far, for there was no communication with the North except by the company's vessels, but he told us he meant to locate a mine he had heard about and thought he could get back before winter set in. He went off with the Aleuts and a few provisions he bought, and that was the last we saw of him until the following summer. Then I made a journey inland to visit a tribe which had brought in no furs, and one night we made camp among a patch of willows. When we were gathering wood I saw that the larger bushes had been hacked down, and thought it had been done by a white man. The next morning we found an empty provision can of the kind we kept, and, later on, bits of charred sticks where a fire had been lighted. That led us to follow up the creek we had camped by; and presently we found the man who had made the fire."

"Dead!" Ruth exclaimed.

"He had been dead for months. All that was left was a clean-picked skeleton bleached by the snow and a few rags of clothes. The significant thing was that the breast-bone was cut through: sharply cleft, as if by an ax."

"How dreadful! You think the Indians killed the man?"

"It looked like it. There may have been a fight over the last of the provisions, which the Aleuts carried off, because I found very few cans and only one small empty flour-bag; but the tools indicated that it was the same man who had visited the factory. I had not even heard his name, and if he had any friends they never learned his fate; but he died rich."

"He had found the gold?" Ruth's eyes were large with excitement.

"Yes," said Osborne. "Not far away, where the creek had changed its bed, there was a shallow hole, part of it filled with ashes, but as the scrub was three or four miles off it was easy to imagine how the man must have worked carrying the half-dry brush to keep a big fire going."

"But why did he want a big fire?"

"To soften the ground. It never thaws deeper than a foot or two beneath the surface, and there were signs that the early winter had surprised him at work. It was obvious that he was a stubborn man, and meant to hold on until the last moment."

"Do you think his companions murdered him for the treasure?"

"No; in those days the Indians cared nothing for gold, though they might have killed the man for a silver fox's skin: furs were our currency. If there was a quarrel it probably began because he insisted on staying when winter was close at hand and the food almost done. For all that I couldn't find the gold he must have got, because there was plenty in the wash-dirt he had left—tiny rounded nuggets as well as grains. It was a rich alluvial pocket that a man could work with simple appliances, and I made up my mind to go back to Snowy Creek some day."

"But you were not alone! What about your companions?"

"I had two half-breeds with Russian blood in them; good trappers, but, except for that, with little more intelligence than the animals they hunted. Gold had no value to them; their highest ambition was to own a magazine rifle."

"But couldn't you have washed out some of the gold?"

"I got a small quantity; but I was the company's servant, and had its business to mind, and we had only provisions enough for the trip. The A.C.C. found the fur-trade more profitable than mining, and did not want its preserves invaded; and nobody suspected how rich the country really was. Anyway, soon after my return, I had a dispute with the chief factor and, fearing trouble, said nothing about my discovery. The office supported the fellow, and I left the A.C.C. with my secret and three or four hundred dollars."

"What did you do then?"

"I'm afraid an account of all my shifts and adventures would be monotonous. Sometimes I had two or three hundred dollars in hand, sometimes I had nothing but a suit of shabby clothes; but when things were at the worst some new chance always turned up, and I wandered about the Pacific slope until I fell in with Clay again."

"Then you didn't go to him when you left the A.C.C.?"

"No; he had done me one good turn, and I couldn't be continually asking favors." Osborne paused and his face turned graver. "Besides, there were respects in which we didn't agree; and in those days I had an independent mind."

"Haven't you now?"

"I've learned that it's sometimes wiser to reserve your opinions," said Osborne dryly. "You can best be independent when you have nothing, because it doesn't matter then whom you offend."

"Was Clay prosperous?" Ruth asked.

"He was getting known as a man who would have to be reckoned with; but he was short of money and was ready for a shot at anything that promised a few dollars. Clay never shirked a risk, but I believe he was honestly glad to see me, and in a moment of expansion I told him about the Snowy Creek mine and the gold that would be waiting for me when I could return."

"Ah! I was waiting until you came to that again. I felt its importance. It was the mine that made you rich and surrounded me with a luxury I was half afraid of at the beginning, wasn't it?"

Miss Dexter came toward them along the terrace and Osborne smiled as he indicated her.

"Your aunt has always been inclined to disapprove of my doings, and I don't suppose she'd be interested in my prospecting experiences. We'll let them stand over till another day."

Ruth agreed, but she had a puzzling suspicion that her father was relieved by the interruption. When Miss Dexter joined them Ruth was forced to follow his lead and confine herself to general conversation. This, however, did not keep her from thinking, and she wondered why her aunt, whose love for her she knew, had shown herself so hypercritical about her father. Caroline was narrow, but she was upright, and it seemed impossible that she could find any serious fault with him. For all that, Ruth wished that his connection with Clay were not quite so close. Clay was not a man of refinement or high principles, and, to do him justice, he did not pretend to be. Ruth had heard his business exploits mentioned with indignation and cynical amusement by men of different temperament. There were, she supposed, envious people who delighted to traduce successful men; but Clay was certainly not free from suspicion, and she would have preferred that her father had chosen a different associate.

CHAPTER X

THE WRECK OF THE KANAWHA

Ruth had time to ponder her father's unfinished story, for a week elapsed before she could persuade him to continue it. Osborne was away for a few days, and when he came home his preoccupied manner suggested that he had business of importance on hand, and Ruth refrained from questioning him. The subject, however, had its fascination for the girl. She had been too young to retain more than a hazy recollection of her father in his struggling days, and she had fallen into the way of thinking of him as the polished and prosperous gentleman whom she had rejoined after a long separation. Now it was difficult to readjust her ideas and picture him as a needy adventurer, taking strange risks and engaging in occupations of doubtful respectability. She was, she hoped, not hypercritical, but she found it hard to reconcile the two sharply contrasted sides of his character.

At last, one evening, when they strolled across the lawn as dusk was falling, she determinedly led up to the subject, regardless of the smile with which he evaded her first questions.

"I don't know why you should be so bent on hearing about the mine," he said. "On the whole, I'd rather forget the thing, because good luck never followed the gold that was taken from Snowy Creek. There seemed to be a curse upon it."

They sat down on a bench beneath a tall, ragged pine, and Osborne lighted a cigar.

"Well," he began, "some time after the Klondyke rush started, when gold had been found freely on American as well as Canadian soil, I went up to Alaska to re-locate the mine. Clay had gone north before this, but not as a miner—he said it was cheaper to let somebody else dig the gold for him. He had a share in a wooden steamboat, started a transport service to several mining camps, and financed prospectors who made lucky finds. Everything he touched prospered, and the man was popular where the canvas towns sprang up; so I was not surprised when I found him unenthusiastic about my project. However, after much persuasion, he agreed to come, and we set off with two hired packers and supplies enough to give us a good chance of success.

"Summer was late that year, and we hauled the hand-sledges two hundred miles over the snow; but I needn't tell you about our journey. We made it with some trouble, and one afternoon came down to the creek, wet and worn out, plowing through belts of melting snow and soft muskegs made by the sudden thaw. I had hide moccasins which were generally soaked and they had given out under the fastenings of the snowshoes. My foot, which had been frost-bitten on the march when I first found the mine, was cut deep, and it cost me a pretty grim effort to hold out for the last few miles. I made it because I couldn't let another night come before I learned my luck. All I had was in the venture, and if it failed I must go back to camp destitute."

"One can understand that you were anxious."

"It was hard to keep cool, but weariness and pain steadied me. I believe I showed no excitement, but I envied the others' calm. I can picture them now: Clay, shuffling along in his old skin-coat and torn gum-boots; the two packers, grumbling at the slush and bent a little by their loads. All round us a desolate wilderness ran back to the skyline; gray soil and rocks streaked with melting snow, out of which patches of withered scrub stuck forlornly. Well, we struck the creek, by compass, near where I intended, for soon afterward I picked up one landmark and Clay another."

"Clay? But he hadn't been there before!"

"You're keen," Osborne observed. "We had often talked over my plans, and he must have known nearly as much about the place as I did. Then one couldn't mistake a prominent strip of rising ground, though it was some distance off when Clay saw it."

"But the mine?"

"We made the spot in the evening, and I got there first, though it hurt me badly to put down my foot, and I've sometimes thought Clay held back to let me pass. Then I had to get a stern grip on my self-control, and for a few moments I stood there with my hands clenched, unable to speak. Where I had left a small hole there was a large one, and a great pile of tailings was thrown up in the bed of the creek. It was obvious that we had come too late."

"How dreadful!" Ruth exclaimed. "After all you had gone through, it must have been almost too hard to bear. What did you do?"

"I can't remember. Clay was the first to speak and I can recall his level voice as he said, 'It looks as if somebody has been here before us, partner!'"

"But how inadequate and commonplace! Didn't he do anything?"

"He sat down on his pack and lighted a cigar; but he was always cool in time of strain. All I remember of my own doings was that some time afterward I fired a stick of dynamite at the bottom of the hole and dug out the bits and half-thawn dirt until it was dark. I knew it was wasted labor, because whoever had found the pocket wouldn't have stopped until he had cleaned it up. Then I threw down my tools and lay among the stones, limp and shivering, while Clay began to talk."

"But who had found the mine?" Ruth interrupted.

"I never learned. But Clay dealt with the situation sensibly. After all, he said, it was only a pocket; a small alluvial deposit. The stream which had brought the gold there had, no doubt, left some more in the slacker eddies, and it might be worth while to look for the mother-lode, where the metal came from. We had food enough to last while we prospected the neighborhood. The next morning we set about it, and, following up the creek, we found gold here and there; but our provisions threatened to run out before we came to the watershed."

"Were any of the pockets as rich as the stolen one?" Ruth asked.

"No," her father answered with a hint of reserve. "Still, we found some gold and got back safely to the coast. For a while I helped Clay, and then he told me he must go south before the ice closed in. We sailed in the vessel that he and some of his friends had bought, and when we rowed off to her one misty day through a heavy surf I did not look forward to a comfortable trip. She was an old wooden steamer that had been whaling, with tall bulwarks and cut-down masts, and the topsail yards she still carried gave her a top-heavy look. The small, dirty saloon and part of the 'tween-decks were crowded with successful miners and others who were at least fortunate in having money enough to take them out of the country before winter set in. None of them, I think, wished to see the North again, and nobody who knew it could blame them. Those who had gold had earned it by desperate labor and grim endurance; those who had none were going back broken men—frost-bitten, crippled by accidents, and ravaged by disease.

"We had some trouble in getting to sea. Several of the crew had deserted, and the rest were half-mutinous because they had been forcibly kept on board. They struck me as a slipshod, unsailorly lot. To make things worse, it was blowing fresh on-shore, and she lay, straining at her cables and dipping her bows, in the long roll, in an open roadstead. They broke a messenger chain that drove the rickety windlass in getting the stream anchor up, and the miners had to help with tackles before they could bring the kedge to the bows. Then she crawled slowly out to sea under half steam, and, although there was not much prospect of it, I hoped she would make a quick passage. The young first mate and one of the engineers seemed capable men, but there was nothing to recommend the rest, and the skipper was slack and too convivial in his habits. He was a little, slouching man, with an unsteady look."

"How did such an old ship get passengers, and why didn't they engage a better crew?" Ruth wanted to know.

"Passengers were not particular during the gold rush, and good seamen were scarce on the Pacific slope. All who were worth anything had gone off to the diggings."

"Oh! Where was the gold she carried kept?"

"In a strong-room under the floor of the stern cabin; that is, the gold that was formally shipped by her, because I believe some of the miners carried as much as possible on their persons and stowed the rest under their bunks. Anyway, you saw men keeping watch while the bedroom stewards were at work, and I imagine it would have been dangerous to mistake one's berth at night. I generally struck a match to make sure of my number. However, for the most part, the passengers seemed an honest lot, and I had more confidence in them than I had in the crew.

"Our troubles began on the first day out, for she burst a pipe in the engine room; but there was no excitement when she stopped and a cloud of steam rushed out of the skylights. Men who had faced the Alaskan winter in the wilds and poled their boats through the rapids when the ice broke up were not easily alarmed.

"'The blamed old boiler's surely blowing. Guess that means another day or two on the road,' one remarked, and the fellow he spoke to coolly lighted his pipe.

"'Well,' he said, 'they've got some sails up there. She'll make it all right if you give her time.'

"She lay a good many hours in the trough of the sea, rolling so wildly that nobody could keep his feet, while a miner and the second engineer strapped the pipe with copper wire and brazed the joint; but the next accident was more serious. She was steaming before a white sea with two topsails set when there was a harsh grinding and the engines stopped with a bang. A collar on the propeller shaft had given way, the bolts had broken, and until it could be mended there was nothing to connect the engines with the screw.

"They set more sail while the engineers got to work; and some hours later Clay and I were sitting in the captain's room. Clay took the accident lightly, but the skipper had a nervous look and had been drinking more than was good for him. There was a bottle in the rack, and Clay was filling a glass when a miner came in. He was a big man with a quiet, brown face and searching eyes.

"'Can your engine crowd fix this thing, Cap?' he asked.

"'They're trying,' said the skipper shortly. 'It may take some time.'

"'What are you going to do while they're at the job?'

"'Head south under sail.' The skipper began to look angry. 'Is there anything else you want to know?'

"'Just this—do you reckon you can handle her all right with the boys you have?'

"The skipper got up with a red face, and I expected trouble, but Clay glanced at the miner and pulled the skipper down.

"'You had better answer him,' he said.

"'If the wind holds, I can keep her on her course until the engines start. That should be enough for you.'

"'Certainly,' said the miner. 'If you'd found the contract too big, we'd have found you boys to help with the shaft or get sail on her. Anyway, if you want them later, you can let me know.' Then he went out and the skipper drained his glass. It was a thing he did too often."

"But could the miner have done what he promised?" Ruth interrupted.

"It's very likely. In fact, I think if we had wanted a doctor, an architect, or even a clergyman, we could have found one among the crowd on board. The fellow certainly found two or three mechanics, and once I crawled into the shaft tunnel to watch them at work. As it was impossible to get the damaged length out, they worked at it in place, crouching awkwardly in an iron tube about four feet wide while they cut slots in the iron. There was hardly room to use the hammer and hold the chisel; black oil washed about the tunnel mixed with salt-water that had come in through a strained gland. Open lamps smoked and flickered close above their heads as she rolled and the air was foul; but they kept it up in turns with the ship's engineers for several days while the weather got worse and the boat lurched along before an angry sea with her canvas set. The decks were wet because the big rollers that came up astern splashed in across her rail. It was bitterly cold and a gray haze shut in the horizon. As the captain could get no sights, he had to make his course by dead reckoning, which is seldom accurate."

"You must have felt anxious with all your gold on board," Ruth said.

"No," replied Osborne, with a moment's hesitation, which she missed. "Clay had insured the vessel and his shipments by her on a kind of floating policy. I believe he had some trouble to effect it, but he managed to get the thing arranged through a broker with whom he had a little influence."

"Clay seems to have a good deal of influence," Ruth thoughtfully remarked. "How does he get it?"

"It's a gift of his," Osborne answered, with a curious smile. "However, to go back to my tale, I knew the gold was insured, because, as joint owner, I had to sign a declaration about its value, which would go by another vessel with the bill of lading. To tell the truth, I was getting more anxious about my personal safety, for the cold and mist and wild weather were wearing on the nerves. At last, the gale blew itself out; but the haze got thicker as the sea began to fall; and one night I was awakened by a shock that threw me out of my berth. As I got a few clothes on I felt her strike again, and when I ran out on the deck, half dressed, it was clear that she had made her last voyage. She lay, canted over, across the sea, with her after-part sinking and the long swell which still ran breaking over her. You could see the smooth slopes of water roll out of the dark and melt into foam that covered half the deck, while the planking crushed in with a horrible sound as the reef ground through her bilge. There was, however, no panic. The miners quietly helped to swing the boats out; and, seeing that she was holding together, I went with Clay and two seamen to open the strong-room. It was reached through a trap in the cabin floor, but some beams in breaking had jammed this fast, and we attacked the deck with bars and axes.

"It was sharply slanted, the poop heaved and worked as the swell roared about it, and a big lamp that still burned hung at an extraor-dinary angle with the bulkhead. I remember that a maple sideboard which had wrenched itself away and slipped down to leeward, lay, smashed to pieces, in a pool of water; but there was no time to lose in looking about. We all worked well, but Clay did more than any of us. He was half dressed, his face was savage and dripping with sweat, and he swung his ax in a fury, regardless of the rest. In fact, his mood puzzled me afterward."

"But his gold was below!" said Ruth.

"It was fully insured," Osborne explained. "I didn't think Clay was likely to make such desperate efforts for the benefit of the under-writers; and he was not acting a part, because when the slant of floor got steeper and we were warned to come out before she slipped off the reef, he shouted reckless offers of money to the men to encourage them to keep on. We might have broken through if we had had a few more minutes, though the strong-room must have been already flooded, but the lamp fell as she reeled when a roller struck her, and we were left in darkness with the water washing about our feet. It drove us out and she was obviously going down when we waded across the after-deck. A boat lay under the quarter, but it was swept clear as soon as I dropped on board, and as we lurched away on the long swell there was a heavy crash. Then a blue light flared up and showed us other boats, and only half the wreck left, looming black amid spouting foam.

"It seemed that nobody had been left behind, and those who could row took the oars in turns through the dreary night. In the dark-ness we missed an island which lay not far off, and it was two days later when we landed on a desolate mainland beach. We were there a fortnight, living, for the most part, on shellfish, and then, fortu-nately, a Canadian sealing schooner ran into a neighboring inlet for water. She took us on board, and, as we filled her up, it was a relief when she transferred us to a wooden propeller off the northern end of Vancouver Island."

"Then the gold was lost?"

"All that was in the strong-room; the miners saved most of theirs. Nobody was blamed for the wreck, the underwriters paid, and when a salvage expedition failed to recover anything, there was an end of the matter. The gold lies at the bottom of the sea, and though I don't know that I'm superstitious, I think that's the best place for it. From the beginning, it brought nobody luck."

"It had a tragic story," Ruth agreed. "I wonder what would happen if somebody fished it up?"

Osborne laughed.

"There's not much fear of that. The wreck must have slipped off the reef soon after we left, because the salvage people found both halves of her in deep water; but the strong tides and the bad weather prevented them from working and they declared that she would be buried in the sand before another attempt could be made."

He turned to her with a smile in his eyes.

"Now, little girl," he said, "you know all about it, and I hope you're satisfied."

"I found it very interesting," Ruth replied with a thoughtful air. "In reality, it was the insurance payment that gave you a start?"

"In a sense." Osborne's tone was grave. "Still, it was not what I'd now consider a large amount, and I've sometimes felt that I wouldn't be sorry for an excuse to give it back."

"I don't suppose Clay ever felt that way," Ruth said.

"One wouldn't imagine so. What Clay gets he keeps. He's not the man to let his imagination run away with him."

Osborne rose and strolled across the lawn, but Ruth sat still in the gathering dark. It was a curious story she had heard, but she thought she could understand her father's feeling regarding the gold. It had brought him bitter disappointment and permanent lameness, as well as hardships and suffering. There was, however, something puzzling in Clay's determined attempt to break into the strong-room while the ship was going to pieces. He was insured against all loss, and he was not the man to take undue personal risks. Then Ruth's thoughts returned to the gold, which had a fascination for her. After all, it was, perhaps, not impossible that it should be recovered. A spell of unusually fine weather or a change in the currents might make another attempt easier. Treasure often had been taken from vessels long after they had sunk. Ruth thought of Jimmy Farquhar, engaged in some mysterious occupation on an island in the North. It seemed extravagant to suppose that he had found the wreck; but it was not impossible. It would be a curious thing if he should bring up from the depth what her father had lost. But her father had said the gold brought bad luck in its train.

The darkness crept up across the lawn and hovered round the girl, enshrouding her, as she thought of Jimmy Farquhar on the lonely island in the North and puzzled over his connection with the ill-fated gold.

CHAPTER XI
FATHER AND SON

Osborne did not go to town on Saturdays, and he and Ruth were sitting in a shady corner of the lawn during the hot afternoon when a cloud of dust whirled up among the firs. The speed with which it streaked the climbing forest had its significance to Ruth, but when a big gray car flashed across an opening her expression changed.

"There's no mistaking Aynsley's trail," Osborne laughed. "He blazes it on the bodies of straying chickens and hogs; but I imagine you noticed that he wasn't alone."

"I did; and I would have been quite as pleased if he had left his father at home."

"So I surmised." Osborne smiled. "It seems to be what the older generation is intended for; but Clay's not the man to take kindly to the shelf and, everything considered, you couldn't blame him. Aynsley's the more ornamental—a fine figure of a man as he sits at the wheel; but his father's the driving force that makes the machine go. So far, his son hasn't made much of anything unless the material was put ready to his hand."

"At least, he has done no harm."

"That's a very negative virtue. It isn't thought highly of in this country."

"I told him not long ago that he ought to work," Ruth replied in unguarded confidence.

"It will be interesting to see if he follows your advice. His friends have been urging the course for several years without much effect."

"He means to take charge of the Canadian mill; but, of course, he may have a number of reasons for doing so," Ruth added hastily.

Osborne made no comment. Of late, he had begun to wonder where her friendship for Aynsley would lead, and although it would not have displeased him had she shown any tenderness for the man, he could discover no sign of this.

He went forward to meet his guests, and when they came out of the house a few minutes later Aynsley went straight across the lawn to greet Ruth and Miss Dexter, who had joined her niece, while Clay and Osborne followed a path which led through the pines. Clay was strongly made and burly, with very dark hair and eyes and a somewhat fleshy face. He looked as if he enjoyed good living; but the alertness of his expression redeemed it from sensuality. He had an air of rakish boldness which rather became him, and his careless dress added to this effect. In white Panama hat, well-cut clothes negligently put on, with a heavy gold watch-chain, diamond studs, and a black silk band round his waist, Clay looked more of a swashbuckler than a sober business man. His appearance was not altogether deceptive, for, although he used modern methods with great shrewdness, he had habits and characteristics more in keeping with the romantic '49.

"Have you held on to those Elk Park building lots?" he asked.

Osborne nodded. "Yes."

"Still got an option on the adjoining frontage?"

"I believe so; the offer wasn't quite formal."

"Then wire and clinch the deal. Do it right now."

"Ah! The municipal improvement scheme is going through?"

"Sure. I got the tip by 'phone as I was leaving. Whatcom serves me pretty well, but there are other fellows to take a hand in the game, and the news will leak out some time this evening. We're an hour or two ahead—that's all. Here, write your message."

Taking a telegram blank from his pocket, he handed it to Osborne; and then swung off his hat with ceremonious gallantry as he came suddenly upon the others through an opening in the pines. Ruth gave him a rather cold bow, for his voice carried well, and she had heard enough to disturb her. She did not expect much from Clay; but it looked as if her father were abetting him in a conspiracy to take an unfair advantage of some civic improvements. She had no justification for questioning either of them; but her aunt, who was seldom diffident, proceeded to deal with the matter boldly when Osborne joined them after dispatching the telegram.

"What's this I hear, Henry?" Miss Dexter asked.

"I can't say. You were not intended to hear anything," Osborne replied with a patient air.

"Then your friend should talk lower. Have you been buying up property the city needs?"

"It's a fairly common practice. I suppose you don't approve of it?"

"Need you ask?" Miss Dexter bristled with Puritanical indignation. "Have you any moral right to tax the people because they want a healthier and cleaner town? Is this the example you would set your daughter?"

Osborne smiled tolerantly.

"It's hardly likely that Ruth will feel tempted to speculate in real estate. Besides, the tax is optional. The people needn't pay it unless they like."

"That's a quibble," Miss Dexter replied shrewdly. "They wouldn't buy your lots at an extravagant price if there was another site available."

"It's unwise to jump at conclusions. As a matter of fact, there are two better sites in the market."

Miss Dexter looked puzzled.

"If that's true," she declared, "the matter's more suspicious than before. There's something not straight."

"I'm afraid there often is," Osborne responded good-humoredly. "Still, while I can't hope for your approval of all my doings, I don't think you have much reason to question my veracity."

"I have none. I beg your pardon, Henry," Miss Dexter said with some dignity. "I'm glad to say that I've always found your word reliable."

"That's something to my credit, anyway." Osborne turned to Clay. "My sister-in-law has no admiration for our modern business ethics."

"There she shows sense," Clay answered with a smile. "I'm old-fashioned enough to believe, ma'am, that the less women have to do with business the better."

"Why?" Miss Dexter demanded sternly.

"You have a better part in life; we look to you to raise the national tone, to protect the family morals, and keep the home clean."

Osborne looked amused, and Aynsley undutifully grinned, but Miss Dexter's expression hinted at rather grim astonishment.

"How is it to be done?" she asked. "What's the use in our cleaning when you men are allowed to muss up things?"

"That sounds logical," Aynsley put in. "I'm afraid we really need reforming."

"You do," Miss Dexter replied with an air of dry amusement which somewhat surprised her niece. "Idle men in particular are bound to make trouble."

"It was the busy ones I was thinking of. My idea is that a man's most dangerous when he's making money."

"What's that?" Clay turned upon his son sternly.

"I believe I heard you agree with Miss Dexter, sir, when she condemned our commercial morality?"

"There's a difference; she's a lady," Clay replied in a decided tone.

Aynsley laughed and turned away with Ruth, who was in a thoughtful mood, for what she had heard deepened her distrust of Clay and made her anxious about his influence on her father. She admitted that, in her inexperience she could not presume to judge what was right for him, but she felt troubled.

"Have you told your father you will take over the mill?" she asked Aynsley.

"Yes; and I believe he was immensely gratified, though he only said he was glad to see I was coming to my senses. However, on thinking it over, I half regret my decision. The old man has money enough for both of us, and, to my mind, driving a car or sailing a yacht is much less risky work than trying to get ahead of the people you deal with."

"But is that necessary? Can't you carry on a business without taking advantage of your rivals and customers?"

"I'm hardly in a position to judge, but from what I've heard it seems difficult. When I take up the mill I've got to make it pay. It would be a bad shake-up for the old man if I only lost the money he put in. He'd feel himself disgraced, and it would be a heavy strain on his affection. Though he tells me I'm a fool pretty often, he's really fond of me."

"Yes," said Ruth; "I've noticed that, and I like him for it. After all, you need some sympathy. The situation's complicated."

"That's so. I'm half afraid I'm not smart enough to grapple with it. Of course, there is such a thing as compromise: you can do your best all round, but make a small concession here and there."

"I'm not sure that would work. Isn't there a risk of the concessions becoming too numerous? It would be safer not to give way at all."

"It sounds a drastic rule. The trouble is that my relatives and friends expect too much of me, and I suspect that some of them are pulling opposite ways."

Ruth felt sorry for him. Though he was careless, he was honest, and she thought he would shrink from anything that was mean and savored of trickery. Now, however, he had to stand a searching test: he would be expected to make the sawmill pay, and Clay would not be satisfied with a small profit. Ruth felt that she had assumed some responsibility in persuading him to undertake an uncongenial task; for if he proved unfitted for it, his troubles would be numerous. For all that, she could not believe that it was impossible to get rich uprightly.

"After all," she said, "you will have every advantage. The best assistants and the latest machinery."

"That's true. But they're liabilities. I mean they'll be scored against me, and I'll have to prove I've made the most efficient use of them. In a way, I'd rather make a start with poorer tools."

"That sounds weak; and you're not often so hesitating."

"It's something to know your limitations," Aynsley answered. "Besides, I feel that I have to do you and the old man credit after the rather reckless confidence you have both shown in me."

"I am sure mine was justified," Ruth said softly.

Aynsley turned to her quickly. She was wonderfully attractive with her slender figure in light summer drapery outlined against the darkness of the surrounding pines; and the dusky background emphasized her fine coloring. Her face, however, was quietly grave. He could see no trace of the tender shyness he longed for, not even a hint of coquetry, which might have warranted some advance. He sometimes thought that Ruth did not know her power and had not quite awakened yet; but it was obvious that she had spoken in mere friendly kindness, and he must be content with that.

"Thank you," he answered in a voice that was slightly strained. "I'll certainly have to pull myself together and see what I can do."

They heard his father calling and, turning back to the lawn, they found Clay ready to go. He had, he explained to Miss Dexter, only called for a word with Osborne, though he found it hard to tear himself away. She heard him with a twinkle in her eyes, and afterward watched him cross the lawn with his jaunty air. Somehow he made a more romantic figure than his handsome son.

"A man of many talents, I think," she said. "One wonders whether he makes the best use of them."

"That depends on one's point of view; and it's not our affair," Osborne remarked.

"It is certainly not mine. How far it may be yours, I can't tell, but a man of that kind doesn't walk alone. Where he goes he drags others after him."

Osborne laughed as the hum of the car rushing along the hillside came back to them.

"The pace he sets is generally hot," he admitted; "but I imagine his son is at present gratifying his love of speed."

As a matter of fact, Clay was then leaning back on the cushions, with his hat jammed tightly on, while he watched Aynsley, whose face was presented to him in clearly cut profile. The car was traveling very fast along one of the rough dirt-roads of the country, throwing up red dust and withered needles and bouncing among the ruts. High overhead there hung a roof of somber foliage, pierced by shafts of glittering light and supported by the columnar trunks of great Douglas firs. There were holes in the uneven surface of the road deep enough to wreck the machine, and though boggy stretches had been laid with small, split logs, these left bare, broad spaces where the wheels sank in the soft soil. Aynsley never slackened speed. He avoided the dangers with judgment and nerve, while the car lurched as it twisted in and out, now clinging to the edge of the bank with tires that brushed the fern, now following a devious track made by wagon wheels. It was an exhibition of fine driving; and Clay, who was a shrewd judge of men, noticed the coolness, courage, and quick decision his son displayed. He took risks that could not be avoided, but he was bold without being rash, and this appealed to his father, who studied him with a puzzled feeling. Considering his strength of character, it was strange that Aynsley had done nothing yet; and Clay was, perhaps, not altogether mistaken in deeming no occupation of importance, unless it was connected with the earning of money. He held that a calling which enriched a man was generally of some benefit to his country.

"I had a letter from Vancouver this morning," he said, as they climbed a hill and the slower pace made conversation possible. "They're putting the new engine in and expect to start the mill in a fortnight."

"I'll be ready then," said Aynsley.

Clay noticed that, although his tone conveyed no hint of eagerness, his expression was resolute. If the boy's task was not quite congenial, he meant to undertake it, which was satisfactory.

"There's another matter I want to talk about. That's a nice girl of Osborne's, though I guess you might do better."

Aynsley turned his head so he could see his father.

"The remark is obviously absurd, sir."

Clay chuckled.

"It's a proper feeling. I find no fault with it. Anyway, I'm glad to see that this time you're looking nearer your own level. I felt a bit worried about you some years ago."

Taken by surprise, as he was, the blood crept into Aynsley's face. He had been infatuated with a girl in a cigar store, and it was disconcerting to learn that his father had known all about the affair. Clay had said nothing, but Aynsley had no doubt that he would have acted had he thought it needful.

"Well," he said with some confusion, "I was at a sentimental age, but I wasn't so foolish as you seem to think. Miss Neston was quite good enough for me, and I'd like you to remember it, since you have mentioned the matter."

"We'll let it go," Clay answered dryly. "I guess you have a different idea of your value now. But you don't seem to be making much progress with Ruth Osborne. I suppose you really want her?"

They had passed the steepest pitch of the hill, but Aynsley threw in the lowest gear and turned quietly to his father.

"You have a rather crude way of putting things; but you can take it that I want her more than anything in the world."

"Very well. I can get her for you."

Aynsley made an abrupt movement, and then said slowly, "I think not. This is a matter in which you can't help me; I want you to understand it."

His resolute manner puzzled Clay, who had not often found him so determined.

"It seems to me that needs an explanation."

"Then I'll try to give you one. You have given me many things for which I'm grateful, and now that you have bought me the sawmill, I'll do the best I can with it. I've allowed you to choose my career; but I think I'm justified in choosing my wife myself."

"You're young," laughed Clay, "or you'd have learned that it's very seldom a man with red blood chooses his wife; in fact, it much oftener happens the other way about. He meets her and that settles him. If you'd been capable of going round with a list of qualifications looking for a girl who could satisfy them, you'd be no son of mine. However, I'm not dictating what you call your choice. I don't object to it; that's all."

"It's enough. How would you get Miss Osborne if I gave you permission?"

Though the question was awkward, Clay smiled. The boy was shrewder than he thought.

"Oh," he said, "I have some influence with Osborne. He owes me several favors."

"A man wouldn't give up his daughter in return for a favor. What is your hold on him?"

"I don't see much reason why you should know."

"You may be right." Aynsley's tone was determined as he continued: "Let's try to understand each other. If Miss Osborne marries me because that's her wish, I'll be a very fortunate man; but it's unthinkable that she should be forced to do so. I can't have any pressure put upon her father."

"When I want a thing, I get after it the best way I can."

"I believe that's true," Aynsley answered with a smile. "In this case, however, the way's important. I must ask you to leave it alone."

"Very well," acquiesced Clay. "As usual, though, I'll be around if you should want me. I guess I haven't failed you yet."

"You have not, Dad," Aynsley replied in an affectionate tone. "Sit tight; I'm going to stir up the machine."

CHAPTER XII

READY FOR THE FRAY

The train was held up on its way to the Canadian frontier by a wash-out farther along the track. Devereux Clay stood in the noon sunshine talking to Osborne at a small wayside station while groups of impatient passengers strolled about the line, stopping now and then to glance at a gap in the somber firs where the rails gleamed in the strong sunshine; the engineer, leaning out from his cab, had his eyes turned in the same direction. There was, however, nothing to be seen but climbing trees, whose ragged spires rose one behind the other far up the steep hillside, and the fragrance the hot noon sun drew out from them mingled with the sharp smell of creosote from the ties. Except for the murmur of voices and the panting of the locomotive pump, it was very quiet in the narrow clearing, and the sound of falling water came up faintly from a deep hollow where a lake glittered among the firs.

Clay leaned against the agent's wooden shack, with his watch in his hand, for time was of value to him just then.

"Twenty minutes yet, from what that fellow said," he grumbled. "Give me a cigar—I've run out—and you needn't wait."

"Oh, I'm in no hurry," said Osborne, glancing toward his automobile, which stood outside the station. "I suppose it's the labor trouble that's taking you to Vancouver?"

"You've hit it," Clay answered in a confidential tone. "I'm a bit worried about things; but I've spent the last two days wondering whether I'd go or not."

He was seldom so undecided, but Osborne thought he understood.

"It looks as if the unions meant business," he said, "and in this agitation against alien labor they seem to have public sympathy. Have you any Japs at the mill?"

"I believe so. That's partly why I'm going. Until I read the papers this morning I thought I'd stay away. I figured it might be better to let the boy worry through alone and see what he could make of it."

"Let him win his spurs?"

"That's right. I told him to sit tight, and so long as he made good I'd foot the bill; but after the big row in Vancouver yesterday, I thought

I'd go along. Still, my notion is to keep in the background unless I find I'm badly wanted."

His manner was half apologetic, and Osborne smiled. Clay was not addicted to hovering in the background when things were happening; but Osborne knew the affection he bore his son.

"It might be wiser for you to be on the spot; the white mob seems to be in an ugly mood," he said. "How is Aynsley getting on?"

"Better than I expected. The boy has the right grip and he's taking hold." Clay turned abruptly and fixed Osborne with his eyes. "I was a bit puzzled about his making up his mind all at once that he'd run the mill. Do you know of anything that might have helped to persuade him?"

"Since you ask, I have a suspicion," Osborne answered.

"So have I; I guess it matches yours. It's like the young fool that a word from a girl who knows less than he does should have more effect than all the reasons I gave him."

"It's not unnatural," Osborne smiled.

"Then suppose we're right in our idea of what this points to? You know my boy."

"I like him. Perhaps I'd better say that if I found that Ruth shared my good opinion, I shouldn't object. But I can't guess her views on the matter."

"I know Aynsley's," Clay said dryly. "We had a talk not long ago, and I offered to see what I could do."

Osborne gave him a searching glance and his expression changed. He looked on his guard.

"So far, you have been able to get your son everything he wished for; but you must understand that you can't dispose of my daughter. Ruth shall please herself."

Clay's eyes gleamed with rather hard amusement.

"It's curious that my boy said much the same thing. In fact, he warned me off. He knows how I've indulged him and seemed to think I might put some pressure on you."

"In the present instance it wouldn't have much effect; but what you say gives me a better opinion of Aynsley than I already had."

"That's all right," Clay rejoined, dropping his hand on the other's arm in a friendly manner. "We certainly can't afford to quarrel, and I don't know that it's unfortunate our children are more fastidious than we are. Anyway, we don't want them to find us out. I'd feel mean if my son disowned me."

Osborne winced at this allusion.

"Aynsley stands prosperity well," he said.

"In my opinion, it's considerably less damaging than the other thing. I'm thankful I've done the grubbing in the dirt for him. I've put him where it's easier to keep clean. So far as I can fix it, my boy shall have a better time than was possible for me. I've put him into business to teach him sense—I don't know a better education for any young man than to let him earn his bread and butter. He'll learn the true value of men and things; and when he's done that and shown he's capable of holding his own, he can quit and do what pleases him. I've no near relations, and there was a time when my distant connections weren't proud of me. Everything I have goes to the boy; and if your daughter will take him, I'd know he was in good hands. If she won't, I'll be sorry, but he must put up with it."

Osborne felt reassured. Clay had his good points, though they were not always very obvious, and perhaps the best was his affection for his son. Before Osborne could reply, Clay glanced again at his watch and resumed his usual somewhat truculent manner.

"If they get me into Vancouver after the trouble begins, I'll see the road bosses in Seattle and have the superintendent of this division fired!" he announced.

At that moment the telegraph began to tick in the shack, and shortly afterward the agent came up to Clay.

"They're through. We'll get you off in five minutes, and I have orders to cut out the next two stops," he said.

While he gave the conductor his instructions a shrill whistle rang through the shadows of the pines and a big engine with a row of flat cars carrying a gravel plow and a crowd of dusty men came clattering down the line. As they rolled into the side-track Clay climbed to the platform of his car, and almost immediately the train started. His face grew hard and thoughtful when he leaned back in a corner seat; and he had emptied the cigar-case his friend had given him before he reached Vancouver, where he hired the fastest automobile he could find.

While his father was being recklessly driven over a very rough road which ran through thick bush, Aynsley sat on a pile of lumber outside the mill with his manager. It was getting dark, the saws which had filled the hot air all day with their scream were still, and the river bank was silent except for the gurgle of the broad, green flood that swirled among the piles. A great boom of logs moored in an eddy worked with the swing of the current, straining at its chains; there was a red glimmer in the western sky, but trails of white mist gathered about the thinned forest that shut the clearing in. Only trees too small for cutting had been left, but the gaps between them were filled with massive stumps. Tall iron stacks, straggling sheds, and sawdust dumps took on a certain harsh picturesqueness in the fading light; and the keen smell of freshly cut cedar came up the faint breeze. But Aynsley had no eye for his surroundings. He was thinking hard.

After a brief experience, he had found, somewhat to his surprise, that his work was getting hold of him. The mechanical part of it in particular aroused his keen interest: there was satisfaction in feeling that the power of the big engines was being used to the best advantage. Then, the management of the mill-hands and the care of the business had their attractions; and Aynsley ventured to believe that he had made few mistakes as yet, though he admitted that his father had supplied him with capable assistants. Now, however, he must grapple with a crisis that he had not foreseen; and he felt his inexperience. There was, he knew, an easy way out of the threatened difficulties, but he could not take it. He must, so far as possible, deal effectively with an awkward situation, and, at the same time, avoid injustice, though that would complicate matters. The problem was not a novel one: he wanted to safeguard his financial interests and yet do the square thing.

"You think the Vancouver boys will come along and make trouble for us tonight, Jevons?" he asked presently.

The young manager nodded.

"That's what I'm figuring on; and it's quite likely the Westminster crowd will join them. They've been making ugly threats. I found this paper stuck up on the door when I made my last round."

Aynsley read the notice.

This is a white man's country. All aliens warned to leave. Those who stay and those who keep them will take the consequences.

"I suppose our keeping the Japs on is their only quarrel with us?"

"It's all they state."

"Well," Aynsley said slowly, "if we give way in this, I dare say they'd find something else to make trouble about. When you begin to make concessions you generally have to go on."

"That's so," agreed Jevons. "It looks to me as if the boys were driving their bosses, who can't pull them up; but those I've met are reasonable men, and when the crowd cools off a bit they'll get control again. They'd give us leave to run the mill if you fired the Japs."

Aynsley frowned.

"I have received their deputations civilly, and during the last week or two I've put up with a good deal. We pay standard wages and I don't think there's a man about the place who's asked to do more than he's able. But I can't have these fellows dictating whom I shall employ!"

"You have some good orders on the books for delivery on a time limit," Jevons reminded him. "You'll lose pretty smartly if we have to stop the mill."

"That's the trouble," Aynsley admitted. "I'd hate to lose the orders; but, on the other hand, I hired these Japs when I couldn't get white men, and I promised their boss I'd keep them until we'd worked through the log boom."

"You might call him up and ask what he'd take to quit. It might work out cheaper in the end."

Aynsley pondered this. Though he had not suspected it until lately, he had inherited something of his father's character. He had seldom thought much about money before he entered the mill, but since then he had experienced a curious satisfaction in seeing the balance to his credit mount up, and in calculating the profit on the lumber he cut. Now he found the suggestion that he should throw away part of his earnings frankly impossible. It was, however, not so much avarice as pride that influenced him. He had taken to business seriously, and he meant to show what he could do.

"No," he said decidedly. "I don't see why I should let the mob fine me for being honest. I'd rather fight, if I'm forced to; and I'm afraid you'll have to stand in."

Jevons laughed.

"I don't know that I'm anxious to back out. I tried to show you the easiest way, as a matter of duty; but there's a good deal to be said for the other course. I don't think there are any union boys still in the mill, and my notion is that the rancher crowd don't mean to quit."

Labor had been scarce that year, and Aynsley had engaged a number of small ranchers and choppers, who, as often happens when wages are high, had come down from their homesteads in the bush. They were useful men, of determined character, and were content with their pay.

"Well," he said, "we may as well ask what the Japs think of doing; but they're stubborn little fellows, and seem to have some organization of their own. Anyway, they whipped the mob pretty badly in Vancouver a day or two ago."

Their leader, being sent for, explained in good English that, as their honorable employer had hired them to do certain work which was not yet completed, they meant to stay. On being warned that this might prove dangerous, he answered darkly that they had taken precautions, and the danger might not be confined to them. Then, after some ceremonious compliments, he took his leave; and Aynsley laughed.

"That settles the thing! They won't go and I can't turn them out. I have some sympathy with the opposition's claim that this is a white man's country; but since they couldn't give me the help I wanted, I had to get it where I could. Now, we'll interview the white crowd."

They found the men gathered in the big sleeping-shed where the lamps had just been lighted. They were sturdy, hard-looking fellows, most of whom owned small holdings which would not support them in the bush, and they listened gravely while Aynsley spoke. Then one got up to reply for the rest.

"We've seen this trouble coming and talked it over. So long as you don't cut wages, we've nothing much to complain of and see no reason for quitting our job. Now, it looks as if the Vancouver boys were coming to turn us out. We'll let them—if they can!"

There was a murmur of grim approval from the rest; and Aynsley, dividing them into detachments, sent them off to guard the saws and booms and engine-house. Then he turned to the manager with a sparkle in his eyes.

"I think we're ready for anything that may happen. You'll find me in the office if I'm wanted."

On entering it he took down a couple of books from a shelf and endeavored to concentrate his attention on the business they recorded. It was the first serious crisis he had had to face, and he felt that hanging idly about the mill while he waited for the attack would be too trying. Somewhat to his surprise, he found his task engross him, and an hour had passed when he closed the books and crossed the floor to the open window.

It was a calm, dark night, and warm. A star or two glimmered above the black spires of the pines, but the mist that drifted along the waterside blurred the tall stacks and the lumber piles. There was no sign of the men; and the deep silence was emphasized by a faint hiss of steam and the gurgle of the river.

Leaning on the sill, Aynsley drank in the soft night air, which struck on his forehead pleasantly cool. He admitted that he was anxious, but he thought he could keep his apprehensions under good control.

As he gazed into the darkness, a measured sound stole out of the mist, and, growing louder, suggested a galloping horse. It approached the mill, but Aynsley did not go down. If anybody wanted him, it would be better that he should be found quietly at work in his office; and he was seated at his table with a pen in his hand when a man was shown in. The newcomer was neatly dressed except that his white shirt was damp and crumpled. His face was hot and determined.

"I've come to prevent trouble," he explained.

"I'm glad to hear it, because, as we both have the same wish, it ought to simplify things," Aynsley responded. "Since yours is the party with a grievance, you'd better tell me what you want."

"A written promise that you won't keep a Jap here after tomorrow morning."

"I can't give it," said Aynsley firmly. "I'll undertake to hire no more and to let these fellows go when they have finished the work I engaged them for, if that will do."

"It won't; I can't take that answer back to the boys. You must fire the Japs right off."

Aynsley leaned forward on the table with a patient sigh.

"Don't you understand that when two parties meet to arrange terms they can't both have all they want? The only chance of a settlement lies in a mutual compromise."

"You're wrong," said the stranger grimly. "The thing can be settled straight off if one of them gives in."

"Is that what you propose to do?"

"No, sir! I don't budge an inch! The boys wouldn't let me, even if I thought it wise."

"Then, as I can't go as far as you wish, there's no use in my making a move," Aynsley answered coolly. "It looks as if we had come to a standstill and there was nothing more to be said."

"I'll warn you that you're taking a big responsibility and playing a fool game."

"That remains to be seen. I needn't keep you, though I'm sorry we can't agree."

He went down with the man, and as they crossed the yard the fellow raised his voice.

"Come out from the holes you're hiding in, boys!" he cried. "Are you going to back the foreigners and employers against your friends?"

Aynsley touched his shoulder.

"Sorry, but we can't allow any speeches of that kind. You have an envoy's privileges, so long as you stick to them, but this is breaking all the rules."

"How will you stop me?" the fellow demanded roughly.

"I imagine you had better not satisfy your curiosity on that point," Aynsley answered. "The man yonder has your horse. I wish you good-night."

The envoy mounted and rode away into the darkness; and Aynsley sought his manager.

"I suspect his friends are not far off," he said. "We had better go round again and see that everything's ready."

CHAPTER XIII
THE REPULSE

The night was dark and the road bad, and Clay leaned forward in the lurching car, looking fixedly ahead. The glare of the head-lamp flickered across wagon ruts and banks of tall fern that bordered the uneven track, while here and there the base of a great fir trunk flashed suddenly out of the enveloping darkness and passed. Where the bush was thinnest, Clay could see the tiny wineberries glimmer red in the rushing beam of light, but all above was wrapped in impenetrable gloom. They were traveling very fast through a deep woods, but the road ran straight and roughly level, and talking was possible.

"You had trouble in the city lately. How did it begin?" Clay asked the driver. "I'm a stranger, and know only what's in your papers."

"The boys thought too many Japs were coming in," the man replied. "They corralled most of the salmon netting, and when there was talk about prices being cut, the white men warned them to quit."

He broke off as the car dropped into a hole, and it was a few moments later when Clay spoke.

"The Japs wouldn't go?"

"No, sir; they allowed they meant to hold their job; and the boys didn't make a good show when they tried to chase them off. Then, as they were getting other work into their hands, the trouble spread. The city's surely full of foreigners."

"You had a pretty big row a day or two ago."

"We certainly had," the driver agreed, and added, after a pause during which he avoided a deep rut, "The boys had fixed it up to run every blamed Asiatic out of the place."

"I understand they weren't able to carry their program out?"

"That's so. I've no use for Japs, but I'll admit they put up a good fight. Wherever the boys made a rush there was a bunch of them ready. You couldn't take that crowd by surprise. Then they shifted back and forward and slung men into the row just where they were wanted most. Fought like an army, and the boys hadn't made much of it when the police whipped both crowds off."

"Looks like good organization," Clay remarked. "It's useful to know what you mean to do before you make a start. Have the boys tried to run off those who are working at the outside mills?"

"Not yet, but we're expecting something of the kind. They'd whip them in bunches if they tried that plan."

This was what Clay feared; it was the method he would have used had he led the strikers. When a general engagement is risky, one might win by crushing isolated forces; and Aynsley's mill was particularly open to attack. It stood at some distance from both Vancouver and New Westminster, and any help that could be obtained from the civic authorities would probably arrive too late. There was, however, reason to believe that the aliens employed must have recognized their danger, and perhaps guarded against it. Clay knew something about Japs and Chinamen, and had a high respect for their sagacity.

He asked no more questions, and as the state of the road confined the driver's attention to his steering, nothing was said as they sped on through the dark. Sometimes they swept across open country where straggling split-fences streamed back to them in the headlamps' glare and a few stars shone mistily overhead. Sometimes they raced through the gloom beside a bluff, where dark fir branches stretched across the road and a sweet, resinous fragrance mingled with the smell of dew-damped dust. The car was traveling faster than was safe, but Clay frowned impatiently when he tried to see his watch. It was characteristic that although he was keenly anxious he offered the driver no extra bribe to increase the pace. He seldom lost his judgment, and the possibility of saving a few minutes was offset by the danger of their not arriving at all.

Presently they plunged into another wood. It seemed very thick by the way the hum of the engine throbbed among the trees, but outside the flying beam of the lamps all was wrapped in darkness. Clay was flung violently to and fro as the car lurched; but after a time he heard a sharp click, and the speed suddenly slackened.

"Why are you stopping?" he asked impatiently.

"Men on the road," explained the driver. "I'm just slowing down."

Clay could see nothing, but a sound came out of the gloom. There was a regular beat in it that indicated a body of men moving with some order.

"Hold on!" he cautioned, as the driver reached out toward the horn. "Let her go until we see who they are. I suppose there's no way round?"

"Not a cut-out trail until you reach the mill."

"Then we'll have to pass them. Don't blow your horn or pull up unless you're forced to."

The car slid forward softly and a few moments later the backs of four men appeared in the fan-shaped stream of light. As it passed them another four were revealed, with more moving figures in the gloom beyond. Most of them seemed to be carrying something in the shape of extemporized weapons, and their advance was regular and orderly. This was not a mob, but an organized body on its way to execute some well-thought-out plan. As the car drew nearer a man swung round with a cry, and the rearmost fours stopped and faced about. There was a murmur of voices farther in front; and, seeing no way through, the driver stopped, though the engine rattled on.

"Let us pass, boys; you don't want all the road," he called good-naturedly.

None of them moved.

"Where are you going?" one asked.

"To the Clanch Mill," answered the driver before Clay could stop him.

The men seemed to confer, and then one stood forward.

"You can't go there tonight. Swing her round and light out the way you came!"

Clay had no doubt of their object; and he knew when to bribe high.

"They'll jump clear if you rush her at them," he said softly. "A hundred dollars if you take me through!"

The car leaped forward, gathering speed with every second; and as it raced toward them the courage of the nearest failed. Springing aside they scrambled into the fern, and while the horn hooted in savage warning the driver rushed the big automobile into the gap.

For a few moments it looked as if they might get through. There was a confused shouting; indistinct, hurrying figures appeared and vanished as the shaft of light drove on. Some struck at the car as it passed them, some turned and gazed; but the men ahead were bolder, or perhaps more closely massed and unable to get out of the way in time.

"Straight for them!" cried Clay.

A man leaped into the light with a heavy stake in his hand.

The next moment there was a crash, and the car swerved, ran wildly up a bank, and overturned.

Clay was thrown violently forward, and fell, unconscious, into a brake of fern. When he came to, he was lying on his back with a group of men standing round him. He felt dazed and shaky, and by the smarting of his face he thought it was cut. When he feebly put up his hand to touch it he felt his fingers wet. Then one of the men struck a match and bent over him.

"Broken any bones?" he asked.

"No." Clay found some difficulty in speaking. "I think not, but I don't feel as if I could get up."

"Well," the man said, "it was your own fault; we told you to stop. Anyhow, you had better keep still a bit. If you're here when we come back, we'll see what we can do."

Glancing quickly round, Clay saw the driver sitting by the wrecked car; and then the match went out. In the darkness the nearest men spoke softly to one another.

"What were you going to the mill for?" one man asked him.

"I had some business there," Clay answered readily. "I buy lumber now and then."

The men seemed satisfied.

"Leave them alone," one suggested; "they'll make no trouble and it's time we were getting on."

The others seemed to agree, for there was some shouting to those in front, and the men moved forward. Clay heard the patter of their feet grow fainter, and congratulated himself that he had obviously looked worse than he felt. Now that the shock was passing, he did not think he was much injured, but he lay quiet a few minutes to recover before he spoke to the driver.

"How have you come off?" he asked.

"Wrenched my leg when she pitched me out; hurts when I move it, but I don't think there's anything out of joint."

"As soon as I'm able I'll have to get on. How far do you reckon it is to the mill?"

"About two miles."

Clay waited for some minutes and then got shakily up on his feet.

"You'll find me at the C.P.R. hotel tomorrow if I don't see you before," he said; and, pulling himself together with an effort, he limped away along the road.

For the first half-mile he had trouble in keeping on his feet; but as he went on his head grew clearer and his legs steadier, and after a while he was able to make a moderate pace. There was no sign of the strikers, who had obviously left him well behind, but he pushed on, hoping to arrive not very long after them, for it was plain that he would be wanted. He was now plodding through open country, but there was nothing to be seen except scattered clumps of trees and the rough fences along the road. No sound came out of the shadows and all was very still.

At last a dark line of standing timber rose against the sky, and when a light or two began to blink among the trees Clay knew he was nearer the mill. He quickened his speed, and when a hoarse shouting reached him he broke into a run. It was long since he had indulged in much physical exercise, and he was still shaky from his fall, but he toiled on with labored breath. The lights got brighter, but there was not much to be heard now; though he knew that the trouble had begun. He had no plans; it would be time to make them when he saw how things were going, for if Aynsley could deal with the situation he meant to leave it to him. It was his part to be on hand if he were needed, which was his usual attitude toward his son.

An uproar broke out as he ran through an open gate with the dark buildings and the lumber stacks looming in front. Making his way to one of the huge piles of lumber, he stopped in its shadow, breathing hard while he looked about.

The office was lighted, and the glow from its windows showed a crowd of men filling the space between the small building and the long saw-sheds. They were talking noisily and threatening somebody in the office, behind which, so far as Clay could make out, another body of men was gathered. Then the door opened, and he felt a thrill as Aynsley came out alone and stood where the light fell on him. He looked cool and even good-natured as he confronted the hostile crowd; nothing in his easy pose suggested the strain Clay knew he must be bearing. As he fixed his eyes on the straight, handsome figure and the calm face, Clay felt that his son was a credit to him.

"I'd hate to see you get into trouble for nothing, boys," Aynsley said in a clear voice. "If you'll think it over, you'll see that you have nothing against the management of this mill. We pay standard wages and engaged foreigners only when we could get nobody else. They'll be replaced by white men when their work is done."

"We've come along to see you fire them out tonight!" cried one of the strikers.

"I'm sorry that's impossible," Aynsley replied firmly.

"See here!" shouted another. "We've no time for foolin', and this ain't a bluffin' match! The boys mean business, and if you're wise, you'll do what they ask. Now, answer straight off: Have we got your last word on the matter?"

"Yes," said Aynsley; "you can take it that you have."

"That's all right," said the spokesman. "Now we know how we stand." He raised his voice. "Boys, we've got to run the blasted Japs off!"

There was a pause and a confused murmuring for nearly a minute. Clay, remaining in the shadow of the lumber, wondered whether it might not have been wiser had he struggled back to Vancouver in search of assistance; but, after all, the police had their hands full in the city, and he might not have been able to obtain it. Besides, he had been used to the primitive methods of settling a dispute in vogue on the Mexican frontier and in Arizona twenty years ago, and, shaken, bruised, and bleeding, as he was, his nerves tingled pleasantly at the prospect of a fight.

When the strikers began to close in on the office Clay slipped round the lumber stack, and was fortunate in finding Jevons, the manager.

"Mr. Clay!" exclaimed Jevons, glancing at his lacerated face.

"Sure," said Clay. "Don't mention that I'm here. My boy's in charge so long as he can handle the situation."

"It's ugly," declared Jevons. "Are you armed?"

"I have a pistol. Don't know that I can afford to use it. What's the program?"

Before Jevons could answer, there was a rush of dark figures toward the office, and a hoarse shout.

"The Japs first! Into the river with them!"

"Steady, boys!" Aynsley's voice rang out. "Hold them, saw gang A!"

A confused struggle began in the darkness and raged among the lumber stacks. Groups of shadowy figures grappled, coalesced into a fighting mass, broke apart, surged forward, and were violently thrust back. There was not much shouting and no shots were fired yet, but Clay was keenly watchful as he made his way from place to place, where resistance seemed weakest, and encouraged the defenders, who did not know him. With rude generalship he brought up men from the less threatened flank and threw them into action where help was needed; but he realized that the garrison was outnumbered and was being steadily pushed back.

They were, however, making a stubborn fight, and the conflict grew fiercer. Yells of rage and pain now broke through the sound of scuffling feet, stertorous breathing, and shock of blows; orders and threats were shouted, and Clay's face grew stern when one or two pistols flashed. He had found a big iron bar and was satisfied with it, but if forced to shoot he would not miss, as he thought the rioters did.

A red glow leaped up from the end of a shed. The blaze spread quickly; there was a sharp crackling, louder than the turmoil it broke in upon, and a cloud of pungent smoke hung above the struggling men. Clay could see their faces now: Japs and white men bunched together, but slowly giving ground, with his son in the midst of the surging, swaying cluster that bore the brunt of the attack.

It struck Clay, as he paused for a moment, that the little, sallow-faced aliens were remarkably cool, though it must be obvious to them that they were not holding their own. He wondered whether they had some plan in reserve. There was, however, no time to ponder this, for a pistol flashed among the rioters. The group that Aynsley led gave back and then drove forward again with a savage rush, while hoarse shouts went up.

"Stand them off while we take him out! Sock the fellow with the pistol; he's plugged the boss!"

Clay suddenly was filled with murderous fury. There was a good deal of the barbarian in him and he had led a hard, adventurous life. His son was shot. The brutes who had brought him down would suffer!

"I'm his father, boys!" he cried. "Follow me and drive the damned hogs into the river!"

The boldest closed in about him, a knot of determined men, small ranchers and prospectors who had long fought with flood and frost in the lonely hills. They were of sterner stuff than the city millhands, and, led by one who would go on until he dropped, they cleft the front of the mob like a wedge. The man with the pistol fired almost in their leader's face, and missed; but Clay did not miss with the bar, and he trod on the fellow's body as he urged on the furious charge.

It was a forlorn hope. Though for a time the men could not be stopped, the rioters closed in behind them, cutting off support. They could not keep up the rush, and presently they gained only a foot or two by desperate struggling. Clay knew their position was now dangerous. The strikers' passions were unloosed and no mercy would be shown; but this did not matter so long as he could leave his mark on some of his foes before they got him down. He fought with a cold fury that helped him to place his blows, and the long bar made havoc among the strikers; but soon he was hemmed in, with his back to a lumber pile, and he knew the end was near. Bruised, dazed, and bleeding, he stood wielding his weapon and sternly watching for a chance to strike.

Suddenly the crowd which pressed upon him gave back and he heard a rush of feet and alarmed shouts. There was a yell that was not made by white men; short, active figures, lithe and fierce as cats, fell with resistless fury upon the retreating foe. The retreat turned into a rout: the strikers were running for their lives, with a swarm of aliens in savage pursuit.

Clay saw that they outnumbered all the Japanese at the mill; but where they came from was not a matter of much consequence. He must rouse himself to take part in the chase, and exact full vengeance from the fugitives. The rioters fled along the bank, scrambled across the log booms, and took to the water; and Clay laughed harshly as he drove some of the laggards in. Whether they could swim or not was their own affair.

He went back to the office with an anxious heart, and a few minutes later he stood beside a camp bed in his son's quarters. He had lost his hat, his city coat was torn to rags, and his white shirt was stained with blood from the gash in his cheek; but he was unconscious of all this. Aynsley lay there, breathing feebly, with a drawn, white face and a small blue mark on his uncovered breast, while an ominous red froth gathered about his lips.

Clay placed his hand on the damp forehead, and the boy half opened his eyes.

"Do you know who I am?" his father asked.

"Sure!" Aynsley smiled feebly. "You said you wouldn't fail me. I suppose you whipped them?"

He turned his head and coughed, and Clay beckoned Jevons.

"Help me raise his shoulders a bit, and then I guess we'd better put some wet bandages on him. As they've cut the 'phone wires, send somebody to the nearest ranch for a horse to bring a doctor from Vancouver."

"I've done so," Jevons told him.

"Then send another man to Westminster, and we'll take the first doctor who gets through or keep them both."

They placed Aynsley in a position in which he could breathe more easily, and Clay gently wrapped him round with wetted rags.

"I don't know if this is the right thing, but it's all I can think of," he said. "We want to keep down any internal bleeding."

After this they waited anxiously for the doctor. Jevons presently crept out to restore order and to see that the fire had been extinguished; and Clay was left alone with his boy. There was no sound in the room where he sat, sternly watching over the unconscious form that lay so still on the bed.

After what seemed an interminable time Jevons opened the door softly.

"Has the doctor come?" Clay asked eagerly.

"Not yet. Any change?"

"None," said Clay. "He can't hear—I wish he could. Who were those fellows who came to the rescue?"

"City Japs, so far as I can learn. It seems they're pretty well organized, and suspecting a raid would be made on their partners here their committee sent a body out. I've been round the mill, and it looks as if a thousand dollars would cover—"

"Get out of here!" Clay exclaimed roughly. "I can't talk about the damage now. Watch for those doctors and bring them in right off!"

Jevons was glad to get away, but it was nearly daybreak when he returned with a surgeon from Vancouver. Shortly afterward the Westminster surgeon arrived, and the two doctors turned Clay out of the room. He paced up and down the corridor, tensely anxious. His own weakness, the ugly gash on his face—everything was forgotten except the danger in which his boy lay. After a while his head reeled, and he stopped and leaned on the rude banister, unconscious of the dizziness.

The first streaks of daylight were sifting into the room when Clay was permitted to enter. Aynsley lay in a stupor, but the doctors seemed satisfied.

"We got the bullet," one of them reported; "but there's still some cause for anxiety. However, we'll do our best to pull him through. Now you'd better let me dress your face: it needs attention."

Clay submitted to his treatment and then sat down wearily in a room below to wait for news.

CHAPTER XIV

FIGHTING FOR A LIFE

Aynsley lay in danger for a long time; and Clay never left the mill. At last, however, the boy began to recover slowly, but when he grew well enough to notice things the scream of the saws and the throb of the engines disturbed him. The light wooden building vibrated with the roar of the machinery; and when the machinery stopped the sound of the river gurgling about the log booms broke his sleep. He grumbled continually.

"How long does the doctor mean to keep me here?" he asked his father one day.

"I can't say, but I understand that you can't be moved just yet," Clay answered. "Aren't you comfortable?"

"Can you expect me to be, with the whole place jingling and shaking? If I'm to get better it must be away from the mill."

"I'll see what the doctor thinks; but there's the difficulty that I don't know where to take you. You wouldn't be much quieter in Seattle. It's curious, now I think of it, that I haven't had a home for a good many years, though I didn't seem to miss it until this thing happened."

Aynsley made a sign of languid agreement. He could not remember his mother, and his father had not kept house within his recollection. For the last few years he had rented luxurious rooms in a big hotel which Aynsley shared with him when not away visiting or on some sporting trip; but Aynsley now shrank from the lack of privacy and the bustle that went on all day and most of the night. There was not a restful nook in the huge, ornate building, which echoed with footsteps and voices, the clang of the street-cars, and the harsh grinding of electric elevators.

"I want to go somewhere where it's quiet," he said.

"Then I guess I'll have to hire a bushman's shack or take you to sea in the yacht. It never struck me before, but quietness is mighty hard to find in this country. We're not a tranquil people."

"I couldn't stand for a voyage," Aynsley grumbled. "She's a wet boat under sail if there's any breeze, and I don't want to crawl about dodging the water. Then the fool man who designed her put the only comfortable rooms where the propeller shakes you to pieces when the engines are going."

On the whole, Clay felt relieved, particularly as Aynsley's hardness to please implied that he was getting better. He had spent some time at the mill and had a number of irons in the fire. It would damage his business if they got overheated or perhaps cooled down before they could be used.

"Well," he suggested, "perhaps Osborne would take us in."

Aynsley's eyes brightened. Osborne's house was the nearest approach to a home he had ever known. It was seldom packed with noisy guests like other houses he visited, and one was not always expected to take part in some strenuous amusement. The place was quiet and beautiful and all its appointments were in artistic taste. He thought of it with longing as a haven of rest where he could gather strength from the pine-scented breezes and bask in Ruth's kindly sympathy.

"That would be just the thing! I feel that I could get better there. Will you write to him?"

"First mail," Clay promised with a twinkle; "but I'm not sure that Ruth's at home. Anyway, I've a number of letters to write now."

"I expect I've been pretty selfish in claiming all your time; but, if Osborne will have me, it will give you a chance of going up to town and looking after things."

"That's so," Clay replied. "As a matter of fact, some of them need it."

The doctor rather dubiously consented to his patient's being moved, and Clay neglected no precaution that might soften the journey. As he feared that the jolting of the railroad cars might prove injurious, a special room was booked on a big Sound steamer, and it was only Aynsley's uncompromising refusal to enter it that prevented his bringing out an ambulance-van to convey him to the wharf. He reached the vessel safely in an automobile, and as she steamed up the Sound he insisted on throwing off his wraps and trying to walk about. The attempt fatigued him, and he leaned on the rail at the top of a stairway from a lower deck when the steamer approached a pine-shrouded island.

A tide-race swirled past the point, flashing in the sunshine a luminous white and green, and Aynsley took his hand from the rail and stood unsupported watching the shore glide by. As he was facing, he could not see an ugly half-tide rock that rose out of the surging flood not far ahead, and he was taken off his guard when the helm was pulled hard over. The fast vessel listed with a sudden slant as she swung across the stream, and Aynsley, losing his balance, fell down a few stairs and struck a stanchion with his side. He clung to it, gasping and white in face, and when Clay ran down to him there was blood on his lips.

"I'm afraid the confounded thing has broken out again," he said.

They carried him into the saloon, and Clay summoned the captain, who came docilely at his bidding. It appeared that there was no doctor among the passengers, and the boat was billed to call at several places before she reached Seattle. None of these stops could be cut out, and the captain suggested that it would be better to land the injured man as intended, and send for assistance by fast automobile. Aynsley nodded feebly when he heard this.

"Put me ashore," he murmured. "I'll be all right there."

An hour later the call of the whistle rang among the pines that rolled down to the beach, and as the side-wheels beat more slowly a launch came off across the clear, green water. Aynsley, choking back a cough, feebly raised himself.

"If Ruth's on board that boat, she mustn't be scared," he said. "I'm going down as if there was nothing wrong."

"You're going down in the arms of the two biggest seamen I can get," Clay replied. "If that doesn't please you, we'll lower you in a slung chair."

Aynsley submitted when he found that he could not get up; and Ruth, sitting with her father in the stern of the launch, started as she saw him carried down the gangway. His face was gray and haggard when they laid him on a cushioned locker, and the girl was moved to pity. But the shock resolved some doubts that had long troubled her. She was startled and sorry for Aynsley, but that was all; she did not feel the fear and the suspense which she thought might have been expected.

Ansley saw her grave face, and looked up with a faint smile.

"I feel horribly ashamed," he said. "If I'd known I'd make a fool of myself—"

"Hush!" Ruth laid her hand on him with a gentle, restraining touch as she saw the effort it cost him to speak. "You must be quiet. We are going to make you better."

"Yes," he said disjointedly. "I've been longing—knew I'd get all right here—but I didn't expect—to turn up like this—"

A choking cough kept him still, and he hurriedly wiped his lips with a reddened handkerchief.

"I am afraid it may be very bad," Clay whispered to Osborne. "Some miles to the nearest 'phone call, isn't it?"

Osborne nodded affirmatively, and as they neared the beach he waved his hand to a man on the lawn.

"Car!" he shouted. "Get her out! I'll tie up the boat."

With some trouble Aynsley was carried into the house, and the doctor who arrived some hours later looked grave when he saw him. The next morning he brought two nurses, and for several days his patient hovered between life and death. He was delirious most of the time, but there were intervals when his fevered brain partly recovered its balance and he asked for Ruth. It was seldom that he spoke to her sensibly when she came, but it was obvious that her presence had a soothing effect, for his eyes followed her with dull satisfaction, and a few quiet words from her would sometimes lull him to the sleep he needed.

Ruth felt her power, and used it for his benefit without hesitation and without much thought about its cause. She was filled with pity and with a curious, protective tenderness for the man, and there was satisfaction in feeling that he needed her. It was her duty and pleasure to assist as far as possible in his recovery. Clay watched her with growing admiration, and sometimes she became disturbed under his searching glance. She felt that he was curious about the motive which sustained her in her task, and this caused her some uneasiness, for she suspected that she might presently have to make it clear to herself and to others. But the time for this had not come. Aynsley was still in danger, and all concerned must concentrate their attention on the fight for his life.

Once when she left his room with an aching head and heavy eyes after a long watch with the nurse, who could not control her fevered patient without the girl's assistance, Clay met her on the stairs, and as he gave her a swift, inquiring glance, she saw that his face was worn.

"Asleep at last," she said. "I think he'll rest for a few hours."

He looked at her with gratitude and some embarrassment, which was something she had never seen him show.

"And you?" he asked. "How much of this can you stand for?"

Ruth did not think the question was prompted by consideration for her. He would be merciless in his exactions, but she could forgive him this because it was for his son's sake. Besides, there was subtle flattery in his recognition of her influence.

"I dare say I can hold out as long as I am needed," she answered with a smile. "After all, the nurses and the doctor are the people on whom the worst strain falls."

"Bosh!" he exclaimed with rough impatience. "I guess you know you're more use than all three together. Why that's so doesn't matter at present; there the thing is."

Ruth blushed, though she was angry with herself as she felt her face grow hot, because she had no wish that he should startle her into any display of feeling; but, to her relief, he no longer fixed his eyes on her.

"My dear," he said, "I want your promise that you'll pull him through. You can, if you are determined enough; and he's all I have. Hold him back—he's been slipping downhill the last few days—and there's nothing you need hesitate about asking from me."

"Though it may not be much, I'll do what I can." Ruth's tone was slightly colder. "But one does not expect—"

"Payment for a kindness?" Clay suggested. "Well, I suppose the best things are given for nothing and can't be bought, but that has not been my luck. What I couldn't take by force I've had to pay for at full market price. The love of a bargain is in my blood. Pull my son through, and whatever I can do for you won't make me less your debtor."

Ruth was silent a moment. She had of late been troubled by a vague uneasiness on her father's account, and with a sudden flash of insight she realized that it might be well to have the man's gratitude.

"After all, I may ask you for a favor some day," she answered, smiling.

"You won't find me go back on my word," he promised.

Strolling to a seat by the waterside, he lighted a cigar and tried to analyze his feelings, which were somewhat puzzling. Aynsley longed for the girl, and Clay approved his choice; he had hitherto given the boy all that he desired, but there was now a difference. While he had a freebooter's conscience, and would willingly have seized by force what would please his son, he felt that Ruth Osborne was safe from his generally unsparing grasp. It was true that Aynsley had demanded a pledge of inaction, but Clay was not sure that this alone would have deterred him. He felt that his hands were tied, and he could not understand the reason. However, Aynsley was young and rich and handsome; he would be a fool if he could not win the girl on his own merits. Then the crushing anxiety Clay had thrown off for a few minutes returned. After all, the boy might not live to prosper in his suit.

It was two or three days later when Clay met the doctor coming downstairs late one evening, and led him into the hall.

"The boy's not coming round," he said shortly. "What do you think? Give it to me straight; I've no use for professional talk."

"I'm frankly puzzled. He's certainly no better, though I've seen some hopeful symptoms. It's no longer what I'll call the mechanical injury that's making the trouble; we have patched that up. His feverish restlessness is burning up his strength; and Miss Osborne is the only person who can calm him. In fact, the way he responds to her is rather remarkable."

"Never mind that!" Clay interrupted. "It isn't what I asked."

"Well, I'm inclined to look for a crisis tonight. If he gets through the early morning, things may take a turn; but a good deal depends on his sleeping, and I've given him all the sedatives I dare. Miss Osborne has promised to keep watch with the nurse, though she looks badly tired."

Clay turned away, and the anxious hours that followed left their mark on him. Men called him hard and callous, but he loved his son, and Aynsley was moreover the object of all his ambitions. Social popularity and political influence had no charms for Clay; commercial control and riches were his aim. He knew his ability as a gatherer, but he did not know how to spend, and, when the boy had made good in the business world, he should have the best that society and culture could give. Now, however, a few hours would determine whether all Clay's hopes must crumble into dust. He trusted the doctor; but, having a strong man's suspicion of medicine, he trusted Ruth Osborne more.

As a matter of fact he was justified, for Ruth did her part that night. It was hot and still, and the door and the window of the sick room were opened. A small, carefully shaded lamp diffused a dim light, and now and then a passing draught stirred the curtains and brought in a faint coolness and the scent of the pines. The tired girl found it wonderfully refreshing as she sat near the bed in a straight-backed chair: she dare not choose one more comfortable lest drowsiness overpower her.

Aynsley was restless, but she thought rather less so than usual, and now and then he spoke feebly but sensibly.

"You won't go away," he begged once in a weak voice, and she smiled reassuringly as she laid a cool hand on his hot, thin arm.

For a while he lay with closed eyes, though he did not seem to sleep, and then, opening them suddenly, he looked round with eagerness as if in search of her.

"That fellow means to get me; he won't miss next time!" he murmured later, and she supposed his wandering mind was occupied with memories of the affray at the mill. Then he added with difficulty: "You'll stand him off, won't you? You can, if you want."

"Of course," Ruth said with compassion and half admiring sympathy, for she was young enough to set a high value on physical courage and manly strength, and her patient, though so pitifully helpless now, had bravely held his post. It was daunting to see this fine specimen of virile manhood brought so low.

When the doctor came in some time later he looked down at Aynsley before he turned to Ruth.

"No sleep yet?" he asked softly.

Aynsley heard him and looked up.

"No," he murmured. "I'm very tired, but I can't rest. How can I when those brutes are burning the gang-saw shed?"

The doctor gave Ruth a warning glance, whispered to the nurse, and went out, passing Clay, who had crept upstairs without his shoes and stood lurking in the shadow on the landing.

"No change," he said, and drew the anxious man away.

It was after midnight now and getting colder. There was no sound in the house, and none from outside, except when now and then a faint elfin sighing came from the tops of the pines. A breeze was waking, and Ruth, oppressed by the heat and fatigue, was thankful for it. She looked at her watch, and then wrapped it in a handkerchief because its monotonous ticking had grown loud in the deep silence. She knew that the dreaded time when human strength sinks lowest was near, and she felt with a curious awe that death was hovering over her patient's bed.

"I can't see," he said very faintly, and stretching out a thin hand searched for touch of her.

She took it in a protecting grasp, and Aynsley sighed and lay quiet. After a while the doctor came in again, noiselessly, and, looking down at the motionless figure, nodded as if satisfied, while Ruth sank into the most comfortable pose she could adopt. It was borne in upon her as she felt his fingers burn upon her hand that she was holding Aynsley's life; and whatever the effort cost her she must not let go. Soon she grew cramped and longed to move, but that was impossible: Aynsley was asleep at last, and it might be fatal to disturb him. Then, though she tried to relax her muscles, the strain of the fixed pose became intolerable; but she called up all her resolution and bore it. After all, the pain was welcome, because it kept her awake, and she was getting very drowsy.

Clay, creeping up again, stopped outside the door. He could not see his son, but he watched the girl with a curious stirring of his heart. The dim light fell on her face, showing the weariness and pity in it, and the man, though neither a sentimentalist nor imaginative, was filled with a deep respect. He could not think it was a woman's tenderness for her lover he saw. There was no hint of passion in her fixed and gentle eyes; hers was a deep and, in a sense, an imper- sonal pity, protective and altogether unselfish; and he wondered, half abashed, how she would have looked had she loved his son. Then, encouraged by her attitude and the quietness of the nurse, he softly moved away.

Day was breaking when the doctor came down into the hall, followed by Ruth, and stopped when Clay beckoned him.

"My news is good," he said. "He's sound asleep, and I think the worst is past."

He moved on, and Clay turned to Ruth, feeling strangely limp with the reaction. The girl's face was white and worn, but it was quiet, and Clay noticed with a pang the absence of exultant excitement.

"It's you I have to thank," he said hoarsely. "I want you to remember that my promise holds good."

"Yes," Ruth answered with a languid smile. "Still, that doesn't seem to matter and I'm very tired."

He moved aside to let her pass, and watched her with a heartfelt gratitude as she went slowly down a corridor.

CHAPTER XV
ILLUMINATION

The scent of the pines was heavy in the languid air. Bright sunshine fell upon the grass, and the drowsy stillness was scarcely broken by the splash of ripples on the beach. Aynsley, now fast recovering, lay in a couch hammock where a patch of shadow checkered the smooth expanse of Osborne's lawn. His face was thin, and his eyes were half closed, though he was by no means asleep. The glare tired him, but his mind was busy and he was tormented by doubts.

Ruth sat near him with a book, from which she had been reading aloud. Her thin summer dress clung in graceful lines to her finely molded figure; the large hat cut off the light from her face, which was quietly serious, and there was a delicacy in its coloring and a curious liquid glow in her eyes.

Aynsley was not an artist, but the picture she made filled him with a sense of harmonious beauty. There was a repose about the girl which generally had its effect on him; but as he watched her Aynsley felt the hard throbbing of his heart. He had admired her greatly since they first met, and it was now some time since appreciation had grown into love; but the man was shrewd in some respects, and had seen that her inclination was not toward him. She was too friendly, too frankly gracious; he would rather have noticed some shy reserve. He had waited with strong patience, until her tender care of him in his illness had given him a vague hope. He feared it might prove illusory, but he could keep his secret no longer, and summoned courage to test his fortune.

"Ruth," he said, "I'll have to get back to the mill next week. Though it has been very pleasant, I've been loafing long enough."

She looked up abruptly, for her thoughts had been far away and he had held no place in them.

"I suppose you must go when you are strong enough," she answered rather absently. "Still, you have not recovered, and perhaps they can get on without you."

This was not encouraging. Her tone was kind, but she had shown no anxiety to detain him, and if she had wished to do so it would have been easy to give him a hint. For all that, he must learn his fate.

"It's possible; in fact, I've a suspicion that they get on better when I'm away; but that is not the point. I've been here some time, and have made a good many demands on you. Now that you have cured me, I have no excuse for abusing your good nature."

"You're not abusing it," she responded in a friendly tone. "Besides, if you need the assurance, I enjoyed taking care of you. Though the nurses really did the work, it's nice to feel oneself useful."

Though she smiled he was not much cheered. The care she had given him was, in a sense, impersonal: she would have been as compassionate to a stranger.

"I can understand," he said. "You are full of kindness, and must, so to speak, radiate it. It's a positive relief to you. Anyway, that's fortunate for me, because I shouldn't have been lying here, almost fit now, if you hadn't taken me in hand."

"That's exaggeration," she replied with a faint blush, which he seized upon as the first favorable sign.

"Not at all," he declared firmly. "You saved my life; I knew it when I wakened up the morning the fever left me, and the doctor practically admitted it when I asked him." He paused and gave her a steady look, though his heart was beating fast. "And since you saved it, my life belongs to you. It's a responsibility you have incurred. Anyway, the life you gave me back when I'd nearly lost it is a poor thing, and not much use to me unless I can persuade you to share it. Perhaps, in good hands, it's capable of improvement."

Ruth was moved. She saw the deep trust and the longing in his eyes, and he had spoken with a touch of humor, which, she thought, was brave because it covered his want of hope. She could not doubt his love, and she knew it was worth much. The knowledge brought the color to her face and disturbed her.

"Aynsley," she said, "I'm sorry, but—"

He made a protesting gesture.

"Wait a minute! You did not know that I loved you. I read that in your friendly candor. I felt that I was aiming too high but I couldn't give up the hope of winning you some day, and I meant to be patient. Now I expect you have got a painful shock; but I'm going away next week—and I was swept off my feet."

"It isn't a shock," she answered with a smile that hid some confusion. "You're too modest, Aynsley; any sensible girl would feel proud of your offer. But, for all that, I'm afraid—"

"Please think it over," he begged. "Though I'm by no means what you have a right to expect, there's this in my favor that, so far as I'm capable of it, you can make what you like of me. Then I'm starting on a new career, and there's nobody who could help me along like you."

Ruth was silent for a few moments, lost in disturbing thought. She knew his virtues and his failings, and she trusted him. Now she realized with a sense of guilt that she had not been quite blameless. She had seen his love for her, and, while she had never led him on, she might have checked him earlier; she could not be sure that she had altogether wished to do so. She was fond of him; indeed, she was willing to love him, but somehow was unable to do so.

"Aynsley," she said, "I'm more sorry than I can tell you; but you really must put me out of your mind."

"It's going to be difficult," he answered grimly. "But I believe you like me a little?"

"I think the trouble is that I like you too much—but not in the way that you wish."

"I understand. I've been too much of a comrade. But if I were very patient, you might, perhaps, get to like me in the other way?"

"It would be too great a risk, Aynsley."

"I'll take it and never blame you if you find the thing too hard." The eagerness suddenly died out of his voice. "But that would be very rough on you—to be tied to a man—" He broke off and was silent for a moment before he looked up at her with grave tenderness. "Ruth dear, is it quite hopeless?"

"I'm afraid so," she said softly, but with a note in her voice which Aynsley could not misinterpret.

"Very well," he acquiesced bravely. "I have to fight this thing, but you shall have no trouble on my account. I find the light rather strong out here; if you will excuse me, I think I'll go in."

Rising with obvious weakness, he moved off toward the house; and Ruth, realizing that he had been prompted by consideration for her, sat still and wondered why she had refused him. He was modest, brave, unselfish, and cheerful; indeed, in character and person he was all that she admired; but she could not think of him as her husband. She pondered it, temporizing, half afraid to be quite honest with herself, until in a flash the humiliating truth was plain and she blushed with shame and anger. The love she could not give Aynsley had already been given, unasked, to another who had gone away and forgotten her.

She knew little about him, and she knew Aynsley well. Aynsley was rich, and Jimmy was obviously poor—he might even have other disadvantages; but she felt that this was relatively of small importance. Somehow he belonged to her, and, though she struggled against the conviction, she belonged to him. That was the end of the matter.

Growing cooler, she began to reason, and saw that she had blamed herself too hastily. After all, though Jimmy had made no open confession, he had in various ways betrayed his feelings, and there was nothing to prove that he had forgotten her. Poverty might have bound him to silence; moreover, there was reason to believe that he was away in a lonely region, cut off from all communication with the outer world. Perhaps he often thought about her; but these were futile speculations, and banishing them with an effort she went into the house.

The next day Clay found Ruth sitting on the veranda.

"So you would not have my boy!" he said abruptly.

"Has he told you?" she asked with some embarrassment.

"Oh, no! But I'm not a fool, and his downcast look was hint enough. I don't know if you're pleased to hear he has taken the thing to heart. It ought to be flattering."

"I'm very sorry." Ruth's tone was indignant. "I think you are unjust."

"And showing pretty bad taste? Well, I'm not a man of culture, and I'm often unpleasant when I'm hurt. I suppose you know the boy had set his whole mind on getting you? But of course you knew it, perhaps for some time; you wouldn't be deceived on a point like that."

"I can't see what you expect to gain by trying to bully me!" Ruth flashed at him angrily, for her conscience pricked her.

Clay laughed with harsh amusement. He had broken many clever and stubborn men who had stood in his way, and this inexperienced girl's defiance tickled him.

"My dear," he said, "I'm not trying to do anything of the kind. If I were, I'd go about it on a very different plan. Aynsley's a good son, a straight man without a grain of meanness, and you could trust him with your life."

"Yes," she answered softly, "I know. I'm very sorry—I can't say anything else."

Clay pondered for a few moments. Her frank agreement disarmed him, but he could not understand his forbearance. He had won Aynsley's mother in the face of the determined opposition of her relatives, and there was a primitive strain in him. Had all this happened when he was younger he would have urged his son to carry Ruth off by force, and now, although the times had changed, there were means by which she could, no doubt, be compelled to yield. Still, although he was not scrupulous, and it might be done without Aynsley's knowledge, he would not consider it. She had saved the boy's life, and he had, moreover, a strange respect for her.

"Well," he conceded, "you look as if you knew your mind, and I guess Aynsley must make the best of it."

Ruth was relieved when he left her, but she was also puzzled by a curious feeling that she was no longer afraid of him. In spite of his previous declaration of gratitude, she had dreaded his resentment; and now that uneasiness had gone. He had said nothing definite to reassure her, but she felt that while he regretted her refusal, she could look upon him as a friend instead of a possible enemy.

During the evening she told her father, who had been absent for a day or two.

"I am not surprised," he said; "I even hoped you would take him. However, it's too late now, and if you hadn't much liking for Aynsley I wouldn't have urged you."

"I was sure of that," Ruth said with an affectionate glance.

"How did Clay take your refusal of his son?"

"I think he took it very well. He paid me a compliment as he went away."

She noticed her father's look of relief, and it struck her as being significant.

"You have reason to feel flattered," he said, "because Clay's apt to make trouble when he is thwarted. For all that, it's unfortunate your inclinations didn't coincide with his wishes."

"Why?" Ruth asked sharply.

Osborne looked amused at her bluntness.

"Well, I really think Aynsley has a good deal to recommend him: money, position, pleasant manners, and an estimable character. Since you're not satisfied, it looks as if you were hard to please."

"I have no fault to find with him," Ruth answered with a blush. "Still, one doesn't make up a list of the good qualities one's husband ought to have."

"It might not be a bad plan," Osborne said humorously; "anyway, if you could find a man to meet the requirements." He dropped his bantering manner. "I'm sorry you dismissed Aynsley, but if you are satisfied that it was best, there's no more to be said."

He turned away, and Ruth pondered what she had heard. It was plain that her father shrank from offending Clay; and that seemed to confirm the vague but unpleasant suspicions she had entertained about their business relations. Somehow she felt that not yet had she got at the bottom of her father's dealings with that man.

CHAPTER XVI

A GHOST OF THE PAST

It was the evening before Aynsley's departure, and he and Clay and the Osbornes were sitting on the veranda. Not a breath of wind was stirring, and the inlet stretched back, smooth as oil and shining in the evening light. The tops of the tall cedars were motionless; not a ripple broke upon the beach; the only sound was the soft splash of water somewhere among the trees.

The heat had been trying all day, and Aynsley glanced languidly at the faint white line of snow that rose above the silver mist in the blue distance.

"It would be cool up there, and that snow makes one long for the bracing North," he said. "This is one of the occasions when I don't appreciate being a mill owner. Tomorrow I'll be busy with dusty books, in a stifling office that rattles with the thumping of engines."

"It's good for a man to work," Miss Dexter remarked.

"No doubt, but it has its disadvantages now and then, as you would agree if a crowd of savage strikers had chased you about your mill. Then, if it weren't for my business ties, I'd send the captain word to get steam up on the yacht, and take you all to the land of mist and glaciers, where you can get fresh air to breathe."

"Wouldn't you miss the comforts, though I dare say you call them necessities, that surround you here? One understands that people live plainly in Alaska."

Miss Dexter indicated the beautifully made table which stood within reach, set out with glasses and a big silver tankard holding iced liquor. Round this, choice fruit from California was laid on artistic plates.

"We could take some of them along; and we're not so luxurious as you think," Aynsley replied. "In fact, I feel just now that I'd rather live on canned goods and splash about in the icy water, like some fishermen we met, than sit in my sweltering office, worrying over accounts and labor troubles."

"Those fishermen seem to stick in your memory," Ruth interposed.

"Is it surprising? You must admit that they roused even your curiosity, and you hadn't my excuse because you hadn't seen them."

"What fishermen were they?" Clay asked.

Ruth wished she had not introduced the subject.

"Some men he met on an island in the North," she said with a laugh. "Aynsley seems to have envied their simple life, and I dare say it would be pleasant in this hot weather. Still, I can't imagine his seriously practising it; handling wet nets and nasty, slimy fish, for example."

"It wasn't the way they lived that impressed me," Aynsley explained. "It was the men. With one exception, they didn't match their job; and so far as I could see, they hadn't many nets. Then something one fellow said suggested that he didn't care whether they caught much fish or not."

"After all, they may have been amateur explorers like yourself, though they weren't fortunate enough to own a big yacht. I don't suppose you would have been interested if you had known all about them."

"Where was the island?" Clay broke in.

Aynsley imagined that Ruth was anxious to change the subject, and he was willing to indulge her.

"I remember the latitude," he said carelessly, "but there are a lot of islands up there, and I can't think of the longitude west."

Clay looked sharply at Osborne, and Ruth noticed that her father seemed disturbed.

"I guess you could pick the place out on the chart?" Clay asked Aynsley.

"It's possible. I don't, however, carry charts about. They're bulky things, and not much use except when you are at sea."

"I have one," said Osborne and Ruth felt anxious when he rang a bell.

She suspected that she had been injudicious in starting the topic, and she would rather it were dropped, but she hesitated about giving Aynsley a warning glance. His father might surprise it, and she would have to offer Aynsley an explanation afterward. Getting up, she made the best excuse that occurred to her and went into the house. She knew where the chart was kept, and thought that she might hide it. She was too late, however, because as she took it from a bookcase a servant opened the door.

"Mr. Osborne sent me for a large roll of thick paper on the top shelf," the maid said.

As she had the chart in her hands, Ruth was forced to give it to the girl, and when she returned to the veranda Aynsley pointed out the island. Ruth saw her father's lips set tight.

"What kind of boat did the fellows have?" Clay asked.

"She was quite a smart sloop, but very small." Aynsley tried to lead his father away from the subject. "At least, that was the rig she'd been intended for, by the position of the mast, but they'd divided the single headsail for handier working. After all, we're conservative in the West, for you'll still find people sticking to the old big jib, though it's an awkward sail in a breeze. They've done away with it on the Atlantic coast, and I sometimes think we're not so much ahead of the folks down East—"

"What was her name?" Clay interrupted him.

Aynsley saw no strong reason for refusing a reply, particularly as he knew that if he succeeded in putting off his father now, the information would be demanded later.

"She was called Cetacea."

Ruth unobtrusively studied the group. Miss Dexter was frankly uninterested; and Aynsley looked as if he did not know whether he had done right or not. Osborne's face was firmly set and Clay had an ominously intent and resolute expression. Ruth suspected that she had done a dangerous thing in mentioning the matter, and she regretted her incautiousness; though she did not see where the danger lay. For all that, she felt impelled to learn what she could.

"Was it the island where you were wrecked?" she asked Clay.

He looked at her rather hard, and then laughed.

"I think so, but the experience was unpleasant, and I don't feel tempted to recall the thing."

Afterward he talked amusingly about something else, and half an hour had passed when he got up.

"I expect it's cooler on the beach," he said. "Will any of you come along?"

They sat still, except Osborne, who rose and followed him, and when they reached a spot where the trees hid them from the house Clay stopped.

"I suppose what you heard was a bit of a shock," he remarked.

"It was a surprise. I don't think you were tactful in making so much of the affair."

"One has to take a risk, and if I'd waited until I had Aynsley alone and then made him tell me what he knew, it might have looked significant. In a general way, the thing you're willing to talk over in public isn't of much account."

"There's truth in that," Osborne assented.

"I have no wish to set the boy thinking," Clay resumed. "I take it we're both anxious that our children should believe the best of us."

His glance was searching, and Osborne made a sign of agreement.

"What are you going to do about it?"

"Trace the sloop. We don't want mysterious strangers prospecting round that reef. When I've found out all I can, the fellows will have to be bought or beaten off."

"Very well; I leave the thing to you."

"Rather out of your line now?" Clay suggested with an ironical smile. "However, I will admit you deserve some sympathy."

"For that matter, we both need it. You're no better off than I am."

"I think I am," Clay replied. "My character is pretty well known and has been attacked so often that nobody attaches much importance to a fresh disclosure; in fact, people seem to find something humorous in my smartness. You're fixed differently; though you slipped up once, you afterward took a safe and steady course."

Osborne lighted a cigar to hide his feelings; for his companion's jibe had reached its mark. He had when poverty rendered the temptation strong, engaged in an unlawful conspiracy with Clay, and the profit he made by it had launched him on what he took care should be a respectable business career. Now and then, perhaps, and particularly when he acted in concert with Clay, his dealings would hardly have passed a high standard of ethics, but on the whole they could be defended, and he enjoyed a good name on the markets. Now a deed he heartily regretted, and would have undone had he been able, threatened to rise from the almost forgotten past and torment him. Worse than all, he might again be forced into a crooked path to cover up his fault.

"We won't gain anything by arguing who might suffer most," he said as coolly as he could.

"No; I guess that's useless," Clay agreed. "Well, I must get on those fellows' trail and see what I can do."

They strolled along the beach for a while, and then went back to the others.

While Clay traced her movements as far as they could be learned, the Cetacea was slowly working north. She met with light, baffling winds, and calms, and then was driven into a lonely inlet by a fresh gale. Here she was detained for some time, and adverse winds still dogged her course when she put to sea again, though they were no longer gentle, but brought with them a piercing rawness from the Polar ice. Her crew grew anxious and moody as they stubbornly thrashed her to windward under shortened sail, for every day at sea increased the strain on their finances and the open-water season was short.

In the sharp cold of a blustering morning Jimmy got up from the locker upon which he had spent a few hours in heavy sleep. His limbs felt stiff, his clothes were damp, and at his first move he bumped his head against a deck-beam. Sitting down with muttered grumbling, he pulled on his soaked knee-boots and looked moodily about. Daylight was creeping through the cracked skylight, and showed that the underside of the deck was dripping. Big drops chased one another along the slanted beams and fell with a splash into the lee bilge. Water oozed in through the seams on her hove-up weather side and washed about the lower part of the inclined floor, several inches deep. The wild plunging and the muffled roar outside the planking showed that she was sailing hard and the wind was fresh.

Jimmy grumbled at his comrades for not having pumped her out, and then shivered as he jammed himself against the centerboard trunk and tried to light the rusty stove. It was wet and would not draw and the smoke puffed out. He was choking and nearly blinded when he put the kettle on and went up on deck, somewhat short in temper. Moran was sitting stolidly at the helm, muffled in a wet slicker, with the spray blowing about him; Bethune crouched in the shelter of the coaming, while white-topped seas with gray sides tumbled about the boat. An angry red flush was spreading, rather high up, in the eastern sky.

"You made a lot of smoke," Bethune remarked.

"I did," said Jimmy. "If you'll get forward and swing the funnel-cowl, which you might have done earlier, you'll let some of it out. I'm glad it's your turn to cook, but you had better spend ten minutes at the pump before you go."

Bethune, rising, stretched himself with an apologetic laugh.

"Oh, well," he said; "I was so cold I felt I didn't want to do anything."

"It's not an uncommon sensation," Jimmy replied. "The best way to get rid of it is to work. If you'll shift that cowl, I'll prime the pump."

Bethune shuffled forward, and, coming back, pumped for a few strokes. Then he stopped and leaned on the handle.

"You really think we'll raise the island today?" he asked.

"Yes. But it isn't easy to shoot the sun when you can hardly see it and have a remarkably unsteady horizon. Then, though she has laid her course for the last two days, I haven't much confidence in the log we're towing."

He indicated the wet line that ran over the stern and stretched back to where a gleam of brass was visible in the hollow of a sea.

"What could you expect?" Bethune asked. "We got the thing for half its proper price, and, to do it justice, it goes pretty well after a bath in oil, and when it stops it does so altogether. You know how to deal with a distance recorder that sticks and stays so, but one that sticks and goes on again plays the devil."

"Talking's easier than pumping," Jimmy said suggestively.

"It is, but I feel like working off a few more remarks. They occurred to me while I sat behind the coaming, numbed right through, last night. I suppose you have noticed how the poor but enterprising man is generally handicapped. He gets no encouragement in taking the hard and virtuous path. It needs some nerve to make a start, and afterward, instead of things getting easier, you fall in with all kinds of obstacles you couldn't reasonably expect. Even the elements conspire against you; it's always windward work."

"I suppose this means you're sorry you came?"

"Not exactly; but I've begun to wonder what's the good of it all. I haven't slept in dry clothes for a fortnight. It's a week since any of us had a decent meal; and my slicker has rubbed a nasty sore on my wrist. All the time I could have had three square meals a day, and spent my leisure reading a dirty newspaper and watching them sweep up the dead flies in the hotel lounge. What I want to know is— whether any ambition's worth the price you have to pay for gratifying it?"

"I should say that depends on your temperament."

"Bethune does some fool-talking now and then," Moran commented from his post at the helm. "When you go to sea for your living, you must expect to get up against all a man can stand for; and if you don't put up a good fight, she'll beat you. That's one reason you'd better get your pumping done before she ships a comber."

With a gesture of acquiescence Bethune resumed his task, and presently went below while Jimmy took the helm. The breeze freshened during the morning, and the sea got heavier, but it dropped in the afternoon, when they ran into a fog belt, which Jimmy thought indicated land. As the days were getting shorter, they set the topsail, and looked out eagerly until a faint gray blur appeared amid the haze, perhaps a mile away. Closing with it, they made out the beach, which Jimmy searched with the glasses after consulting his notebook.

"Luff!" he called to Bethune. "Now steady at that; I've got my first two marks." Then he motioned to Moran. "Clear your anchor!"

A few minutes afterward he completed his four-point bearing, and the Cetacea stopped, head to wind, with a rattle of running chain. The sea was comparatively smooth in the lee of the land, and ran in a long swell that broke into a curl of foam here and there. Bethune took up the glasses and turned them on the beach.

"It is some time since high-water, and we ought to see her soon," he said. "I'm trying to find the big boulder on the point." He paused and put down the glasses. "Do you see anything?"

"No," said Moran gruffly; "she should be showing."

"That's true," Bethune agreed. "The tallest timber used to be above water when the top of the boulder was just awash, and now its bottom's a foot from the tide."

Jimmy said nothing, but seizing the dory savagely, he threw her over the rail and jumped into her with a coil of rope. Moran followed and lowered a bight of the rope while Jimmy rowed. Some minutes passed, but they felt nothing, and Bethune watched them from the sloop with an intent face. It looked as if the wreck had broken up and disappeared. Then as the dory turned, taking a different track, the rope tightened and Moran looked up.

"Got her now! She's moved, and there may not be much of her holding together."

Jimmy stopped rowing, and there was silence for a moment or two. It would take time to unpack and fit the diving pumps, and sunset was near, but neither of them felt equal to bearing the strain of suspense until daybreak.

"It may blow in the morning," Jimmy said.

"That's so," agreed Moran, pulling off his pilot coat. "I'm going down."

There was a raw wind, the tide ran strong, and the water was chilled by the Polar ice; but Moran hurriedly stripped off his damp clothes and stood a moment, a finely poised figure that gleamed sharply white against gray rocks and slaty water. Then he plunged, and the others waited, watching the ripple of the tide when the sea closed over him. Some moments passed before his head broke the surface farther off than they expected. Jimmy pulled toward him, and after a scramble, which nearly upset the craft, he got on board and struggled into his clothes. Then he spoke.

"She's there, but so far as I can see, she's canted well over with her bilge deep in the sand."

Jimmy and Bethune were filled with keen relief. They might have increased trouble in reaching the strong-room, but it was something to know that the wreck had not gone to pieces in their absence.

Jimmy picked up the end of the rope and tied on a buoy. Then he pulled back to the sloop, where Bethune cooked a somewhat extravagant supper.

CHAPTER XVII

THE STRONG-ROOM

When Jimmy went on deck the next morning, fog hung heavily about the land and the slate-green sea ran with a sluggish heave out of belts of vapor. The air felt unusually sharp and the furled mainsail glistened with rime. This was disturbing, because they must finish their work, or abandon it, before winter set in; but Jimmy reflected that it was some weeks too soon for a severe cold snap. While he watched the smoke from the stove funnel rise straight up in a faint blue line, he heard a splash of oars and Bethune appeared in the dory.

"I took the water breaker off before you were up," he said as he came alongside. "There was ice on the pool. It struck me as a warning that we had better lose no time."

"That's obvious," returned Jimmy. "Hand me up the breaker. We'll get the pumps rigged first thing."

Breakfast was hurried. The weather was favorable for work, and they could not expect it to continue so. In an hour the sloop had been warped close to the wreck and Jimmy put on the diving dress. He was surprised to feel the half-instinctive repugnance from going down which he thought he had got rid of; but this could not be allowed to influence him, and he resolutely descended the ladder. In a few minutes he reached the wreck, and found one bilge deeply embedded; but the opposite side was lifted up, and a broad strip of planking had been torn away. Jimmy could see some distance into the interior, and his lamp showed that the stream had washed out part of the sand which had barred their way to the bulkhead cutting off the strong-room. This had been strained by the working of the wreck, and it seemed possible to wrench the beams loose.

He attacked the nearest with his shovel, using force when he found a purchase, but the timber proved to be firmly mortised in. He lost count of time as he struggled to prize it out, and did not stop until he grew distressed from the pressure. His heart was beating hard and his breath difficult to get, but the beam still defied him. Making his way out of the hold, he stumbled forward toward the ladder; and when his comrades removed his helmet on board the sloop, he sat still for a few moments to recover. It was inexpressibly refreshing to breathe

the keen, natural air. At last he explained what he had found below, and added:

"My suggestion is that we bore out an opening for the saw; then we could cut the stanchion through and prize the cross-timbers off."

"The trouble is that we haven't a big auger," Bethune objected. "You often run up against a difficulty of the kind when you're using tools: the thing you want the most is the one you haven't got."

"Mortise-chisel might do," said Moran. "How thick's the timber?"

"Three or four inches. By its toughness I imagine it's oak or hackmatack."

"Then, there's a big job ahead," grumbled Bethune; "and my experience is that as soon as you drive a chisel into old work you come upon a spike. Unfortunately, we haven't a grindstone."

"Quit your pessimism and find the chisel!" snapped Moran. "I'm going down."

They watched the bubbles that marked his progress rise to the surface in a wavy line and then stop and break in a fixed patch. Rather sooner than they expected the bubbles moved back; and Moran looked crestfallen when they took off his diving dress.

"Did you cut out much stuff?" Bethune asked.

"No," said Moran, holding up the chisel; "this is what I did. Came across a blamed big spike at the second cut."

Bethune giggled. Even Jimmy grinned. There was a deep notch in the edge of the tool.

"Your philosophy isn't much good," Moran said grumpily. "It helps you to prophesy troubles, but not to avoid them. We'll have to spend some time in rubbing that nick out."

"I'll try the engineer's cold-chisel," Bethune replied. "With good luck, I might cut the spike."

He took the tool and an ordinary carpenter's chisel down with him; and the edge of the chisel was broken when he returned.

"I've cut the spike, and dug out about an inch of the wood," he reported. "Why are you frowning, Jimmy?"

"It looks as if we may spend a week over that timber. These confounded preliminaries sicken me!"

"They're common." Bethune launched off into his philosophy. "If you undertake anything that's not quite usual, half your labor consists in clearing the ground; when you get at the job itself, it often doesn't amount to much."

"Chuck it!" Moran interrupted. "Jimmy, it's your turn."

Jimmy stayed below as long as he could stand it, hacking savagely with broken chisels at the hard wood, and scraping out the fragments with bruised fingers; then he came up and Moran took his place. It was trying work, and grew no easier when, by persistent effort, they made an opening for the saw. The tool had to be driven horizontally at an awkward height from the sand, and the position tired their wrists and arms. Still, the weather was propitious, which was seldom the case, and they toiled on, until exhaustion stopped them when it was getting dark. Then Moran sent Bethune ashore to look for stones with a cutting grit, and they sat in the cabin patiently rubbing down the nicked tools, while the deck above them grew white with frost.

It cost them two days to break the beam, and on the evening they succeeded there was a sharp drop in the temperature.

Jimmy was cooking supper when Moran called him up on deck and pointed seaward.

"See that?" he said. "Seems to me we've got notice to quit."

Searching the western horizon, where the sea cut in an indigo streak against a dull red glow, Jimmy made out a faintly glimmering patch of white. Taking up the glasses, he saw that it was low and ragged, and fringed on its windward edge by leaping surf. This showed it was of some depth in the water, and he recognized it as a floe of thick northern ice.

"Yes," he answered gravely; "we'll have to hurry now."

They spent the next week attacking the bulkhead. Jimmy thought it would have resisted them only that it had obviously been built in haste and here and there the strengthening irons had wrenched away through the working of the hull. They lost no time, but the work was heavy, and tried them hard.

It was late in the afternoon, and blowing fresh enough to make diving risky, when Jimmy prepared to go down for what he hoped would be the last attempt; but stopping a few moments he looked anxiously about. Gray fog streamed up from seaward in ragged wisps, and the long swell had broken into short, white-topped combers, over which the sloop plunged with spray-swept bows, straining hard at her cables as the flood tide ran past.

"We might hold on for another hour," Bethune said hopefully; but breaking off he pointed out to sea. "That settles it," he added. "If it's any way possible, we must cut the bulkhead tonight."

A tall, glimmering shape crept out of the fog about a mile away. It was irregular in outline, and looked like a detached crag, except that it shone with a strange ghostly brightness against the leaden haze. It came on, sliding smoothly forward with the tide, another mass which was smaller and lower rocking in its wake; and then a third crept into sight behind. The men gazed at them with anxious faces; then Jimmy held out his hand for the helmet.

"They'll ground before they reach us, but the sooner I get to work the better," he said.

A bent iron plate hung from a tottering beam when he crawled up to the after end of the hold, and he savagely tried to wrench it out with a bar. The effort taxed his strength, but when he felt that he could keep it up no longer the timber yielded, and he fell forward into the gap. It cost him some trouble to recover his balance, and while he crouched on hands and knees, the disturbed water pulsed heavily into the dark hole. Lifting his lamp, he saw that the floor was deep in sand; and out of the sand two wooden boxes projected. He found that he could not drag them clear, and it seemed impossible to remove them without some tackle, but in groping about he came upon a bag. It was made of common canvas, and had been heavily sealed, though part of the wax had broken away, but on lifting it Jimmy found the material strong enough to hold its contents.

He sat still for a moment or two, his heart beating with exultant excitement. The sand was much deeper at the other side of the small, slanted room. He could not tell what lay beneath it; but he could see two boxes, and he held a heavy bag. Gold was worth about twenty dollars an ounce, and value to a large amount would go into a small compass. It looked as if wealth were within his grasp.

The effects of the continued pressure made themselves felt, and Jimmy hastily picked his way out of the hold. He had some trouble in getting up the ladder, which swung to and fro, and when he reached the deck he saw Moran busy forward, shortening cable. Bethune released him from his canvas dress, and lifted the bag.

"You got in?" he cried.

"Yes; here's a bag of gold. I saw two boxes, and expect there are others in the sand."

Bethune clenched his hand tight.

"And we can't hold on! It's devilish luck, I say! She has dragged the kedge up to the stream anchor, and is putting her bows in. Still,

I'm going to make a try."

Glancing at the sea, Jimmy shook his head. The combers were getting bigger with the rising tide and the sloop plunged into them viciously, flooding her forward deck, and jarring her cable.

"No," he said. "I had trouble in reaching the ladder, and she might drag to leeward before you could get back. The thing's too risky."

Moran, coming aft, felt the bag, and looked at the diving dress with longing, but he supported Jimmy's decision.

"I surely don't want to light out, but we'll have to get sail on her."

Crouching in the spray that swept the bows, they laboriously hauled in the chain with numbed and battered hands, and, leaving Bethune to hoist the reefed mainsail, coiled the hard, soaked kedge warp in the cockpit. Then they set the small storm-jib, and the Cetacea drove away before the sea for the sheltered bight.

"We'd have known how we stood in another hour," Bethune grumbled, shifting his grasp on the wheel to ease his sore wrist.

They were too tensely strung up to talk much after supper, for the weight of the bag was sufficient to indicate the value of its contents, and they thought it better not to break the seals. Jimmy grew drowsy, and he had lain down on a locker when Moran opened the scuttle-hatch.

"Now that it's too late to dive, the wind's dropping and coming off the land," he said.

Jimmy went to sleep, and it was daybreak when he was wakened by an unusual sound. It reminded him of breaking glass, though now and then for a few moments it was more like the tearing of paper. He jumped up and listened with growing curiosity. The noise was loudest at the bows, but it seemed to rise from all along the boat's waterline. Moran was sleeping soundly, but when Jimmy shook him he suddenly became wide awake.

"What is it?" Jimmy asked quickly.

"Ice; splitting on her stem."

"Then it's too thin to worry about."

"That's the worst kind," Moran replied, slipping into his pilot coat. "Get your slicker on; I'm going out."

There was not much to be seen when they reached the deck. Clammy fog enveloped the boat, but Jimmy could see that the surface of the water was covered by a glassy film. He knew that heavy ice is generally opaque and white, but this was transparent, with rimy streaks on it that ran to and fro in irregular patterns. As the tide drove it up the channel, it splintered at the bows, throwing up sharp spears that rasped along the waterline. Still, it did not seem capable of doing much damage, and Jimmy was surprised at Moran's anxious look.

"Shove the boom across on the other quarter!" Moran said sharply.

Jimmy moved the heavy spar, the boat lifted one side an inch or two, and Moran, lying on the deck, leaned down toward the water. Jimmy, dropping down beside him, saw a rough, white line traced along the planking where the water had lapped the hull. It looked as if it had been made by a blunt saw.

"She won't stand much of this," Jimmy said gravely, running the end of his finger along the shallow groove made by the sharp teeth of the splitting ice.

"That's so. I've seen boats cut down in a tide. The trouble is, the stream sets strong through the gut, except at the bottom of the ebb."

Jimmy nodded. This was his first experience of thin sheet-ice, but he could understand the dangerous power it had when driven by a stream fast enough to break it on the planking, so that its edge was continually furnished with keen cutting points. He could imagine its scoring a boulder that stood in its way; while, instead of changing with flood and ebb, the tide flowed through the channel in the sands in the same direction, as tidal currents sometimes do round an island.

Bethune came up and looked over the side. A glance was enough to show him their danger.

"What's to be done?" he asked.

"I don't quite know," said Moran, with a puzzled air. "The ice gathers along the beach, and the patches freeze together as the tide sweeps them out. She'd lie safe where the stream is pretty dead, but there's no place except this bight where we'd get shelter from wind and sea."

"It's plain that we can't stay here, and we'd better get off as soon as possible," said Jimmy. "We can hang on to the wreck unless it blows, but I want the breakers filled before we start."

"It will take us some time," Bethune objected. "I feel I'd rather get up those boxes from the hold."

"So do I," Jimmy rejoined. "But I'm taking no chances when there's a risk of our being blown off the land."

"The skipper's right," declared Moran. "We'll go off with the dory, while he drops her down with the tide."

They helped to shorten cable, and, after breaking out the anchor, pulled the dory toward the beach through the thin ice, while the sloop drifted slowly out to sea. Jimmy was relieved to hear the unpleasant crackle stop, and he leisurely set about making sail, for the wind was light. He must have canvas enough to stand off and on until the others rejoined him.

He found the waiting dreary when he reached open water, for he was filled with keen impatience to get to work. The gold lay in sight in the hold of the wreck, and an hour or two's labor was all that was required to transfer it to the sloop. And it was obvious that this must be done at once, because the drift ice was gathering in the offing, and an on-shore breeze might suddenly spring up. They had nowhere to run for shelter, now that the only safe haven was closed to them. Still, Jimmy felt that he had done wisely in exercising self-control enough to send for the water.

It was almost calm and very cold. Sky and water were a uniform dingy gray, and the mist, which had grown thinner round the land, still obscured the seaward horizon. Once Jimmy thought he made out an ominous pale gleam in a belt of haze, but when it trailed away before a puff of fitful breeze, he saw nothing. For two hours he sailed to and fro in half-mile tacks, finding just wind enough to stem the tide; and then, when his patience was almost exhausted, he felt a thrill of relief as he heard the measured splash of oars. A few minutes later the dory came alongside, and Bethune handed up the casks.

"We had to break the ice with a big stone, and I hardly thought we'd get through," he said. "It froze up again while we carried the first load down."

"It doesn't matter so much now," Jimmy replied. "If all goes well, we should be away at sea by daybreak tomorrow."

While they stowed the breakers the wind dropped, and Jimmy, watching the sails shake slackly, made a gesture of fierce impatience.

"The luck is dead against us! It looks as if we should never get at that gold! There's a two-knot stream on her bow, and she'll drift to leeward fast."

"Then we'll tow her!" Moran said stubbornly. "Get into the dory; you haven't carried those breakers, and I'm not used up yet."

Though Jimmy had rested since the previous evening, he found the work hard. He had suffered from his exertions under water during the past week, and the tide ran against them, and the long heave threw a heavy strain upon the line as the sloop lifted. The smaller craft was often jerked back almost under her bowsprit, and it needed laborious rowing to straighten out the sinking line. Still, they made progress, and at last dropped anchor beside the wreck early in the afternoon.

"Now," said Moran, "I guess we'll go down unless you want your dinner before you start. We haven't had breakfast yet."

Bethune laughed and looked at Jimmy.

"Could you eat anything?" he asked.

"Not a bite! I don't expect ever to feel hungry until we get those boxes up. Lash the ladder while I couple the pipe to the pump!"

Bethune was the first to go down. When he came back after an unusually long stay, he reported that he had been unable to extricate the nearest box, though he had cleared the sand from it before he was forced to ascend. Jimmy took his place, and worked savagely, dragging out the box and moving it toward the bulkhead, but in the confined space, which was further narrowed by some broken timbers, he could not lift it through the opening. While he tried, with every muscle strained, a piece of timber shifted in the sand beneath his feet; and Jimmy lost his balance and fell forward, putting out his lamp.

He felt smaller and less buoyant when he got up, his breath was hard to get, and he grew uncomfortably hot. Then it flashed upon him with a shock of unnerving fear that his air-pipe was foul, and for a moment he grappled sternly with his dismay. There was no time to lose, but he must keep his head. Passing his hand over the canvas dress, which felt ominously slack, he fumbled at the lamp. As he did so a wavering beam of light shot out, shining uncertainly through the water; and he supposed that in falling he must have broken the circuit by pressing the switch. Lifting the lamp, he saw that the tube was bent sharply round a ragged timber, and while his heart throbbed painfully and his breath grew labored, he moved back and reached for it; but he found his hands nerveless and his legs unsteady, and when he stooped to loose the line his head reeled and he pitched forward across the timber, grasping the line as he fell.

CHAPTER XVIII
BOGUS GOLD

Cold as it was, Jimmy lay for a long time on the sloop's deck when he had been stripped of the diving gear. How he had crawled out of the hole and climbed the ladder was not clear to him; he thought that he must have untangled the line as he fell and have been driven forward by an overpowering longing for the upper air.

He found some trouble in explaining to Moran what had happened, for he felt limp and shaky yet. And he shuddered at the thought of going down again.

"When we once get the box out of the hold," he said, "there should be no trouble in swinging it on board."

Moran smoked out a pipe before he took his turn. When the copper helmet disappeared, Jimmy got a firm grip on the signal line; and while he waited he looked about.

The days were rapidly shortening, and the light was growing dim. The horizon seemed to be creeping in on them, obscured by smoky fog, which stirred and wreathed about as the wind sprang up. Small ripples were splashing round the sloop, and the swell was steeper.

"I hope Hank will manage to sling that box," Jimmy said to Bethune, who nodded as he steadily turned the pump.

"We may get another turn or two, but that will be all. There's a breeze behind the heave that's working in."

Neither of them said anything further, but waited with what patience they could summon until Moran came up.

"I got the box out of the hold before I was beat; the next man shouldn't have much trouble in hitching a sling round it," he said, and glanced out to sea as he added significantly: "He'd better get through mighty quick."

A gust of wind rent the fog, and a long, low mass, shining a dead, cold white, appeared in the gap. Then, while the haze streamed back, another pale streak showed up on the opposite bow.

"They're all around us!" Jimmy exclaimed hoarsely.

The men were not easily daunted, and they had borne enough in the North to harden them, but the sight was strangely impressive, and their courage sank. This was a peril with which none of them except

Moran had grappled; and he had no cause for thinking light of it. The pack-ice was gathering round the island, hemming them in, and the sloop would be crushed like an eggshell unless she could avoid its grip. Then, to make things worse, a blast of bitter air whipped the men's anxious faces, and the sea broke into short, angry ripples.

"We have got to quit," said Moran despondently. "But I surely want that box."

"You shall have it, if I can get the sling on," Bethune replied. "Help me on with the dress as quick as you can."

He flung a hasty glance about. A long raft of ice with ragged edges was drifting nearer, and the fog, disturbed by the rising breeze, rolled across the sea in woolly streamers.

"It looks as if I had to finish the job this time," he said with a harsh laugh. "I no longer have the cheap hotel to fall back on."

When he had been down for some time, Jimmy, turning the pump in obedience to the plucking of the signal line, began to wonder when he would come up. Bethune seemed particular about his air supply, and Jimmy surmised that he found it needful to move the case along the bottom to get a clear lead for the lifting line because the Cetacea had altered her position. Moran put his hand on the crank when required, but at other times he stood motionless, watching the ice with an imperturbable brown face. Indeed, Jimmy, as a relief from the tension, began to speculate about his comrade and wonder what he thought. Though they had toiled hard and faced many perils together with mutual respect and confidence, he felt that he knew very little about the man. Moran's reserve and stolid serenity were baffling. When strenuous action was required he could be relied upon, but even then he was seldom hurried, and his movements somehow suggested that his splendid frame was endowed with unreasoning, automatic powers. For all that, Jimmy knew that such a conception of his friend was wrong. He had seen the cool judgment and indomitable courage that controlled the man's strength in time of heavy stress.

All this, however, was not of much consequence. Jimmy fixed his eyes upon the frothing patch of bubbles that broke the troubled surface of the swell. It was stationary, and Bethune had already stayed below an unusual time. He was not in difficulties, because when Jimmy jerked the line he got a reassuring signal in reply. It looked as if the man expected to bring up the case.

In the meanwhile the ice was driving nearer, propelled by wind and tide, and its low height suggested that it had formed in some shallow bight. If this were so, it might not ground before reaching the sloop. Still, its progress was not rapid, and Jimmy did not think there was any urgent need to recall Bethune, particularly as he must finish his task or abandon it.

At last the bubbles began to move back. It was difficult to follow them because the swell was streaked with foam, but although they were occasionally lost for a few moments, they reappeared. Then the top of the ladder swung against the rail and soon the copper helmet rose out of the sea. Bethune flung an arm on deck and grasped a cleat, but he seemed to have some difficulty in getting any farther, and they dragged him on board. His face was livid when they released him, and he lay back on the skylight without speaking for some moments. Then he gasped painfully:

"The case is slung; I had to move it clear of her. Heave up!"

They sprang to the line he had brought and hauled it in; Jimmy trying to control his fierce impatience. Care was needed lest the sling get loose in dragging along the sand. At last the line ran perpendicularly down, and they were encouraged by the weight they had to lift. Even Moran showed excitement as a corner of the box broke the surface. Throwing himself down, he swung it on board with a powerful heave. Then he and Jimmy dropped down limply on the deck and gazed at their treasure. The box was thick and bound with heavy iron, the wood waterlogged; but, making allowances for that, it obviously contained a large quantity of gold. Jimmy felt exultant, but after a time Bethune disturbed his pleasant reflections.

"Look at the ice!" he exclaimed.

The floe was bearing down on them, and in the distance, half hidden by the fog, a taller mass seemed to have stranded on the reef, for the spray was leaping about it and there was a great splash as a heavy block fell off. Moran glanced at the floe and ran forward. Jimmy joined him and they hurriedly got the chain cable in; then, with Bethune's help, they reefed the mainsail and stowed the folding ladder and pumps below, but they had a struggle to lift the kedge anchor. It seemed to have fouled some waterlogged timber below; but they would not sacrifice it by slipping the warp, because they knew it might be a long time before they could come back. When they finally broke it out Bethune had already hoisted the mainsail. There was no time to lose, for the fog was getting thicker in spite of the rising wind, and a glimmering mass of ice had crept up threateningly close. Moreover, the light was going and the sea getting up. Hurriedly setting a small jib, they stood out for open sea.

"Make the best offing you can," directed Jimmy, leaving Moran at the helm. "I'll get the stove lighted, and after supper we'll open the case."

It was nearly twenty-four hours since he had eaten anything and he was beginning to feel faint from want of food. Indeed, he had some difficulty in getting the fire to burn and was conscious of an annoying, slack clumsiness. When the meal was ready he called Bethune down and handed out Moran's share.

"I've been extravagant, but we have earned a feast tonight," he said exultantly.

They ate hungrily while the water splashed beneath the floorings and the lamp swung at erratic angles as the Cetacea rolled; and Bethune made no objection when Jimmy afterward lighted his pipe. The case lay against the centerboard trunk, but they did not feel impatient to open it. This was a pleasure that would lose nothing by being deferred; they were satisfied to sit still in the warm cabin and gloat over their success.

"Strictly speaking, we have no right to break into the thing," Bethune said; "and it might perhaps lay us open to suspicion; but I'm afraid I can't keep my hands off until we get home. Get out the tools, Jimmy."

Jimmy did so, and then, opening the scuttle, called to Moran.

"We're going to look inside the box. Is it safe for you to come down?"

Moran seemed to make a negative sign, though Jimmy could hardly see him. It had grown dark, and thick fog was driving past the boat, while the spray that beat in through the weather shrouds indicated that she was sailing hard. Dropping back below, Jimmy closed the scuttle and took up a hammer. His fingers shook and he felt his nerves tingle as he drove a wedge under the first band.

"I wish we'd cleaned out the strong-room; but we can come back, and we have got enough to wipe off our debt and give us a luxurious winter," he said happily. "It will be a change to put up at a good hotel—we might even make a trip to California; and if Jaques can get somebody to run the store we will bring him and his wife to town."

"It's not a very ambitious program," Bethune laughed. "I dare say we can carry it out; though we don't know yet what our share will come to."

"I'll stand out for half," declared Jimmy with a determined air. "In fact, we'll make a bargain before we deliver up the stuff."

Working eagerly, he soon started the band and inserted a chisel under a board. In a few moments he prized it loose, and thick folds of rotten canvas were exposed.

"There seems to be a lot of packing," Bethune remarked. "There's a seal here we'll have to break; but we have smashed one already. Don't waste time. Rip it open!"

Jimmy used his knife, and plunged his hand into the case. He was surprised by the feel of its contents.

"It seems to be in small ingots," he said.

"That's curious, because there's no smelter in the country. Slash the wrapping to bits and let's see it!"

Jimmy did so and then uttered an exclamation as he dropped the object he took out. It was dark-colored, and fell with a dull thud.

"It's lead!" he cried.

Tilting the case in savage anger, Jimmy shook out a number of small gray lumps. They scattered about the floorings, and when he gashed one with his knife the metal cut soft and showed a silvery luster. He dropped the knife and his face grew hard and white. There was tense silence for a moment, and then Jimmy, rousing himself with an effort, flung the scuttle back.

"Hank!" he called, and his voice was strangely hoarse.

It seemed that Moran recognized the urgent tone, for they felt by the change of motion that he was altering the boat's course, but with characteristic coolness he neglected no seamanlike precaution. Jimmy heard the jib being hauled aback and the mainsheet got in, and she was hove to, rising and falling with an easy lurch, when Moran dropped through the scuttle. He stooped over the box, and after a time looked up with a heavy frown.

"Some crook has worked off a low-down trick on us!" he said.

"On the underwriters first, but that's no matter," replied Bethune, who was struggling against the shock. "Slit one of the bags, Jimmy, and let's see if it's all the same."

Jimmy took the bag he had found in the wreck, and when he cut it open a few coarse, yellow grains ran out.

"That looks all right, but there's not very much of it; and the bag

Hank brought up isn't large," he said gloomily.

"You want to sew it up before you lose the stuff," advised Moran, sitting down on the box. "Now, if there's anything to be fixed, we had better get it settled. She's carrying all the sail she wants and I can't leave her long."

"Are we to go back?" Bethune asked. "We haven't emptied the strong-room, and what we have left behind may be genuine."

"Can't do it," Moran said grimly. "The way the wind is, the drift ice will be packed solid along the shore tomorrow."

They sat silent for a while. There was only one thing to be done, but they shrank from indicating it and owning their defeat. At last Jimmy made a gesture of resignation.

"Square away; our course is south," he said.

Moran nodded silently and went up through the scuttle, and Jimmy threw himself down on the locker while Bethune lighted his pipe. Neither of them spoke until they heard a rattle of blocks and the rush of water along the lee side showed that the Cetacea had swung round.

"Our plans for the winter won't materialize," Bethune said; "we'll be glad to put up at a dollar hotel if we're lucky enough to get taken on at a mill. However, we can talk about this tomorrow; I don't feel quite up to it now."

After a curt sign of agreement, Jimmy pulled a damp sail over him and, although he had not expected to do so, presently went to sleep.

When Moran wakened him to take his turn at the helm it was blowing hard and bitterly cold. Settling himself as far as he could in the shelter of the coaming, he began his dreary watch. Long, white-topped seas raced after the sloop, ranging upon her weather quarter, while the spray she flung aloft beat in heavy showers on Jimmy's slicker. He could scarcely see her length ahead, and knew that he was running a serious risk if there was ice about; but he thought she would not be much safer if he hove her to, and, fixing his eyes on the compass, he let her go.

After exhausting toil and many hardships, their search had failed, and he was too jaded and depressed to wonder whether it would ever be resumed. They were going back bankrupt; he could not see how they were even to retain possession of the sloop. At the best, they could make no use of her until the spring. The outlook was black, and what intensified the gloom was that Jimmy now recognized that since Bethune had first broached the scheme he had been buoyed up by a faint but strongly alluring hope. He had not allowed his mind to dwell on it, but it had hovered in the background, beckoning him on. After all, there had been a certain chance that their project would succeed, and in that case his share of the salvage should have been sufficient to set him on his feet. There were many openings in western Canada for a man with energy and means enough to give him a start, and Jimmy did not see why he should not prosper. Then when he had begun to make progress he might renew his acquaintance with Ruth Osborne.

He had thought of her often, and looking back on their voyage, he ventured to believe that he had to some extent won her favor. He recollected trivial incidents, odd words and glances, which could not have been altogether without their significance. Could he lift himself nearer her social level, it was not impossible that he should gain her love. The thought of this had driven him stubbornly on.

Now he had failed disastrously. He was going back a ruined man. The best he could hope for was that by stern self-denial and rough work on the wharves or in the sawmills, he might earn enough to discharge his debt to the storekeeper who had trusted him. Beyond that there was nothing to look forward to. He must try to forget Ruth.

Jimmy's heart sank as he sat shivering at the helm while the bitter spray whirled about him and the sloop lurched on through the darkness, chased by foaming seas.

CHAPTER XIX
A DANGEROUS SECRET

A cold snap had suddenly fallen over the northern half of Vancouver Island, and tall pines and unpaved streets were white with frozen snow. A chilling wind swept round Jaques' store and rattled the loose windows; tiny icicles formed a fringe about the eaves; but the neat little back room, with its polished lamp and its glowing stove, seemed to Jimmy and his comrades luxuriously bright and warm. Supper had been cleared away, and the group sat about the table discussing what could now be done, after the failure of the second attempt to recover the gold.

Jaques leaned his head on his hand, with his elbow resting on the table; Mrs. Jaques sat opposite him, her eyes fixed intently on Bethune, who was the spokesman for the party. Jimmy, with a gloomy expression, gazed toward the one window, where a frozen pine bough occasionally scraped against the pane with a rasping sound that was heard above the rattle of the sashes. Moran, with a downcast face, sat where the lamplight fell full upon him.

There was silence for a few moments, broken only by the cheery crackle of the stove. Then Jaques spoke.

"We might as well thrash the thing out from the beginning," he said. "The first matter to be decided is what had better be done with your boat."

"That raises another point," asserted Bethune. "What we do with her now depends on our plans for the future, and they're not made yet."

"Then suppose we consider that you're going back to try again in the spring?"

Jimmy looked at Mrs. Jaques, and fancied that her expression was encouraging.

"You're taking it for granted that we can get out of debt. If such a thing were possible, we'd haul her up and strip her for the winter with the first big tides."

"Not here," Jaques said pointedly. "For one thing, she'd be spotted, and you'll see why you had better avoid that if you'll listen."

"I see one good reason now," Bethune answered with a rueful

grin. "You're not our only creditor, and the other fellow isn't likely to show us much consideration."

"Let that go for the present. Do you know any lonely creek some distance off where she'd lie safe and out of sight?"

"I dare say we could find one," Jimmy replied.

"Then I'm going to talk. Some time after you left, a man from Victoria called on me. Said he was an accountant and specialized on the development of small businesses. He'd undertake to collect doubtful accounts, show his clients how to keep their books, and buy on the best terms, or sell out their business, if they wanted; in fact, he said that some of his city friends thought of trying to make a merger arrangement with the grocery stores in the small Island ports."

"No doubt it seemed an opportunity for getting a good price for your store," Bethune suggested.

"I wasn't keen. Things had improved since you were here, and trade was looking up. However, I showed the man my books, and I saw that he was especially interested when he came to your account. Asked me did I know that you were a remittance man who had forfeited his allowance and that your partner was a steamboat mate who'd been fired out of his ship. I told him that I was aware of it; and he said the chances were steep against your making good. Then he gave me some useful hints and went away."

"That's interesting," Bethune commented. "Did you hear anything more from him?"

"I did; not long ago he sent me an offer for my business as it stands, with all unsettled claims and liabilities. When I got a Vancouver drummer I know to make inquiries, he said that it ought to be a safe proposition—the money was good."

"Ah! It looks as if somebody thought us worth powder and shot. Did you take his offer?"

"No, sir! I stood off, for two reasons. I knew that the buyers either foresaw a boom in the Island trade, in which case it would pay me to hold on, or they'd some pretty strong grounds for wanting to get hold of you. On thinking it over, I didn't see my way to help them."

"Thanks. I wonder whether Mrs. Jaques had any say in the matter?"

"She certainly had," Jaques admitted fondly. "She thought it wouldn't be the square thing to give you away, and that to see you through might be the best in the end."

"We're grateful; but I'm not sure that she was wise. It's obvious that there was something crooked about the wreck, and what you have told us implies that some men with money are anxious to cover up their tracks. I suspect they've grown richer since the bogus gold was shipped, and might be willing to spend a good sum to keep the matter dark. The fellow who called on you probably knew nothing of this; he'd be merely acting for them on commission."

None of the others spoke for the next minute. The situation demanded thought, for they were people of no consequence, and they did not doubt that men with means were plotting against them.

"You seem to have got hold of a dangerous secret," Mrs. Jaques said, breaking the silence.

"An important one, at least," Bethune agreed. "It might, perhaps, get us into trouble; but our position's pretty strong. I'll admit, though, that I can't see what use we had better make of it."

Mrs. Jaques watched him closely.

"I suppose it has struck you that you might make a bargain with the people who insured the gold? They'd probably pay you well if you put the screw on them."

Jimmy started and frowned, but Bethune motioned to him to be silent.

"I wonder whether you really thought we'd take that course, ma'am?" he asked.

"No," she smiled; "I did not. But what's the alternative?"

"We might go to the underwriters and see what we could get from them. I suppose that's what we ought to do; but I'd rather wait. If we can clean out the strong-room, we'll have the whole thing in our hands."

"In your hands, you mean."

"No; I meant what I said. My suggestion is that your husband should relinquish his claim on us, and take a small share in the venture. If he'd do so, we could go back next spring. It's a proposition I wouldn't make before, but things have changed, and we want another man."

"Well," said Jaques, "I half expected this, and I've been doing some figuring. The mills are booked full of orders for dressed lumber, there's a pulp factory going up, and I'm doing better now that trade's coming to the town. Still, I see a risk."

"So do I," Bethune replied. "We're three irresponsible adventurers without a dollar to our credit, and we have men of weight and business talent up against us. It's possible that they may break us; but I think we have a fighting chance." He turned to Mrs. Jaques. "What's your opinion?"

"Oh, I love adventure! And somehow I have confidence that you'll make good."

"Thank you! It's evident that the opposition can do nothing at the wreck when we're on the spot, and the ice will keep the field for us while we're down here; but we must get back before they can send a steamer in the spring. In the meanwhile, we have the bags of gold to dispose of."

"That's a difficulty," said Jaques. "They certainly ought to be handed to the underwriters."

"Just so; but as soon as we part with them we give our secret away. We must stick to them and say nothing until we finish the job."

"Wouldn't it be dangerous? You have cut one bag and broken into the box. If the fellows who are working against you found that out, they'd claim you had stolen the gold. Then you'd be in a tight place."

"The experience wouldn't be unusual," Bethune answered with a laugh. "We must take our chances, and we'll put the stuff in your safe. What most encourages me to go on is that there were several different consignments of gold sent by the steamer and insured, and I can't take it for granted that all the shippers were in the conspiracy. There's no reason to suspect the contents of the remaining cases."

"You hadn't made out the marks when I last asked you about them," Jimmy broke in.

"No; they're hardly distinguishable; but I now think I have a clue. I'm inclined to believe the case was shipped by a man named Osborne. His name's in the vessel's manifest, and he has been associated with her owner for a long time. I found that out when I was considering the salvage scheme."

Jimmy started.

"His Christian name?"

"Henry. I understand he has a house on the shore of Puget Sound. You look as if you knew him!"

Jimmy said nothing for a few moments, though he saw that the others were watching him curiously. Bethune's suggestion had given him a shock, because it seemed impossible that the pleasant, cultured gentleman he had met on board the Empress should be guilty of common fraud. Besides, it was preposterous to suppose that Ruth Osborne could be the daughter of a rogue.

"I do know him; that is, I met him on our last voyage. But you're mistaken," he said firmly.

"It's possible," Bethune admitted. "Time will show. I've only a suspicion to act on."

"How do you mean to act on it? What do you propose to do?"

Bethune gave him a searching glance.

"Nothing, until we have emptied the strong-room and we'll have to consider what's most advisable then. In the meanwhile, I expect the opposition will let us feel their hand; there may be developments during the winter." He turned to Jaques. "We'll lay the sloop up out of sight with the next big tides and then go south and look for work. In the spring we'll ask you to grubstake us, and get back to the wreck as soon as the weather permits. I think that's our best plan."

The others agreed, and soon afterward the party broke up. As they went back to the boat Bethune turned to Jimmy.

"Do you feel inclined to tell me what you know about Osborne?" he asked.

"I only know that you're on the wrong track. He isn't the man to join in a conspiracy of the kind you're hinting at."

Bethune did not reply, and they went on in silence down the snowy street. Jimmy found it hard to believe that Osborne had had any share in the fraud, but a doubt was beginning to creep into his mind. For a few minutes he felt tempted to abandon the search for the gold; but he reflected that he was bound to his comrades and could not persuade them to let the matter drop. Besides, if by any chance Bethune's suspicion proved correct, he might be of some service to Miss Osborne. No matter what discovery might be made, she should not suffer; Jimmy was resolved on that.

Leaving port the next day, they found a safe berth for the sloop; and when they had hauled her up on the beach they walked to a Siwash rancherie, where they engaged one of the Indians to take them back in a canoe. Reaching Vancouver by steamboat, they had some trouble in finding work, because the approach of winter had driven down general laborers and railroad construction gangs from the high, inland ranges to the sheltered coast. There was, however, no frost in the seaboard valleys, and at last Jimmy and his friends succeeded in hiring themselves to a contractor who was clearing land.

It was not an occupation they would have taken up from choice, but as their pockets were empty they could not be particular. The firs the choppers felled were great in girth, and as Moran was the only member of the party who could use the ax, the others were set to work sawing up the massive logs with a big crosscut. Dragging the double-handled saw backward and forward through the gummy wood all day was tiring work, while, to make things worse, it rained most of the time and the clearing was churned into a slough by the gangs of toiling men. When they left it to haul out a log that had fallen beyond its edge they were forced to plunge waist-deep into dripping brush and withered fern.

For all that, Bethune and Jimmy found the use of the crosscut easy by comparison with their next task, for they were presently sent with one or two others to build up the logs into piles for burning. The masses of timber were ponderous, and the men, floundering up to the knees in trampled mire, laboriously rolled them into place along lines of skids. Then they must be raised into a pyramid three or four tiers high, and getting on the last row was a herculean task carried out at the risk of being crushed to death by the logs overpowering them and running back.

Jimmy and Bethune stuck to it because they had no other recourse, toiling, wet through, in the slough all day and dragging themselves back, dripping, dejected, and worn out, to the sleeping shack at night. The building was rudely put together, and by no means watertight. Its earth floor was slimy, the stove scarcely kept it warm, while it was filled with a rank smell of cooking, stale tobacco, and saturated clothes. The bunks, ranged like a shelf along the walls, were damp and smeared with wet soil from the garments the men seldom took off; and Jimmy was now and then wakened by the drips from the leaky roof falling on his face. He felt that once he was able to lay them down he would never wish to see a cant-pole or a crosscut-saw again.

But the deliverance he longed for came in a way he did not antici-pate.

CHAPTER XX

HOUNDED

Clammy mist hung about the edge of the clearing, veiling the somber spires of the pines, but leaving the rows of straight trunks uncovered below a straight-drawn line. It was a gloomy morning. Jimmy, standing with Bethune and several others beside a growing log-pile, stopped a moment to rest his aching muscles. He was wet through, and his arms and back were sore from the previous day's exertions. Two strong skids, placed so as to form an inclined bridge, led to the top of the log-pile and the soil between them was trodden into a wet, slippery mess in which it was difficult to keep one's footing. A length sawed off a massive trunk lay across the ends of the skids, and Jimmy and his companions were trying to roll it into its place on top of the previously laid tier.

Getting their poles beneath it they forced it upward, little by little. When they got half-way, a pole slipped, and for a few anxious moments the men strained every muscle to prevent the mass from rolling back, while their companion found a fresh rest for his pole. The log must be held: they could not jump clear in time. Breathing hard, with the sweat dripping from them, they raised it a foot or two, until it seemed possible to lift it on to the lower logs by a strenuous effort. They made the attempt; and one of the skids broke. Laying their shoulders beneath the mass, they struggled with it for their lives. If it overpowered them, they would be borne backward and crushed. With one support gone, it seemed impossible that they could lift it into place. For a few moments they held it, but did no more, though Jimmy felt the veins swell on his forehead and heard a strange buzzing in his ears. His mouth was dry, his heart beat painfully, and he knew he could not stand the cruel strain much longer. But there was no help available. They must conquer or be maimed.

"Lift! You have got to land her, boys!" cried somebody in a half-choked voice. And they made their last effort.

For a moment the mass hung in the balance, and then rose an inch. Again they hove it upward before their muscles could relax, and now its weight began to rest upon the lower logs. Another thrust rolled it slowly forward—and the danger was past.

Though the incident was not of an unusual character, Jimmy sat down limply in the wet fern to recover breath, and he was still resting when the foreman came up and beckoned him.

"We'll not want you and your partner after tonight," he said abruptly.

Jimmy looked at him in surprise.

"As you haven't found any fault with us, might one ask the reason?"

"You might; but I can't tell you. There it is—you're fired. I've got my orders."

The Canadian is often laconic, and Jimmy nodded.

"Very well," he said; "we'll go now. This isn't a luxurious job."

"As you like," replied the foreman. "The boss's clerk is in the shack; I'll give him your time."

Jimmy followed him to the office and drew his pay, but the clerk seemed unable to explain his dismissal.

"I guess it's because we can't get our value out of the boys in this rain," he said evasively.

"But why single us out?" Jimmy persisted. "I don't know that I want to stay; but I'm curious. Our gang has put up as many logs as the others."

"I've no time for talking!" the clerk exclaimed. "Take your money and quit!"

Bethune drew Jimmy away and they crossed the clearing to where Moran was at work. He showed no great surprise when he heard their news.

"Well," he said, "I'll finish the week here and then follow you to the city. We'll need the money."

"All right," Bethune agreed; "if you get the chance of staying; but that's doubtful. You know where to find us."

They went back to the sleeping shack to get their clothes.

"What did you mean when you said he might not have the chance?" Jimmy asked.

"I have a suspicion that Hank will get his time in the next day or two. The boss wouldn't want to make the thing too obvious, and Hank's a good chopper. There are some awkward trees to get down where he's working."

"But why should they want to get rid of him—or us?"

Bethune smiled grimly.

"I think we're marked men. We'll find out presently whether I'm right."

Bethune's forebodings proved correct, for only a few days elapsed before Moran joined him and Jimmy in Vancouver. After spending a week in searching for employment they got work with a lumber-rafting gang and kept it for a fortnight, when they were dismissed without any convincing reason being given.

On the evening after their return to the city they sat in a corner of the comfortless lobby at the hotel. It was quiet there because the other boarders lounged in tilted chairs before the big windows with their hats on and their feet supported by the radiator pipes, watching the passers-by.

"I came across the fellow we got the pumps from this afternoon," Jimmy remarked. "The last time I saw him he was fairly civil, but he's turned abusive now. Wanted to know when we were going to pay him the rest of his money, and made some pointed observations about our character."

"That won't hurt us," laughed Bethune. "As we have nothing to give him and the sloop's safely hidden, he can't make much trouble. I heard something more interesting. An acquaintance of mine mentioned that they had a big lot of lumber to cut at the Clanch mill and wanted a few more men. If we could get a job there, we might hold it."

"It seems to me we can't hold anything," Jimmy grumbled. "Why that?"

Bethune chuckled in a manner that indicated that he knew more than he meant to tell.

"Boldness often pays, and I imagine that our mysterious enemies won't think of looking for us at the Clanch mill. We'll go out there tomorrow."

They found it a long walk over a wet road, for soon after they left the city rain began to fall. On applying at the mill gate, they were sent to the office, and Jimmy was standing, wet and moody, by the counter, waiting until a supercilious clerk could attend to him, when an inner door opened and a young man came out. Jimmy started as he recognized the yachtsman they had met on the island; but Aynsley moved forward with a smile.

"This is a pleasant surprise! I'm glad you thought of looking me up."

"As a matter of fact, we are looking for work," Bethune said laconically.

Aynsley laughed and indicated the door behind him.

"Go in and sit down. I'll join you in a minute or two, and we'll see what can be done."

They entered his private office, which was smartly furnished, and, being very wet, felt some diffidence about using the polished hardwood chairs. The throb of engines and the scream of saws made it unlikely that their conversation could be overheard, and Jimmy turned to Bethune with a frown.

"You made a curious remark about boldness paying, when you suggested coming here. Did you know that young man was in charge?"

"No; it's an unexpected development. But I'll confess that I knew the mill belonged to his father."

"Clay?" Jimmy exclaimed. "The owner of the wreck?"

"Her late owner. She belongs to the underwriters now. It seems to me the situation has its humorous side; I mean our getting a job from the man who's been hunting us down."

"You suspected Osborne not long ago," Jimmy said shortly.

"They're partners; but, from what I've gathered, it's more likely that Clay's the man who's on our trail. We helped him to follow it by registering with an employment agent—and that makes me wonder whether it would be an advantage to change our names?"

"I'll stick to mine!" said Jimmy; and Moran declared his intention of doing the same.

"After all, it's a feeble trick and not likely to cheat the fellow we have to deal with," Bethune agreed. "He has obviously got a pretty accurate description of us."

"But would a man of his kind spend his time in tracking us? And wouldn't it lead to talk?"

Bethune laughed.

"He'll act through agents; there are plenty of broken-down adventurers in Vancouver who'd be glad to do his dirty work. These cities are full of impecunious wastrels; I was one myself."

"Perhaps we'd better clear out," suggested Jimmy. "I'd hate to take the fellow's pay."

"You needn't feel diffident. If it's any consolation, the mill foreman will get full value out of you. However—" Bethune broke off as Aynsley came in.

"The fishing doesn't seem to have been very profitable," he said, putting a box on the table. "Have a cigar."

"All we caught hardly paid for the net," Bethune replied. "On the whole, I don't think we'll smoke. Perhaps we had better not, so to speak, confuse our relations at the start. You see, though we didn't know you were the manager, we came along in the hope that you might have an opening for three active men."

"If I hadn't, I'd try to make one," Aynsley answered. "However, as it happens, we do need a few extra hands; but I'm afraid I've only rough work to offer."

"It couldn't be much rougher than we've been doing. I believe we can make ourselves useful; and that Hank here could move more lumber in a day than any man in your mill. But of course you're under no obligation to take us."

"We'll let that go; I need help. You can begin with the stacking gang, but something better may turn up. Now tell me something about your northern trip."

Bethune told him as much as he thought advisable, and, although he used tact, Aynsley gave him a keen glance now and then, as if he suspected some reserve. Before Aynsley could make a comment, Bethune stood up.

"I've no doubt you're a busy man," he said, "and we mustn't waste your time. Shall we make a start in the morning?"

"You can begin right now."

Aynsley rang a bell and handed them over to his foreman.

For some weeks the men remained contentedly at the mill. The work was hard, but the pay was fair, and the boarding arrangements good, and Aynsley seldom failed to give them a pleasant word as he passed. Indeed, Jimmy felt a warm liking for him; and it was not by his wish but by Bethune's that their respective stations as employer and workmen remained clearly defined.

One day, when Aynsley had been absent for more than a week, the foreman came to them.

"I'm sorry you'll have to quit," he said. "We're paying off several of the boys."

"Quit!" Jimmy began indignantly; but he caught Bethune's warning look and added lamely, "Oh, well; I suppose it's by Mr. Clay's orders?"

"No, sir," the foreman answered unguardedly; "Mr. Aynsley had nothing to do with it. He didn't even know—" He broke off abruptly. "Anyhow, you're fired!"

He turned away from them quickly; and Bethune, sitting down on a pile of lumber, took out his pipe.

"Since I've got my notice with no reason given," he drawled, "I don't see why I should exhaust myself by carrying heavy planks about. Of course you noticed his statement that Mr. Aynsley was not responsible—though the fellow was afterward sorry he had made it. I'm of the opinion that there's something to be inferred from his use of our employer's Christian name, particularly as a big automobile stood at the gate for two hours yesterday. I shouldn't be surprised to learn that Clay, senior, had examined the pay-roll."

"What's the blamed hog aiming at in getting after us like this?" questioned Moran.

Bethune looked thoughtful.

"He may wish to drive us out of the country; but I'm more inclined to believe he means to wear us out, and then make some proposition when he thinks we're tame enough."

"He'll be badly disappointed if he expects we'll come to terms!" Jimmy strode up and down, his face flushed with anger. "Anyway, I can't believe that Aynsley knows anything about this."

"He doesn't." Bethune smiled grimly. "I know by experience how the scapegrace son tries to conceal his escapades from his respectable relatives, but I rather think the unprincipled parent who doesn't want his children to find him out is more ingenious. All this, however, isn't much to the purpose; we'll have the boys down on us unless we clear the lumber from the saws."

They left the mill the next morning and tramped back to Vancouver in a generally dejected mood.

"What's to be done now?" asked Jimmy as they reached the outskirts of the city.

"How about going down into the States and trying our luck?" Bethune suggested. "We'd at least be out of Clay's reach—anywhere but Seattle."

"What—run!" Jimmy exclaimed indignantly. "I stay right here!"

"Me too!" grunted Moran.

Bethune laughed.

"Well, how about turning and charging the enemy? I'll admit that I'd enjoy a good fight right now—physical or verbal."

"Won't do," objected Moran; "we won't be well armed until we know just what those other boxes in the strong-room contain. Before we get a chance to find out, I've an idea our enemy himself will make a move."

And he did.

CHAPTER XXI

JIMMY'S EMBARRASSMENT

Jimmy's courage had fallen very low, dragging with it the last remnants of hope and ambition. Every loophole of escape from poverty seemed closed against him. For days he had tramped the streets of Vancouver, making the rounds of the wharves and mills in search of work, and had found nothing. He loathed the dreary patrol of the wet streets; he abhorred his comfortless quarters in the third-rate hotel; and the curt refusals that followed his application for a humble post were utterly disheartening. Worse than all, he felt that he had drifted very far from the girl who was constantly in his thoughts. He had almost lost hope of the salvage scheme's succeeding, but he was pledged to his comrades, and they meant to try again if they could finance another venture with Jaques' assistance. They must pick up a living somehow, and, if possible, save a few dollars before the time to start arrived.

One gloomy afternoon Jimmy stood outside an employment bureau among a group of shabbily dressed, dejected men, some of whom were of distinctly unprepossessing appearance. One had roughly pushed him away from the window; but he did not rouse himself to resent it. He felt listless and low-spirited, and to wait a little would pass the time. Besides, he thought he had read all the notices about men required which the agent displayed, and had offered himself for several of the posts without success. He got his turn at the window at last, and left it moodily; but when he reached the edge of the sidewalk he stopped suddenly and the blood rushed to his face. Ruth Osborne was crossing the street toward him.

Jimmy looked around desperately, but it was too late to escape; he could only hope that Miss Osborne would pass without recognizing him. He did not want her to see him among the group of shabby loungers. His own clothes were the worse for wear, and he knew that he had a broken-down appearance. The employment bureau's sign suggested what he was doing there, and he would not have the girl know how low he had fallen. He had turned his back toward her and pulled his shabby hat low down over his eyes, when her voice reached him.

"Mr. Farquhar!"

Jimmy turned, thrilled but embarrassed, and Ruth smiled at him.

"I can't compliment you upon your memory," she said.

Jimmy saw that the other men were regarding them curiously. He was not surprised, for Ruth had a well-bred air and her dress indicated wealth and refinement, while his appearance was greatly against him; but it was insufferable that those fellows should speculate about her, and he moved slowly forward.

"I think my memory's pretty good," he answered with a steady glance.

"That makes your behavior worse, because it looks as if you meant to avoid me."

"I'll confess that I did; but I'm not sure that you can blame me. No doubt you saw how I was employed?"

Ruth's eyes sparkled and there was more color than usual in her face.

"I do blame you; it's no excuse. Did you think I was mean enough to let that prevent me from speaking to you?"

"Since you have asked the question, I can't imagine your being mean in any way at all," Jimmy answered boldly. "I'm afraid I was indulging in false sentiment, but perhaps that wasn't unnatural. We all have our weaknesses."

"That's true; mine's a quick temper, and you nearly made me angry. I feel slighted when people I know run away from me."

"One wouldn't imagine it often happens. Anyhow, I've pleaded guilty."

"Then, as a punishment, you must come with me to our hotel and tell us of your voyage to the North. My father will not be back until late, but I think you'll like my aunt."

Jimmy looked surprised.

"You knew I was in the North?"

"Yes," she answered, smiling. "Does that seem very strange? Perhaps you find it easy to let a pleasant acquaintance drop."

"I found it very hard," Jimmy said with some warmth.

Then he pulled himself up, remembering that this was not the line he ought to take. "After all," he added, "it doesn't follow that a friendship made on a voyage can be kept up ashore. A steamboat officer's privileges end when he reaches land."

"Where he seems to lose his confidence in himself. You're either unusually modest or unfairly bitter."

"It's not that. I hope I'm not a fool."

Ruth felt half impatient and half compassionate. She understood why he had made no attempt to follow up their acquaintance; but she thought he insisted too much upon the difference between their positions in the social scale.

"I suppose your father learned where I had gone?"

"No; it was Aynsley Clay who told me. My father certainly asked one of the Empress mates what had become of you, but learned only that you had left the ship. You must remember Aynsley, the yachtsman you met on the island."

"Yes," said Jimmy incautiously. "My partners and I worked in his mill until a week or two ago. Then we were turned out."

"Turned out? Why? I can't imagine Aynsley's being a hard master."

"He isn't. We got on very well. I don't believe we owe our dismissal to him."

Ruth started. She was keen-witted and quick to jump to conclusions. Jimmy's statement bore out certain troublesome suspicions, and she remembered that she had forced Aynsley to speak about him in Clay's presence. Perhaps she was responsible for his misfortunes; she felt guilty.

"Then whatever you were doing in the North was not a success?" she suggested.

"It was not," Jimmy answered with some grimness.

Ruth studied him with unobtrusive interest. It was obvious that he was not prospering, and he looked worn. This roused her compassion, though she realized that there was nothing that she could do. The man's pride stood between them.

"I'm sorry," she said gently. "You may be more fortunate another time. I suppose you have some plans for the future?"

She seemed to invite his confidence, and he saw that her interest was sincere. It was unthinkable that she should have any knowledge of the conspiracy between her father and Clay, but he could not speak to her openly. Loyalty to his friends prevented his taking such a course, because she might inadvertently mention what she had heard, and it was impossible to ask her to keep it secret from her relatives.

"They're indefinite," he answered. "I expect we'll find something that will suit us by and by."

She saw that he was on his guard, and felt hurt by his reserve, particularly as she had made several advances which he would not meet. Then, glancing down a street that led to the wharf, she saw, towering above the sheds, a steamer's tunnel and a mast from which a white and red flag fluttered.

"That's your old boat; she came in this morning," she said. "I wonder whether we might go on board? After the pleasant trip we had in her, I feel that I'd like to see the ship again."

"As you wish," said Jimmy, with obvious hesitation.

Ruth regretted the mistake that she had made, because she thought she understood his reluctance. He looked as if he had come down in the world, and would no doubt find it painful to re-visit the boat on board of which he had been an officer.

"Perhaps there isn't time, after all," she said. "I told my aunt when I would be back at the hotel, and we are almost there. She will be glad to talk with you."

Jimmy glanced at the building and stopped. Several luxuriously appointed automobiles were waiting in front of it, and a group of well-dressed people stood on the steps. He felt that he would be out of place there.

"I'm afraid I must ask you to excuse my not coming in," he said.

"But why? Have you anything of importance to do just now?"

"No," said Jimmy with a smile; "unfortunately I can't give that as a reason. I wish I could."

"You're not very flattering, certainly."

"I'm sorry. What I meant was that I'd kept you rather long already, and of course one can't intrude."

She looked at him steadily, offering him no help in his embarrassment.

"You're very kind," he said with determined firmness. "But I don't intend to take advantage of that by coming in."

"Very well," she acquiesced; and, giving him her hand, she let him go.

The calmness with which she had dismissed him puzzled Jimmy as he went away. He wondered whether he had offended her. He had, no doubt, behaved in an unmannerly way, but there was no other course open. Indeed, it was fortunate that he had kept his head, and she might come to see that it was consideration for her that had influenced him. Then he reflected bitterly that she might not trouble herself any further about the matter and that it would be more useful if he resumed his search for something to do.

But Ruth did trouble herself. That evening she and her father were sitting in the rotunda of the big hotel with Aynsley and Clay. The spacious hall was lavishly decorated and groups of well-dressed men and women moved up and down between the columns and sat chatting on the lounges. Some were passengers from the Empress and some leading inhabitants of the town who, as is not uncommon in the West, dined at the hotel. Outside there was obviously a fall of sleet, for the men who came in stamped their feet in the vestibule and shook wet flakes from the fur-coats they handed to a porter.

Perhaps it was the air of luxury, the company of prosperous people, and the glitter of the place, that made Ruth think of Jimmy walking the wet streets. The contrast between his lot and the comfort she enjoyed was marked, and she felt disturbed and pitiful. This, however, could not benefit Jimmy; and, although he had rather pointedly avoided any attempt to presume upon their friendship or to enlist her sympathy, she longed to offer him some practical help. She must try to find out something about his affairs, using subtlety where needed; while generally frank, she was not repelled by the idea of intriguing, so long as her object was good. It was obvious that in Clay she had a clever man to contend against; but this rather added to the fascination of the thing, and she had some confidence in her own ability.

"I met Jimmy Farquhar this afternoon," she said abruptly, speaking to her father.

"The Empress's mate? What is he doing in Vancouver, and why didn't you ask him in?"

"He wouldn't come. I gathered that he'd been having rather a hard time lately."

The remark she had made at a venture had not been wasted. Her father's easy manner was not assumed; it was natural, and convinced her that he was not connected with Jimmy's misfortunes. This was a relief, but she had learned something else, for, watching Clay closely, she had seen him frown. The change in his expression was slight, but she had expected him to exercise self-control and she saw that he was displeased at the mention of Farquhar. This implied that he had a good reason for keeping his dealings with Jimmy in the dark.

"Then I must try to overcome his objections if I run across him," said Osborne. "I liked the man."

"The C.P.R. pick their officers carefully," Clay remarked with a careless smile at Ruth. "Still, the fellow didn't show much taste when he refused your invitation."

"I really didn't feel flattered," Ruth said lightly, wondering whether he had imagined that he might learn something from an unguarded reply.

"I guess he's not worth thinking much about. You wouldn't have had to ask me twice when I was a young man, but it's my opinion that the present generation have no blood in them."

"I believe that's an old idea," Ruth laughed. "Your father may have thought the same of you."

Clay was quick to seize the opportunity for changing the subject.

"You're not right there," he chuckled. "My folks were the props of a small, back-East meeting house, and did their best to pound the wildness out of me. It wasn't their fault they didn't succeed, but I'd inherited the stubbornness of the old Puritan strain, and the more they tried to pull me up the hotter pace I made. That's why I've given Aynsley his head, and he trots along at a steady clip without trying to bolt."

Ruth paid little attention to what he was saying. She was puzzling about Clay's connection with Jimmy's affairs, searching for some reason for Clay's evident attitude. She was not sorry when he and Osborne rose and turned toward the smoking-room, for she wanted to question Aynsley.

"Why did you turn Jimmy Farquhar out of your mill?" she asked as soon as they were alone.

Aynsley was taken by surprise.

"As a matter of fact, I didn't turn him out."

"Then did he and his friends go of their own accord?"

"No," said Aynsley with some awkwardness; "I can't say that they did."

"Then somebody must have dismissed them. Who was it?"

He could not evade the direct question, for he had none of his father's subtlety, but he felt a jealous pang. Ruth would not have insisted on an answer unless she had an interest in one of the men. Farquhar was a good-looking fellow with taking manners; but Aynsley erred in imagining that she was concerned only about Jimmy. The girl saw that there was more in the matter and she was feeling for a clue.

"The old man came along when I was away and cut down the yard gang," he explained. "He's smart at handling men economically, and thought I was paying too much in wages."

"But why did he pick out those three? Didn't they work well?"

Aynsley felt confused; but he would not seek refuge in deceit.

"So far as I could see, they were pretty smart; but I'm not so good a judge. Anyway, he didn't explain."

"Then you asked him about it?"

"Yes," Aynsley answered lamely. "Still, I couldn't go too far. I didn't want him to think I resented his interfering. After all, he bought me the mill."

Ruth saw that he suspected Clay's motive. So did she, but she did not think he could tell her anything more, and, to his relief, she changed the subject.

CHAPTER XXII

A WARNING

In the luxuriously appointed smoking-room of the hotel Clay leaned forward in the deep leather chair into which he had dropped and looked keenly at Osborne.

"Tell me how you are interested in this fellow Farquhar," he demanded.

"I don't know that I am much interested," Osborne replied. "He was of some service to us during our voyage from Japan, and seemed a smart young fellow. It merely struck me that I might give him a lift up in return for one or two small favors."

"Let him drop! Didn't it strike you that your daughter might have her own views about him? The man's good-looking."

Osborne flung up his head, and his eyes narrowed.

"I can't discuss—"

"It has to be discussed," Clay interrupted. "You can't have that man at your house: he's one of the fellows who were working at the wreck."

"Ah! That makes a difference, of course. I suppose you have been on their trail, but you have told me nothing about it yet."

"I had a suspicion that you didn't want to know. You're a fastidious fellow, you know, and I suspected that you'd rather leave a mean job of that kind to me."

"You're right," Osborne admitted. "I'm sure you would handle it better than I could; but I'm curious to hear what you've done."

"I've gone as far as seems advisable. Had the fellows fired from several jobs and made it difficult for them to get another; but it wouldn't pay to have my agents guess what I'm after." Clay laughed. "Farquhar and his partners are either bolder or smarter than I thought; I found them taking my own money at the Clanch Mill."

"You meant to break them?"

"Sure! A man without money is pretty harmless; but wages are high here, and if they'd been left alone, they might have saved enough to give them a start. Now I don't imagine the poor devils have ten dollars between them."

"What's your plan?"

"I don't know yet. I thought of letting them find out the weakness of their position and then trying to buy them off; but if I'm not very careful that might give them a hold on me."

Osborne looked thoughtful.

"I wonder whether the insurance people would consider an offer for the wreck? I wouldn't mind putting up my share of the money."

"It wouldn't work," Clay said firmly. "They'd smell a rat. I suppose you felt you'd like to give them their money back."

"I have felt something of the kind."

"Then why did you take the money in the first instance?"

"You ought to know. I had about two hundred dollars which you had paid me then, and I wanted to give my girl a fair start in life."

"And now she'd be the first to feel ashamed of you if she knew."

Osborne winced.

"What's the good of digging up the bones of a skeleton that is better buried!" he said impatiently. "The thing to consider is the wreck. If we could buy it we could blow it up."

"We can blow it up, anyway. That is, if we can get there before the Farquhar crowd. We have steam against their sail, and I've made it difficult for them to fit out their boat. Unless I find I can come to terms with the fellows, I'll get off in the yacht as soon as the ice breaks up."

"Your crew may talk."

"They won't have much to talk about; I'll see to that. Now, I don't know what claim insurers have on a vessel they've paid for and abandoned for a number of years, but I guess there's nothing to prevent our trying to recover her cargo, so long as we account for what we get. It's known that the yacht has been cruising in the North, and what more natural than that we should discover that a gale or a change of current had washed the wreck into shallow water after the salvage expedition gave her up? If there had been anything wrong, we'd have made some move earlier. Very well; knowing more about the vessel and her freight than anybody else, we try what we can do. If we fail, like the salvage people, nobody can blame us."

"You'd run some risk, for all that," Osborne said thoughtfully.

"I can't deny it. If Farquhar and his friends were business men, I'd feel uneasy. He has cards in his hand that would beat us; but he doesn't know how many trumps he holds. If he did know, we'd have heard from him or the underwriters before this."

"It seems probable," Osborne agreed. "All the same, I wish the winter was over and you could get off. It will be a relief to know that she is destroyed."

"You'll have to wait; but there won't be much of her left after we get to work with the giant-powder," Clay promised cheerfully.

They talked over the matter until it got late; and the next morning the party broke up, the Osbornes returning home and Aynsley going back to his mill. Clay, however, stayed in Vancouver and visited a doctor who was beginning to make his mark. There were medical men in Seattle who would have been glad to attend to him, but he preferred the Canadian city, where he was not so well known. He had been troubled rather often of late by sensations that puzzled him, and had decided that if he had any serious weakness it would be better to keep it to himself. Hitherto he had been noted for his mental and physical force, and recognized as a daring, unscrupulous fighter whom it was wise to conciliate, and it might prove damaging if rumors that he was not all he seemed got about.

His work was not finished and his ambitions were only half realized. Aynsley had his mother's graces, for Clay's wife had been a woman of some refinement who had yielded to the fascination the handsome adventurer once exercised. The boy must have wealth enough to make him a prominent figure on the Pacific Slope. Clay knew his own limitations, and was content that his son should attain a social position he could not enjoy. This was one reason why he had been more troubled about Farquhar's salvage operations than he cared to admit. His personal reputation was, as he very well knew, not of the best, but his business exploits, so far as they were known to the public, were, after all, regarded with a certain toleration and would be forgotten. The wreck, however, was a more serious matter, and might have a damaging effect on his son's career if the truth concerning it came out. This must be avoided at any cost. Moreover, with his business increasing, he would need all his faculties during the next few years, and the mysterious weakness he suffered from now and then dulled his brain. In consequence, he was prudently but rather unwillingly going to see a doctor.

The man examined him with a careful interest which Clay thought ominous, and after questioning him about his symptoms stood silent a few moments.

"You have lived pretty hard," he commented.

"I have," said Clay, "but perhaps not in the way that's generally meant."

The doctor nodded as he studied him. Clay's face showed traces of indulgence, but these were not marked. The man was obviously not in the habit of exercising an ascetic control over his appetites, but he looked too hard and virile to be a confirmed sensualist. Yet, to a practised eye, he showed signs of wear.

"I mean that you haven't been careful of yourself."

"I hadn't much chance of doing so until comparatively recent years," Clay replied with a grim smile. "In my younger days, I suffered heat and thirst in the Southwest; afterwards I marched on half-rations, carrying a heavy pack, in the Alaskan snow; and I dare say I got into the habit of putting my object first."

"Before what are generally considered the necessities of life—food and rest and sleep?"

"Something of the kind."

"You work pretty hard now?"

"I begin when I get up; as a rule, it's eleven o'clock at night when I finish. That's the advantage of living in a city hotel. You can meet the people you deal with after office hours."

"It's a doubtful advantage," said the doctor. "You'll have to change all that. Have you no relaxations or amusements?"

"I haven't time for them; my business needs too much attention. It's because I find it tries me now and then that I've come here to learn what's wrong."

The doctor told him he had a serious derangement of the heart which might have been inherited, but had been developed by his having taxed his strength too severely.

Clay listened with a hardening face.

"What's the cure?" he asked.

"There is none," said the doctor quietly. "A general slackening of tension will help. You must take life easier, shorten your working hours, avoid excitement and mental concentration, and take a holiday when you can. I recommend a three months' change with complete rest, but there will always be some risk of a seizure. Your aim must be to make it as small a risk as possible."

"And if I go on as I've been doing?"

The doctor gave him a keen glance. He was a judge of character, and saw this was a determined, fearless man.

"You may live three or four years, though I'm doubtful. On the other hand, the first sharp attack you provoke may finish you."

Clay showed no sign of dismay. He looked thoughtful rather than startled, for something had occurred to him.

"Would you recommend a voyage to a cold, bracing climate, say in the spring?"

"I'd urge it now. The sooner the better."

"I can't go yet. Perhaps in a month or two. In the meanwhile I suppose you'll give me a prescription?"

The doctor went to his desk and wrote on two slips of paper which he handed to Clay. He had told him plainly what to expect, and could do no more.

"The first medicine is for regular use as directed; but you must be careful about the other," he cautioned. "When you feel the faintness you described, take the number of drops mentioned, but on no account exceed it. The dispenser will mark the bottle."

Clay thanked him and lighted a strong cigar as he went out, then remembered that he had been warned against excessive smoking, and hesitated, but the next moment he put the cigar back in his mouth. If the doctor's opinions were correct, this small indulgence would not matter much. With good luck, he could bring all his schemes to fruition in the next year or two; he had no intention of dropping them. He had been warned, but he had taken risks all his life, and he had too much on hand to be prudent now. Still, it would do no harm to have the prescriptions made up. He looked around for a quiet drugstore. Nobody must suspect that his career was liable to come to a sudden termination.

CHAPTER XXIII

THE FIRST ATTACK

Clay made no marked change in his mode of living, and shortly after his visit to the doctor he engaged in a struggle with a group of speculators who opposed one of his business schemes. They were clever men, with money enough to make them troublesome enemies, and Clay realized that he must spare no effort if he meant to win. He beat them and determined to exact a heavy indemnity, but the battle was stubbornly fought and during the month it lasted he had little rest by night or day. Long after the city offices were closed he entertained his supporters in his rooms at the hotel, and, rising early, altered and improved his plans before the business day began.

To his delight, he felt no bad effects; he was somewhat limp and lazy, but that, no doubt, was a natural reaction from the strain. He could now, however, afford to take a few days' rest, and he telegraphed Aynsley that he would spend the week-end at Osborne's house, which was always open to both. Enjoying the first-fruits of his victory, in the shape of some tempting offers, shortly before he left his office, he traveled down the Sound in high content, and, to complete his satisfaction, he learned on arriving that Aynsley had secured some large and profitable orders for lumber.

Dinner was served early on the Saturday evening, and Clay, finding that he had an excellent appetite, ate and drank more than usual. He was quite well, he told himself, but had had an anxious time and needed bracing. Miss Dexter watched him with disapproval when, after dinner was finished, he stood in the hall with a large glass in his hand. The man had a high color, but his eyes had a strained look and his lips a curious bluish tinge. He appeared to be quite sober, which caused her some surprise, but he was talking rather freely and his laugh was harsh. She thought he looked coarse and overbearing in his present mood.

The large hall was tastefully paneled in cedar, a fire of pine logs burned on the open hearth, and small lamps hung among the wooden pillars. A drawing-room and a billiard-room, both warmed and lighted, opened out of it, but Osborne left his guests to do what they liked best, and nobody seemed inclined to move. Ruth and Aynsley were talking near the hearth, Miss Dexter had some embroidery in her hands, and Osborne lounged in a deep chair beside the table. Clay, with the now empty glass in his hand, leaned negligently upon the table, feeling well satisfied with himself. His manners were not polished, but he was aware of it, and never pretended to graces he did not possess. He smiled when he caught Miss Dexter's censorious glance.

"I'm often in trouble, ma'am, and find I can't fight on coffee and ice-water," he explained humorously.

"Perhaps that's one of their advantages," Miss Dexter replied. "But as we're not quarrelsome people, you ought to enjoy a few days' peace."

"That's so. I guess I warmed up over telling your brother-in-law about my latest battle." He turned to Osborne. "Frame and Nesbitt were in this morning, ready to take what I'd give them on their knees. Fletcher came and tried to bluff, but he wilted when I cracked the whip. I have the gang corralled, and they'll go broke before they get out."

Clay's rather obvious failings included an indulgence in coarse vainglory, though he had generally the sense to check it when it might prove a handicap. Now, however, he was in an expansive mood, inclined to make the most of his triumph.

"The joke is that they were plumb-sure they'd squeeze me dry," he went on. "Got hold of a tip about the development land purchase plan and never guessed I'd planted it for them. Morgan cost me high, and his nerve is bad, but he's a cute little rat, and works well in the dark."

"I thought the opposition had bought him," Osborne said.

"So they did," Clay chuckled. "Now they want his blood, and I believe Denby's mad enough about it to have him sandbagged. That plays into my hand, because the fellow will stick to me for protection. If he tries to strike me for extra pay, I've only to threaten I'll throw him to the wolves. Guess the way they're howling has scared him pretty bad."

"Have you begun the clean-up yet?"

"Washed out the first panful before I came away," Clay replied in miners' phraseology. "Ten thousand dollars for two small back lots. It's all good pay-dirt, carrying heavy metal."

"In a way, I'm sorry for Fletcher. He's had a bad time lately, and, as he has got into low water, I'm afraid this will finish him."

"He joined the gang. Now he has to take the consequences."

Clay saw that Miss Dexter was listening with disapproval. He was not averse to having an audience and he had spoken loudly.

"If you saw the people who'd conspired to rob you come to grief through their greediness, what would you do about it, Miss Dexter?" he asked.

"I should try not to gloat over their downfall," she answered with some asperity.

"Looks better," Clay agreed. "But when I have the fellows down, it seems prudent to see that they don't get up again too soon."

Miss Dexter studied him. Admitting that modesty would have become him better, she did not believe he was boasting at random. There was power in the man, though she imagined he did not often use it well. She disliked his principles, and he frequently repelled her, but sometimes she felt attracted. He had, she thought, a better side than the one he generally showed.

"Does it never pay to be merciful?" she asked.

"Very seldom. In my line of business you have, as a rule, to break or be broken hard. It's a hard fight. I keep the rules of the ring. Sometimes they're pretty liberally interpreted, but if you go too far, you get hustled out and disqualified. In this country the stakes are high, but I've been through the hardest training since I was a boy, and I've got to win." He paused with a glance toward Aynsley. "Sounds pretty egotistical, doesn't it? But I know my powers, and I can't be stopped."

His forceful air gave him a touch of dignity and redeemed the crude daring of his boast. Osborne looked at him curiously, but Miss Dexter felt half daunted. She thought his attitude grossly defiant; the inordinate pride he showed would bring its punishment.

"It sounds very rash," she said. "You don't know what you may have to contend with."

Clay laughed harshly.

"I've some suspicion; but there comes a time, often after years of struggle, when a man knows he has only to hold on and win the game. Curious, isn't it? But he does know, and sets his teeth as he braces himself for the effort that's going to give him the prize."

He spoke with vehemence, the color darkening in his face. Miss Dexter wondered whether the last glass of whisky and potass had gone to his head; but the flush suddenly faded and his lips turned blue. Osborne was the first to notice it. Jumping up, he grabbed Clay by the arms and shoved him toward the nearest chair. Clay fell into it heavily, and began fumbling at his vest pocket, but he soon let his hand drop in a nerveless manner. The next moment Aynsley was at his side. The hall was large, and the boy had been sitting some distance off, but he did not run and he made no noise. He had inherited his father's swiftness of action, and Ruth, following in alarm, noticed the lithe grace of his movements. The girl's impressions were, however, somewhat blurred, and it was not until afterward that the scene fixed itself vividly in her mind.

"Perhaps we'd better get the car out," Aynsley said quickly. "We may want it if this is going to last."

Osborne rang a bell and there was silence for a few moments while they waited, uncertain what to do. Clay's face was livid and his eyes were half shut. He seemed unconscious of their presence, and they imagined that he was struggling against the weakness that was mastering him. His lips were tight set, his brows knit, and his hand was firmly clenched. Osborne gave an order to a servant, who immediately disappeared, and then Clay's tense pose relaxed. He sank back in the chair, loose and limp, as if all power had suddenly gone out of him.

The change was more startling to those watching than the first attack. They had long known his strength and resolution; but now he lay inert, with head falling forward, a bulky, flaccid figure, suddenly stripped of everything that had made him feared. He was grotesque in his helplessness, and Ruth had a curious feeling that there was something unfitting, almost indecent, in their watching him. It appeared, however, that he was conscious, for when Osborne held a glass to his lips he feebly moved his head in refusal, and his slack fingers began to fumble at the pocket again.

"There's something he wants there!" Ruth said sharply. "Perhaps it's something he ought to take!"

Aynsley thrust his hand into the pocket and brought out a small bottle.

"Six drops," he read out and was about to lift his father's head when Miss Dexter stopped him.

"No," she said; "you'll spill it. Wait for a spoon."

She brought one and with some trouble they administered the dose. For a while there was no visible result, and then Clay sighed and with a slack movement changed his pose. A little later he opened his eyes and beckoned.

"The medicine!" Aynsley requested in a hoarse voice.

"No," said Miss Dexter firmly. "He has had six drops."

Aynsley yielded, for it was plain that his father was recovering. A moment later Clay raised himself in his chair and looked at Miss Dexter with a feeble, apologetic smile.

"Sorry I made this disturbance."

"Are you feeling better?" Aynsley asked.

"Quite all right in a minute." Clay turned to Osborne. "It would be bad manners to blame your cook; guess the fault was mine. Got breakfast early, and had no time for lunch."

Though he had made a hearty dinner, the explanation he suggested did not satisfy the others, and Ruth thought it significant that he had made it so promptly. They did not, however, trouble him with questions, and after a while he rose and walked to another chair.

"The car won't be needed," Aynsley said to Osborne.

"The car?" Clay interposed. "What did you want it for?"

"We had thought of sending for a doctor," Aynsley answered deprecatingly.

Clay frowned.

"Shucks! You're easily scared; I wouldn't have seen him. Where's that bottle?" He slipped it hastily into his pocket and turned to Ruth. "Very sorry all this happened; feel ashamed of myself. Now I wonder whether you'll give us some music."

They went into the drawing-room, and Clay chose an easy chair at some distance from the others. He cared nothing for music, but he felt shaky, and he was glad of an excuse for sitting quiet. Moreover, he wanted time to think. It looked as if the doctor, whom he had begun to doubt, had after all been right. He had had a warning which he could not neglect; and as he rather vacantly watched the girl at the piano it was borne in upon him that she had probably saved his life. The others had thought him insensible, but she had guessed that he was feeling for the remedy which had pulled him round.

It was a pity she had refused Aynsley, but he bore her no ill-will, although he was generally merciless to those who thwarted him. He would have liked to thank her, but that was inadvisable, for he must not admit that he had had a dangerous attack. Then it struck him that if he were seriously threatened, it might be well to take precautions. There was a good offer he had received for some property he wished to sell, but he had not answered because all the terms were not settled, and he did not wish to seem eager. It might be better to close the matter now. When he had thanked Ruth for the song, he quietly made his way to Osborne's writing-room.

It was necessary to write several letters, and he found his fingers nerveless and composition difficult. Indeed, he laid the pen down and then resolutely took it up again. He was not going to be beaten by a bodily weakness, and nobody must notice that his writing was shaky. He tore up the first letter and wrote it again in a firm, legible hand, though the sweat the effort cost him gathered on his forehead. His schemes must be completed and all his affairs straightened out before he gave in. The man was ruthless and unscrupulous, but he had unflinching courage and an indomitable will.

In the billiard-room Osborne was talking to Aynsley.

"What do you think about your father?" he asked.

"I'm anxious. Of course, he made light of the matter, and, so far as I know, he's never been troubled in this way before, but I didn't like his look."

"It struck me as significant that he'd seen a doctor," Osborne remarked. "The bottle proves that. From the careful directions about the dose it must have been made up from a prescription. Anyway, he's been overdoing it lately, and perhaps you had better go along and see what he's about. If he's attending to any business, make him stop and bring him down."

Aynsley entered the writing-room and left it in a few minutes, rudely dismissed. Coming down, he made an excuse for taking Ruth into the hall.

"I know you'll do me a favor," he begged.

"Of course. I suppose it concerns your father?"

Aynsley nodded.

"He's writing letters, and I'm afraid it will do him harm. He looks far from fit, but he's in a most contrary mood, and ordered me out when I hinted that he'd better stop. Knowing what he's capable of, I thought I'd better go."

He spoke lightly, but Ruth saw the uneasiness he wished to conceal.

"Do you think I could persuade him?"

"I'd like you to try. Anyway, he won't be rude to you; and I've a suspicion that you have some influence over him. You ought to be flattered, because nobody else has."

Ruth went to the writing-room and stood beside Clay with a reproachful smile. She felt pitiful. The man looked ill.

"We really can't allow you to leave us in this way," she said. "Besides, it's too late to think of business matters."

"I suppose Aynsley sent you," he answered with grim bluntness. "It would be better if you took him in hand instead of me. The boy wants looking after; he's got no nerve."

"You ought not to blame him for feeling anxious about you. However, I'm your hostess and I don't think you are treating me well. When I tell you to put away those papers you can't disobey."

Clay gave her a steady look.

"Anything you ask me will be done," he said. "But, as a favor, will you give me another five minutes?"

"Of course. But you might exceed it, so I think I'll wait."

Before the time had quite elapsed Clay closed the last envelope with a firm hand, and a few minutes later they entered the drawing-room and Aynsley gave Ruth a grateful glance.

When Clay returned to Vancouver he called at once on the doctor; and when he left his face was grim, for he had been plainly told that he was worse, and must change his mode of life at once; but this was more than Clay could consent to do. He had money in a number of ventures, none of which had yet achieved the success he looked for. Time was needed before he could bring them to the desired consummation, and if he sold out now it must be at a sacrifice of the handsome profit that might otherwise be secured. He would be left with only a moderate fortune, and he meant to be rich. Ambitious as he was for his son, he had also a keen reluctance to leaving his work half finished. In fact, it was obvious that he must hold on for a year or two longer.

Moreover, the doctor had warned him against increasing the dose of the restorative, which Clay admitted having done. The powerful drug had braced him up when he suffered from reaction after any unusual strain and he had come to regard it as a reliable standby. Now he must curtail its use, and he would feel the deprivation. Then, since he was running some risk, it was advisable to take precautions. First of all, the wreck must be destroyed. If he should be cut off suddenly, no evidence must be left behind to spoil his son's career. Aynsley must bear an untarnished name.

The first step would be to get Jimmy Farquhar and his companions out of the way—to buy them off if possible; if not—A hard look crept into Clay's eyes, and he sat down at once and wrote a short note to Jimmy.

CHAPTER XXIV
THE GIRL IN THE BOAT

Trade was slack in the Pacific province, and men from the interior flocked down to the coast and overflowed the employment bureaus. This made it unusually hard for Jimmy and his friends to find work. For a month they had done almost nothing, only an odd job now and then; they were in arrears with their hotel bill; and the future looked anything but bright to them.

After supper one evening they sat in the lobby of their shabby hotel in a gloomy mood. Jimmy had found temporary work, and since early morning had been loading a vessel with lumber in a pouring rain. All day he had been wet through, and he was tired and sore. He had grown thin, and had a gaunt, determined look.

"What's this?" he exclaimed, examining Clay's envelope, which had just been handed to him. "I have no acquaintances in Vancouver who use expensive stationery." He read the note and then looked up with a surprised frown. "It's from Clay! He asks me to meet him in the smoking-room of his hotel. It's the big, smart place they've lately opened."

"Oho!" said Bethune. "I've been expecting this. I suppose you mean to go?"

"What's your opinion?"

"Perhaps it might be wiser to take no notice of the invitation; but I don't know. I'd like to see the fellow and hear what he has to say. It's curious that we haven't met him yet, though we have felt his influence."

"Anyway, I'm not going alone. I might make a mess of things; he's evidently a cunning rogue. If you think it's wise to see him, you'll have to come."

"We'll all go," said Bethune with a grin. "I believe he knows us already, and he won't get much out of Hank."

"I'm sure not great at talking," Moran agreed. "Now, if he tried to have us sandbagged, and you told me to get after him—"

"It hasn't come to that yet," Bethune laughed. "The fellow's more refined in his methods, but they're quite as dangerous." He looked at the note. "However, it's nearly time, and we may as well make a start."

Clay looked up in surprise from his seat at a small table when the three walked in, and he felt half amused at Moran's steady, defiant stare. This, he thought, was a strange companion for Bethune, whom he at once recognized as the business leader of the party. Jimmy he dismissed, after a searching glance, as less dangerous. He was the practical seaman, no doubt, but it was his partner's intelligence that directed their affairs.

"Sit down," Clay said, taking out his cigar-case. "I wrote to Mr. Farquhar, but I'm glad to see you all. Will you have anything to drink?"

"No, thanks," Jimmy answered quickly; and added, "I'm afraid it's rather an intrusion, but as we go together, I thought I might bring my friends."

Clay understood his refusal as a declaration of hostility, but he smiled.

"As you prefer," he said, lighting a cigar and quietly studying his callers.

The room was large and handsome, with an inlaid floor, massive pillars, and pictures of snow-clad mountains on the walls. It was then almost unoccupied, and that added to the effect of its size and loftiness, but two very smart and somewhat supercilious attendants hovered in the background. Farquhar and his friends were shabbily dressed, and Clay had hoped that they might feel themselves out of place and perhaps embarrassed by his silence, but there was no sign of this. Indeed, they seemed very much at ease. Bethune's expression was slightly bored, while Moran glanced about with naïve curiosity. For all that, they looked worn, and there was something about them which suggested tension. They had felt the pressure he had skilfully brought to bear, but whether it had made them compliant or not remained to be seen.

"Well," Clay began, "we must have a talk. You have undertaken some salvage operations at a wreck in the North?"

"Yes," Jimmy answered concisely.

"You don't seem to have been very successful."

"I dare say our appearance proves it," Bethune smiled. "As a matter of fact, we haven't cleared our expenses yet."

Clay did not know what to think of this frankness; he imagined that if the man had any wish to extort the best terms he could, he would have been less candid. He saw that he must be cautious, for he had done a risky thing in asking Farquhar to meet him. He would rather have left the fellow alone and tried to destroy the wreck before they reached it; but he knew that he might not live to do so. He had had his warnings and he could not leave the matter open.

"It's obvious that, as the salvage people abandoned the vessel, something has happened to give you a chance," he said. "However, as you can't have money enough to buy a proper outfit, you're not likely to make much use of the opportunity. You want steam and the best diving gear, and I guess you found them too expensive."

"We might do better if we had them," Bethune admitted.

"Very well; are you willing to take a partner?"

There was uncompromising refusal in Jimmy's face, but he did not speak, and Clay surmised that Bethune had given him a warning kick under the table. Bethune, in fact, had done so, and was thinking hard. To refuse would imply that they expected to succeed and that the salvage could be easily accomplished with such poor apparatus as they could obtain; but this was not advisable, because it would encourage Clay to anticipate them.

"We might consider a sleeping partner who'd be content with his profit on the money he supplied," he said.

"That means you intend to keep the practical operations in your own hands?"

"Yes," Bethune answered; "you can take it that it does."

"Then the arrangement wouldn't suit me. I know more about the vessel than you do, and I've been accustomed to directing things. But I'll bid you five thousand dollars for your interest in the wreck."

"Strictly speaking, we have no interest that we could sell."

"That's true; but I'll buy your knowledge of how she lies and the best way of getting at her cargo. Of course, after you have taken the money you'll leave her alone."

"It's tempting," Bethune said thoughtfully. "But perhaps we had better be frank. I understand that you were one of the owners, and, as the underwriters paid you, I don't see what you would gain."

"All the gold on board her wasn't insured."

Bethune looked hard at him and Clay smiled. "It's true. Then, there's no reason why I shouldn't have a try at the salvage. I'm open to make a shot at anything that promises a moderate profit."

"I suppose there is no reason," Bethune agreed slowly. "Would you go up to ten thousand dollars?"

"No, sir!" Clay said firmly. "I stick to my bid."

"Then I'm sorry we can't make a deal." Bethune turned to the others. "I suppose that's your opinion?"

"Of course," said Jimmy; and Moran nodded.

Clay was silent for a few moments. He would gladly have given ten thousand dollars to settle the matter, but he doubted whether Bethune would take it; and to bid high would rouse suspicion. It looked as if he had accomplished nothing, but he had found out that his opponents were more capable than he had imagined, and he decided that it would be safer to put no further pressure on them. He did not wish them to learn that he was the cause of the trouble they had had in finding employment, as it would indicate that he had some strong reason for preventing their return to the wreck.

"Well," he said, "it's a pity we can't come to terms, but I can make no fresh suggestion. You're up against a pretty big undertaking."

"So it seems," Bethune answered pleasantly. "We'll have to do the best we can. And now, as we mustn't take up your time, I'll bid you good-night."

Clay let them go, and as they went down the street Jimmy turned to Bethune.

"What do you think of the interview?" he asked.

"A drawn game. Neither side has scored; but I've learned two things. The first is that he has no suspicion that we have found the bogus case."

"How do you infer that?"

"From his view of our character. You must recollect that we're hard-up adventurers whom he wouldn't expect to be scrupulous. He'd conclude that if we had found anything suspicious we'd have let him know and tried to sell our secret. He was waiting for some hint, and I was careful to give him none."

"What's the next thing?"

"That he'll try to clean out the wreck before we get there. It was the only reason he let us go. I dare say you noticed how careful he was not to show any anxiety to buy us off. It's curious, but I really think he spoke the truth when he said all the gold was not insured."

"If it had been a straight deal, with nothing behind it, I think I'd have taken the five thousand dollars," Jimmy said. "He won't have much trouble in getting ahead of us when the ice breaks up. It will cost something to fit out the sloop, and our pockets are empty."

"Oh, there's time yet," Bethune replied with a cheerful laugh. "Something may turn up."

Fortune favored them during the next week, for Bethune secured a post as hotel clerk, and Moran went inland to assist in repairing a railroad track which a snowslide had wrecked. Soon afterward Jimmy shipped as deck-hand on a Sound steamboat and was lucky in attracting the attention of one of the directors who was on board by the cool promptness with which he prevented an accident when a passenger gangway broke. The director had a talk with him, and, learning that he was a steamship officer, placed him in charge of a gasolene launch which picked up passengers at unimportant landings and took them off to the boats. The work was easy, and paid fairly well; and Jimmy had held his post for a month with some satisfaction when he went off to meet a north-bound steamer at dusk one evening.

He had no passengers and it was blowing fresh with showers of sleet. Savage gusts whipped the leaden water into frothing white, and as he drew out from the shore the ripples which chased the launch grew larger. When he passed a headland they changed into short, breaking seas, and the craft plunged wildly as she crossed a strong run of tide. Here and there an island loomed up dimly, but the shore had faded into the haze. When Jimmy first joined her, the boat had carried another hand, but the man had gone and had not been replaced because trade was slack in winter. Jimmy thought that he might have trouble in getting his passengers on board; but they were not likely to be numerous, and the steamer would run into shelter behind an island.

He was late, for his engine was not working well, but there was no sign of the steamer when he stopped, and the boat lay rolling with the spray blowing across her rail. It rattled on Jimmy's slickers and stung his face, but the cold was mild by comparison with what he had endured in the North, and he sat in the shelter of the coaming, glancing up the Sound every now and then. Presently a sleet-storm broke upon him, and when it blew away a blinking white light and a colored one broke out of the driving cloud. Jimmy lighted a blue flare and, starting the engine, headed for the end of the island. When he stopped, the steamer was close ahead, a lofty, gray mass, banded with rows of lights. She rolled as she crossed the tide-stream, and he could see the foam about her big side-wheels and the smoke that swept from her inclined stacks. It did not look as if she were stopping, and he was about to get out of her way when a deep blast of her whistle broke through the turmoil of the sea. In another minute he was abreast of the gangway and caught the rope thrown down, though he kept the launch off at a few yards' distance.

The ladder was lowered, and hung banging awkwardly against the vessel's side; and while Jimmy waited with his hand on the tiller a deck-hand ran down to the lowest step and flung a valise into the boat, and then turned to assist a woman who followed him. Jimmy could not see her well, but he noticed that she was active and not timid, which was reassuring, and he cautiously sheered the launch closer in.

"Give me your hand and jump!" he cried.

She did as he directed, and when she was safe on board he stood looking up at the gangway.

"That's all!" somebody shouted; and when he let the rope go, the side-wheels churned and the steamer forged ahead while the launch slid clear of her with propeller rattling.

Jimmy pulled up a canvas hood which covered part of the cockpit and lighted a lantern under it before he turned to his passenger.

"If you sit here, you'll be out of the wind and spray. Where are you going?"

"To Pine Landing." She gave a start when Jimmy stooped over the engine where the light fell upon him. "You!" she cried. "Mr. Farquhar!"

He gazed at her in surprise, with his heart throbbing. Though she had turned her head quickly and the light was not good, he thought he had seen a flush of color in her face.

"It was too dark to recognize you until you spoke, Miss Osborne," he said as coolly as he could. "Then, I didn't expect to see you here."

"Our house is scarcely a mile from the Landing."

"The pretty place in the woods? I didn't know it was yours. I've seen it from a distance, but have never been there."

"I think you are to blame for that," she said.

"Until a few weeks ago, I was living on the Canadian side." Jimmy laughed as he added: "Besides, I hadn't many opportunities for making visits."

Ruth glanced at him with quick sympathy, remembering how he had looked when she had last seen him; but he was doing something to the engine and his face was hidden.

"How did you come to be in this boat?" she asked.

"I'm her captain, but just now I wish I were an engineer," he answered humorously. "She's not running as she ought to do, and I'm afraid you'll have rather a long trip. In fact, I think we had better go round behind the island where there's smoother water. Will your people be anxious because you're late?"

"They don't expect me until tomorrow. Some friends were traveling by the boat, and I thought I could get home before it was dark."

Jimmy thrilled at her nearness, but he knew that he must steel himself against her charm. Her friends were his enemies and he could not involve her in any difficulties with them. He must wait until fortune favored him, if it ever did so. But the waiting was hard.

"You didn't tell me how you happen to be running this boat," she reminded him with a smile.

"Well, you see, I didn't want to leave this neighborhood," Jimmy explained slowly, picking his words. "My partners and I have a plan which we can't put into execution yet, and it prevents us from going too far from Vancouver. I'm not sure that anything will come of it, but it might. One lives in hope."

Ruth was relieved by his answer. It had been painful to think of his following some rough occupation, and, worse still, wandering about the city in search of work. Though she felt sorry for him, it made her indignant. She hated to imagine his being content to live among the broken men she had seen hanging about the dollar hotels.

"Mr. Farquhar," she said, "even in this country it is hard for a man to stand alone, and I think there are times when one is justified in taking a favor from one's friends. Now, you were very kind on board the Empress, and I'm sure my father—"

He made an abrupt movement, and she stopped, and just then the launch plunged her bows into a breaking sea and a shower of spray blew inside the hood.

"It's impossible," he said firmly a few moments later. "I suppose I'm stupidly independent; but there are my partners to consider. They expect me to see our plans through. After all, they may turn out as we hope."

"And then?"

"Then," he answered carelessly, "I don't think I'll carry any more lumber or drive this kind of boat."

Ruth felt baffled and inclined to be angry. She had had impecunious admirers who did not consider her father's money a disadvantage. Jimmy's was, of course, a more becoming attitude, but she thought he adhered to it too firmly. Then, as she remembered his worn look and his threadbare clothes when she met him in Vancouver, she was moved to pity. The trouble was that it could not be shown. She could not offer him sympathy which he did not seem to want.

"I hope that you will succeed in your venture," she said.

"Thank you," he answered; "we'll do our best. Now I must keep a look-out, for there's a rock in the channel."

There was strain in his voice, and she was glad to see that his reserve cost him something; but she saw the need for caution when a gray mass of stone loomed out of the darkness close at hand with the sea spouting about it. After that she made no further attempt to talk, and they went on in silence, both sensible of constraint and yet not wishing the voyage at an end.

When they swung round a rocky point, Jimmy stopped the engine, and the launch ran in toward a small wooden pier. Dark pines rolled down to the water, and the swell broke angrily upon the beach and surged among the piles. There was nobody about, but Jimmy caught a trailing rope abreast of a few steps where the water washed up and down, while the launch ground against the weedy timber.

"I'll get out and help you up," he said.

Ruth hesitated when she saw him stand knee-deep on the lowest step, holding out his hand; but there was no way of getting ashore dry without his assistance. The next moment he had thrown his arm about her and stood, tense and strung up, trying to preserve his balance. She knew that it would be ridiculous to let herself fall into the sea, and she yielded to his grasp, sinking down into his arms with her head on his shoulder. He staggered as he reached the next slippery step, and she clung closer to him in alarm; then, as she thrilled at the contact, she felt his heart beat and his muscles suddenly grow tense. He caught his breath with a curious gasp, and Ruth knew that it was not caused by the physical effort he had to make. She lay still, not inert but yielding, until he gently set her down out of reach of the water. She was glad that the darkness hid her burning face; and Jimmy stood curiously quiet, with his hand clenched.

No words were needed. Both knew that something had happened to them during the last few moments; something which might be ignored but could not be forgotten. They were no longer acquaintances; the tie of friendship had broken with the strain and could be replaced only by a stronger bond.

Ruth was the first to recover.

"My valise is in the boat," she said, with a strange little laugh.

For a tense moment Jimmy was silent. Then:

"Yes," he replied; "I forgot it." He sprang down and returned with the bag. "I'm afraid you'll have to send for it and go home alone. The launch would get damaged if I left her here, and I couldn't take her alongside your landing tonight."

"It isn't very far through the woods," Ruth said, and hesitated a moment before she gave him her hand. "I'm glad I met you, and I will look forward to hearing of your success."

Jimmy dropped her hand quickly and jumped back on board, but Ruth stood still until the launch vanished into the darkness. Then she started homeward with her nerves tingling and her heart beating fast. She knew what Jimmy felt for her, and she wondered when the time would come when he could avow it openly.

CHAPTER XXV
PAYING A DEBT

Aynsley, sitting near an open window in his office, laid down his pen and looked out with a sense of satisfaction. A great raft of lumber was ready to start down the river, and men were scrambling about it loosing the mooring-chains. The pond was full of logs lately run down on a freshet, and the green flood swirled noisily past them. Its color indicated that the snow was melting fast on the lofty inland ranges, and sweet resinous scents rose from the stacks of cedar where the sunshine struck hot upon them. A cloud of smoke streamed across the long sheds and streaked the pines behind the mill with a dingy smear; and the scream of saws and the crash of flung-out boards filled the clearing. All this suggested profitable activity; and Aynsley's satisfaction deepened as he glanced at some letters which a clerk handed him. They contained orders, and he foresaw that he would soon have to increase the capacity of the mill. He was thinking over a scheme for doing so when his father was shown in. Clay smiled at his surprise, and sat down in the nearest chair, breathing heavily.

"Why don't you locate on the ground-floor instead of making people walk up those blamed awkward steps?" he asked.

"I can see better from here what's going on," Aynsley explained. "I find it saves me a little money now and then."

Clay beamed upon him.

"There was a time when I didn't expect to hear you talk like that. However, you have a pretty good mill-boss and secretary, haven't you? Do you think you could leave them to look after matters for a little while?"

"I suppose I could," Aynsley answered dubiously. "They know more about the business than I do; but, for all that, I'd rather be on the spot. Things seem to go wrong unless you look closely after them."

"They do; you're learning fast, my son. It looks as if the mill is getting hold of you."

Aynsley took a plan of some buildings from a drawer.

"What do you think of this?" he asked. "We could keep the new saws busy, but the job would cost about twenty thousand dollars. Could you let me have the money, or shall I go to the bank?"

Clay inspected the plan carefully.

"It's a good scheme," he declared. "If trade keeps steady, you'll soon get the cost back. I could lend you the money easily but perhaps you'd better try the bank. You've got to stand by yourself sooner or later; and it seems to me that you're getting pretty steady on your feet. Guess you're not sorry now I made you work?"

Aynsley pondered the question. In some respects the business was not to his taste, but in spite of this it was rapidly engrossing his attention. There was a fascination in directing, planning for the future, and bringing about results.

"No," he said. "In fact, I'm getting a good deal more satisfaction out of it than I expected."

"That should help you in another matter. You won't take your not getting Osborne's girl quite so hard."

For a few moments Aynsley sat still with knitted brows. It was his habit to be honest with himself, and he saw that to some extent his father was right. He thought of Ruth with deep tenderness and regret, and he believed that he would always do so, but the poignant sense of loss which he had at first experienced had gone. He did not think that he was fickle or disloyal to her, but his new interests had somehow dulled the keenness of his pain.

"I suppose that's true," he answered quietly.

"Your real trouble will begin when you see her getting fond of another man. What are you going to do about it then?"

Aynsley winced.

"It's rather hard to speak about, but, if the fellow's fit for her, I'll try to bear it and wish them well."

"You'll make good," Clay commented with dry approval. "But I've been getting off the track. You have been sticking to your work pretty closely, and, as things are going, you can leave it without much risk. I want you to take me North for a few weeks in the yacht. The doctor recommends the trip."

It struck Aynsley that his father was not looking well. He had lost his high color, his face had grown pouchy under the eyes, and he had a strained, nervous look. Aynsley had some business on hand which demanded his personal attention, but he recognized his duty to his father. Then, the North had its fascination, and the thought of another grapple with gray seas, smothering fog, and biting gales appealed to him.

"Very well," he said. "When do you want to go?"

"As soon as we can get away. Next week, if possible. You had better tell the captain to get his crew and coal on board."

Aynsley called his secretary, and when Clay left he had arranged to meet him at Victoria in a fortnight.

The time was, however, extended; for on getting the yacht ready for sea some repairs to rigging and engines were found needful, and these took longer than the skipper expected. At last Clay received word that they would be finished in a few days, and he paid a visit to Osborne. Reaching the house in the evening, he sat talking with his host in the library after dinner. A shaded lamp stood on a table laid out with wine and cigars, but this was the only light and beyond its circle of illumination the large room was shadowy. The floor was of polished wood, but a fine rug stretched from near the table to the door, where heavy portières hung. The men spoke in quiet, confidential voices as they smoked.

"The Farquhar gang have separated, and I've lost track of them, but if they can scrape up three or four hundred dollars between them I'll be surprised," Clay said. "They're going to have some trouble in fitting out their boat; and she's a very small thing, anyway. Though the delay has worried me, we should get up there long before they do, and we only need a few days of fine weather to finish the job."

"There's some risk in your taking the diver and Aynsley," Osborne cautioned. "You may have some difficulty in keeping both in the dark."

"It oughtn't to be hard. I take the owner's berth with the small sitting-room attached, and everything we bring up will go straight in there—and I'll keep the key. The diver's business ends when he puts the stuff on deck, and after it's stowed nobody will touch it but myself."

"Aynsley may want to see it, and ask questions."

"Then he won't be gratified. I have him pretty well drilled, and he knows when to stop. Besides, I'll find him useful. When anything needs talking over, I'll have him to consult with instead of a paid man. The skipper's more of a sailing-master. Aynsley takes command."

"Still, you can't keep everything from him," Osborne persisted. "It seems to me there are too many people who must, to some extent, be taken into your confidence. That's where Farquhar has the advantage. He has only two partners, whom he can rely upon."

"Shucks! You get to imagining trouble! Some of the gold is there all right, and, if it's needful, I can make a show with that. For all that, I'd like a companion who knew as much as I did, and I feel a bit sore because I have to go without. It's your place to see me through, but you've got so blamed fastidious lately."

"I'm not going," Osborne answered softly, for Clay had raised his voice. "I've had enough to do with the wreck."

Clay indicated the handsome room and its rich fittings with a wave of his hand.

"You have had your share of the plunder, and you hadn't a shack to call your own when I first got hold of you. Now, when I'm up against an awkward job, you go back on me. However, if I wanted you—"

He broke off, looking up sharply as a draught of colder air entered the room; and Osborne, turning with a start, saw Ruth standing on the rug. Her face was in shadow, for she was outside the direct illumination of the shaded lamp, but so far as he could discern, her attitude was easy and natural.

"Walter has just come back with the car and brought this telegram," she said. "I thought it might be important."

Osborne was partly reassured by her voice. She spoke in her normal tone, but he wished he could see her better.

"Thank you," he said, opening the envelope. "We'll have finished our talk before very long."

Ruth went out in silence, and Clay looked hard at Osborne.

"Could she have heard?"

"I don't think so. I hope not."

"I'd soon have found out if it had been a man," Clay said grimly. "Anyhow, all she could have picked up wouldn't give her much of a clew."

He was wrong. Ruth's suspicions had already been aroused, and now Clay had justified them out of his own mouth. She knew that he was going north where Jimmy, who had spoken of some plan for improving his fortune, had been engaged at the wreck. Clay had mentioned a share of the plunder, so something was far from straight. Worse still, he seemed to have been urging her father to go with him.

It had cost her an effort to maintain her composure when she gave him the telegram, and her face was pale when she went downstairs and sat in a corner of the empty hall. Ruth had had a shock. Until lately she had given her indulgent father her wholehearted affection and respect. His life had long been hard, but she believed he had at last achieved success by courage and integrity. Then she began to distrust his association with Clay, and by degrees perplexing doubts had grown up. She was imaginative, and when she began to form a theory, odd facts that had accidentally come to her knowledge had fitted in. Vessels, she knew, were sometimes lost by their owners' consent and frauds perpetrated on the underwriters. It was horrible to think that, but what Clay had said indicated something of the kind.

Then, as she recovered from the shock, she felt pitiful, and tried to make excuses for her father. He must have been hard pressed when he yielded to temptation, and his partner had, no doubt, placed it in his way. She was filled with a desire to protect him. He must be saved from the evil influence that had led him into wrong. She remembered that Clay had declared he owed her a debt of gratitude. She would remind him of it. He must release her father from whatever hold he had on him; she had a curious confidence that he would do so if she begged it.

She waited, nerving herself for the effort, until he came downstairs and then she beckoned him into the empty drawing-room.

"I suppose my father's busy?"

"Yes; he has a letter to write."

Clay leaned carelessly on a chair-back, watching her as she stood quietly confronting him. The intentness of her expression and her stillness were significant. She suspected something, and he was sorry for her; if he could remove her suspicions, he would do so.

"Then he won't be down for some minutes," she said. "I have something to say—you have been trying to make him go North with you?"

"No; not exactly. I'm not sure I could make him; he's pretty determined. Don't you want him to go?"

"No!" she cried. "You mustn't take him! And in future you must leave him alone. I can't let you force him to do things he hates!"

Clay smiled at her vehemence.

"It looks as if you suspected me of leading him astray. Now, in a sense, that's hardly fair to either of us. Don't you think your father has a will of his own?"

"I know you have some power over him, and I beg you not to use it."

Clay pulled out a chair.

"I think you had better sit down while we talk this thing over. To begin with, your father and I are old friends; we have faced hard times together and shared very rough luck. It seems to me that gives us some claim on each other."

"That is not what I mean," Ruth said firmly.

Clay was determined to spare her as far as he could.

"Then, if you suspect some other influence, I'd better warn you that you're too young and inexperienced to form a reliable opinion. You hear something that startles you, and, without understanding it, you make a blind guess. Take it from me that your father is known as one of the straightest business men in this State." He paused and laughed. "In fact, he's getting too particular for me. I'm 'most afraid I'll have to drop him."

"That is what I want you to do; I mean as a business partner."

"Then you wouldn't quite bar me out as a private acquaintance?"

"No," Ruth answered slowly. "Somehow, I feel that you might prove a good friend."

"Thanks. Now I want you to listen. I'm not going to defend my commercial character. I've taken up a good many risky deals and put them through, fighting the men who meant to down me as best I could; but all my business hasn't been a raid on somebody else's property. In fact, you can't play the bold pirate too often. Very well; now and then, when I was doing an innocent trade, I wanted a respectable associate as a kind of guarantee, and asked your father to stand in. He's known as a straight man, and my having him helped to disarm suspicion; I'll admit that I found him useful in that respect. I hope I've said enough to satisfy you?"

Though his manner was humorous, Ruth felt somewhat comforted. His explanation sounded plausible, and she was glad to make the most of it; but it did not banish all her doubts.

"I don't want him to have anything to do with your northern trip," she persisted.

"Why?"

Ruth hesitated, and Clay felt moved to sympathy. There was distress and perplexity in her face, but what touched him most was something in her manner that suggested confidence in his ability to help her.

"I'm afraid; I feel that no good can come of it," she said with an appealing look. "You mustn't let him have any part in it."

"Very well." Clay leaned forward, speaking in an earnest tone. "Set your mind at rest. You have my word that your father shall have no share in what I hope to do at the wreck. What's more, he doesn't know all my plans about her. There's nothing in them that can injure him; on the contrary, if I can carry them out, it will be to his benefit, in a way that he doesn't expect and that you could find no fault with."

Ruth felt that he was speaking the truth; giving her a pledge of greater importance than she could gage. His manner had impressed her, and she was conscious of keen relief.

"Thank you," she said, getting up. "You must forgive my frankness—it seemed needful."

"It's a compliment, because it shows that, after all, you have some faith in me." He added, with a smile, "You won't regret it."

Ruth left him with a lighter heart. She did not know whether she had been too hard on Clay or not, but she felt that she could trust him.

CHAPTER XXVI
AN UNEXPECTED DELAY

As soon as Aynsley joined her at Victoria, the handsome schooner-yacht, with its auxiliary engines, got under way. For the first day or two the wind was fair, but although she spread a good deal of canvas, Clay insisted on keeping up a full head of steam.

"She'd slip along fast enough with her propeller disconnected and the gaff-topsails set," Aynsley expostulated. "Keeping the fires going is a waste of coal."

"I'm willing to meet the bill," Clay replied. "Guess I'm used to hustling, and I like to feel I'm getting there."

"We may get there too soon," Aynsley persisted. "I expect we'll find ice about the island."

"Then we can wait until it clears. Keep her going at her best clip to please me."

Aynsley promised to do so, though his father's eagerness made him thoughtful. As a matter of fact, Clay was tensely impatient to begin work on the wreck. He had so far never spoiled an undertaking by undue haste, but he had now a foreboding that if he delayed his attempt he might be too late. His life was threatened, and he must finish the work he had on hand while there was an opportunity.

When they lost sight of Vancouver Island the wind drew ahead, and, furling sail, the yacht proceeded under steam. For two days she made a satisfactory run, and then, as the breeze freshened and the sea got up, her speed slackened and, burdened by her heavy masts, she plunged viciously through the white-topped combers. The weather did not improve, and on the third afternoon Clay stood on the sloppy after-deck impatiently looking about. Gray mist obscured the horizon, and long ranks of frothing seas loomed up ahead. The vessel lurched over them, rolling wildly, burying her bows in the foam, which swept in across her low bulwarks and poured out through the waist gangway in streaky cataracts. The sooty cloud from her funnel streamed far to leeward, and Clay could feel her engines throbbing; but he saw that she was making poor speed, and he beckoned to Aynsley, who came aft and joined him.

"I've been watching that log since lunch, and she's doing very badly," he said, indicating the dial of a brass instrument on the taff-rail. "There's hardly sea enough to account for it, and they seem to be firing up."

"Saltom is having some trouble with his condenser," Aynsley explained. "As you're anxious to get on, he didn't want to stop, but the vacuum's falling."

"Then I'll go down and see him; but I'm not an engineer, so you'd better come along."

They climbed down a greasy iron ladder, and found a man in over-alls kneeling beside a big iron casting in the bottom of the engine room. Near by piston-rod and connecting-rod flashed with a silvery glimmer between the throbbing cylinders and the whirling cranks that flung a shower of oil about, and floor-plates and frames vibrated in time to the rhythmic clangor. The engineer held an open lamp, its pale flame flickering to and fro as the vessel rolled, while he watched the index of the vacuum gage.

"You have lost half an inch since I was down," said Aynsley, stooping beside him.

"She's surely worrying me," replied the engineer. "I'll have to let up on feeding from the hot-well before long, and we haven't too much fresh water."

"Are you satisfied it's not the air-pumps?"

"Can't see anything wrong with them. I suspect there's something jambing the main inlet-valve, and the tubes may be foul, though those I took out last season were clean."

"Why didn't you scrap the blamed condenser if you doubted it?" Clay broke in. "I haven't cut your bills, and this boat has got to go when I want her."

His tone was sharp, and the man looked up with a start.

"I don't waste my employer's money," he began; but Clay cut him short.

"Let that go! She won't run, you say. What are you going to do about it?"

Aynsley was surprised. Clay had a quick temper, but he generally knew how to keep it in check, and now his voice was hoarse with rage.

"I'd like to stop her right away and see what's wrong, but it's a long job to strip a surface-condenser and these castings are heavy to move about."

"She'd fall off into the trough of the sea when her propeller stopped, and the rolling would make his work very difficult," Aynsley explained.

"Well," Clay said shortly, "what do you suggest?"

"I'd like a day or two to overhaul her in, up some inlet where we'd get smooth water," the engineer replied.

"Do you know of a suitable place?" Clay asked Aynsley.

"Yes; but it's a little off our course, and would take a day to reach."

Clay turned with a frown to the engineer.

"He'll sail her in, but if you're not through in forty-eight hours, I'll fire you and scrap this machine!" Then he touched Aynsley's arm. "Leave him to it, and give your orders to Hartley."

They went up on deck, and Aynsley saw his father light a cigar and then savagely throw it away; and when he came back after speaking to the skipper Clay was standing in the deckhouse with a small bottle and a wineglass in his hand. He looked at his son angrily, and Aynsley, recognizing the bottle, hastily went out.

A few minutes later the yacht swung off her course to the east, and they set the foresail and two jibs. At midnight, when it was blowing hard, the engines stopped, and they hoisted the reefed mainsail. Aynsley was surprised to see Clay on deck, but he did not speak to him, for Clay's manner indicated that he was in a dangerous mood.

When day broke the schooner was sailing fast, close-hauled, with her lee channels in the water and the white seas breaking over her weather bow. Aynsley found his father sitting at the foot of the mainmast, which was the only dry spot. It looked as if he had been on deck since midnight.

"She's getting along fast, but Hartley thinks she's carrying more sail than is prudent," Aynsley remarked. "There's a big strain on the weather rigging, and I imagine it would be safer to heave her to and shorten sail."

"Let her go," said Clay. "The fellow who designed her specified the best Oregon sticks for masts, and I remember paying high for them. Now they've got to stand up to it."

"Very well," Aynsley acquiesced; but when the breeze still freshened he stayed on deck, watching the growing list of the vessel as, hard pressed by the canvas and half buried in foam, she plunged furiously through the breaking seas.

During the morning the wind veered to the east, breaking the schooner off her course, so that they were forced to make long tacks, and it was late when a great range of forest-shrouded hills rose up ahead. Rocky points and small islands broke the line of beach, and as they closed with it Aynsley climbed the fore rigging with his glasses. There was a gap in the belt of surf three or four miles off, which he knew was the spot he sought, and coming down, he had a consultation with the skipper before he explained the situation to Clay.

"So far as we can calculate from the tables, the tide had been ebbing for about two hours," he said. "That means the stream will be setting strongly out of the inlet, and we'll have the wind against us going in. I know the place pretty well, because I once sheltered there, but Hartley wasn't with me then, and after looking at the chart he's a bit nervous about trying it on the ebb."

"How long would you have to wait for water on the flood?"

"About nine hours. You see there's a rocky patch in the entrance, and not much room to tack. Then Saltom wants to put her on the beach, and we'd have to wait until near high-water unless we go in at once. Still, it's a very awkward place."

"Take her in and chance it!"

As she drew nearer, Aynsley stood in the rigging, studying the shore through his glasses. He could see by the wet belt above the fringe of surf that the water had fallen; and the inlet had a forbidding look. On the starboard side of its mouth the tops of massive boulders showed through the leaping foam; to port there was a rocky shoal; and beyond these dangers a deep, narrow channel ran inland between the hills. The wind blew straight down it, lashing the water white.

"We'll want speed; you'd better give her the whole mainsail," he advised the skipper when he came down.

For a few minutes the crew were busy shaking out the reef, and then as the yacht buried her lee bulwarks Aynsley took the wheel. The sea was smoother close in along the land, but she was hard pressed by her large spread of sail, and the water that leaped in across her bows flowed ankle-deep across the steeply slanted deck. The tall masts bent to leeward, the weather shrouds hummed, and her crew stood with bent legs at their stations on the inclined wet planking, ready to seize the sheets. Forward, a dripping seaman swung the lead in the midst of the spray cloud that whirled about her rigging, and his voice came faintly aft through the roar of parted water.

"Seven fathom!" He missed a cast, and his next cry was sharper.

"Shoaling, sir! And a quarter six!"

There was silence for a few moments while he gathered up his line, and the yacht raced in toward the beach.

"By the deep, four!" he called.

"Ready about!" shouted Aynsley, pulling at his wheel. "Helm's a-lee!"

There was a furious thrashing of canvas as she rose to an even keel, while rocks and pines closed in on one another as her bows swung round. Then she started on the opposite tack, heading for the entrance, with the boulders not far to leeward and the tide on her weather bow. It carried her back, the trailing screw hampered her, and when a wild gust hove her down until the sea boiled level with her rail Clay, holding on by a shroud, glanced sharply at his son.

Aynsley was gazing fixedly ahead, his face set but cool, though the foam that surged among the boulders seemed rushing toward them. Clay was not much of a seaman but he could see that they were gaining little; but he had confidence in his son. The leadsman had found bottom at three fathoms and still Aynsley did not bring her round. There was a slack along that shore, and he meant to make the most of it, though it looked as if she must strike in the next few moments.

She swayed upright suddenly, swung, and drove away on the other tack toward a confused white seething, where stream and shore-running sea met upon the shoal. They were close upon it when she came round again; and five minutes later she was racing back, with the ominous white patch on her lee bow, but not far enough for her to clear it. On the opposite side a tongue of beach ran out, narrowing the entrance. It looked impossible for them to get in, and during the few moments while she sped toward the rocks Clay was conscious of a new respect for his son.

Aynsley had shown himself no fool in business, he was a social favorite, and now he was altogether admirable as he stood, composed but strung up, at the yacht's helm. His finely proportioned figure was tense, his wet face was resolute, and there was a keen sparkle in his eyes. The boy was showing fine nerve and judgment. Clay was proud of him. This strengthened his determination to safeguard his son's career. Aynsley must bear an honored name; it was unthinkable that reproach should follow him on account of his father's misdoings.

Aynsley shouted to the skipper, who was anxiously watching the shore.

"There's not much room! I'll let her shoot well ahead before I fill on her. See the boys are handy with the fore-sheets!"

As he pulled the helm down, Hartley gave an order, and the schooner, coming round, drove forward, head to wind, with canvas banging. It was a bold but delicate maneuver, for Aynsley had to trust that her momentum would carry her through the dangerous passage against the tide. If it failed to do so, and she lost her speed before he could cant her on to a new tack, there was no way of saving her from the rocks. The skipper stood with set lips amidship just clear of the jerking foresail-boom; the crew forward, the slack of the fore-sheets in their hands; and Clay, leaning on the rail aft, watched his son. Aynsley's pose was alert but easy; he looked keen but confident with his hands clenched upon the wheel.

"Lee sheets!" he cried, pulling the wheel over sharply.

Her head swung slowly round, and the shaking canvas filled; she gathered way, and when her deck slanted the boulders were sliding past abeam. Coming round again, she left them astern, and drove forward swiftly into clear and sheltered water. Ten minutes afterward they ran the headsails down, and Aynsley ran her gently on to the beach. There she would have to stop until Engineer Saltom finished his repairs.

CHAPTER XXVII

ON THE BEACH

Late on a gloomy evening Jimmy and his friends sat down for a few minutes' rest on the beach of a lonely island on the northern coast. With the help of Jaques they had fitted out the sloop, and had sailed much earlier in the year than was prudent, fearing that Clay might arrive ahead of them. The voyage proved trying, for they spent days hove to while the sloop was blown to leeward by bitter gales, and they were now and then forced to run off their course for shelter. Still, they stubbornly fought their way north. The strong breeze that Clay's schooner-yacht had met badly buffeted the smaller boat. In driving her to windward through a steep head-sea the heavy strain upon the shrouds started a leak under her channel plates, and after a long spell of steady pumping the men reluctantly decided to seek a sheltered harbor, where the damage could be repaired.

This had not proved a difficult task, for some caulking was all that was required, but in order to reach the leak they had to lay her on the beach, and Jimmy thought it a desirable opportunity for filling up the water-breakers. Taking them ashore in the dory, they carried the small craft up; and after getting the water they set out for a walk across the island, because the sloop would not float until nearly high tide. The island was barren except for a few clumps of stunted trees, but they enjoyed the ramble, and were now feeling tired by the unusual exercise, as well as hungry, because they had not troubled about taking any lunch.

Picking a sheltered spot, Bethune lighted his pipe and languidly looked about. Dingy clouds were driving across the island, and the leaden water broke with an angry splash among the stones. There had been a light breeze from seaward when they went ashore, but it had changed, and now blew moderately fresh off the land. It was very cold, with a rawness that penetrated. Bethune shivered.

"We ought to be getting on board," he said; "but I wish we had a paid crew to carry down the breakers and row us off. And I'd enjoy my supper better if I didn't have to cook it myself. It's curious how luxurious tastes stick to you."

"If you'd been a lobster fisher, you wouldn't have had any," Moran remarked.

"I expect that's true," Bethune laughed. "No doubt it depends on the way one is brought up; but you don't often surprise us with these reflections. Anyway, I can't help thinking of our opponent sitting at the saloon table on board his yacht with a smart steward waiting to bring him what he wants, while we squat over our tin plates in the cubby-hole with our knees against the centerboard trunk and our heads among the beams. It's a painful contrast."

"The sooner you finish moralizing and make a move, the sooner we'll get supper," Jimmy reminded him.

"I wish it was Hank's turn, only that one doesn't have much pleasure in eating the stuff he cooks. Still, it will be a comfort to work with the stove upright, and not to have to hold the things on. That's why I was waiting until the tide lifted her."

"She's afloat now," said Moran.

Bethune, looking up, saw that this was correct, for the sloop's mast began to move across the rocks in the background. Then there was a rattle of chain, and she drifted faster.

"Taking up the slack of her cable," said Jimmy. "We'd better get on board. I didn't give her much scope because I wanted to keep her off the stones."

"Wait until I've smoked my pipe out," Bethune said lazily; and they sat still for a few minutes.

The sloop brought up, sheering to and fro in the eddying gusts. When Moran turned to look at her he jumped up with an exclamation.

"She's off again!"

They watched her mast, and saw a gap open between it and a boulder. It was obvious that she was moving out to sea.

"The wind has changed since we left!" exclaimed Jimmy. "When she swung, she got a turn of her cable round the anchor-fluke and pulled it up."

"We'd better run for the dory!" Bethune cried, setting off along the shore.

"No use!" Jimmy called after him. "There isn't time." He jerked off his heavy sea-boots as he added: "She's dragging her cable along the bottom now, but it won't check her long."

The others saw that he was right. The water got deeper suddenly below the half-tide line, and when the boat had picked up her anchor her progress would be rapid.

"It's too cold for swimming, and you can't catch her!" Bethune expostulated breathlessly.

"I must do the best I can," said Jimmy, flinging off his jacket and plunging into the water.

They left him and ran along the beach, stumbling among the stones. It was some distance to the dory, and darkness was coming on. The Cetacea would drift to leeward fast, and they feared that she would be out of sight before they could begin the chase, but they might be in time to pick up their exhausted comrade. There was no doubt that he soon would become exhausted, because the water was icy cold, and a short, troubled swell worked into the bay. Besides this, the horror of their position lent them speed. It looked as if they would be left without food or shelter from the inclement weather on the desolate island. They had not even a line to catch fish with, and Bethune remembered that he had only three or four loose matches in his pocket.

He fell into a hollow between two boulders, hurting his leg, but was up again in a moment, making the best speed he could, with Moran clattering among the rocks a yard or two behind. Fortunately, the tide was almost up to the dory when they reached her. Thrusting her off they jumped on board and rowed with savage determination, pulling an oar each. The light craft lifted her bows and leaped forward in time to their powerful strokes, but a steeper swell was working in against the wind as the tide rose, and the long undulations checked her. Though the air was keen, the sweat dripped from the men as they rowed with throbbing hearts and labored breath, turning their heads for a glance forward every now and then.

They could not see their comrade, but that was hardly to be expected: a man's head is a small object to distinguish at a distance in broken water. The Cetacea, however, was still visible, and she did not seem to be much farther offshore. It was possible that Jimmy had got on board, and that they might overtake her before she felt the full force of the wind. The hope put fresh heart into them, and they strained every muscle to drive the dory faster across the irregular heave.

When Jimmy plunged into the icy water he gasped as it closed about him. The cold took away his breath and paralyzed his limbs, and he let his feet fall with an unreasoning desire to scramble out again. This, however, lasted only for a moment; before he could touch bottom he overcame the impulse, and, throwing his left hand forward, struck out vigorously. His was not a complex character, and his normal frame of mind was practical rather than imaginative, but he had been endowed with certain Spartan virtues. Moreover, he had learned in the sailing ships that what is needful must be done, no matter how the flesh may shrink.

Now, though he could not think collectively, he knew that it was his business to overtake the sloop. He could swim better than either of his comrades, and he set about his task with the unreflecting stubbornness that generally characterized him when an effort must be made. His mind was fixed on his object, and not on the risk he ran.

After the first half-minute the shock began to pass, and he suffered less, but he dully realized that he was making very poor progress. His clothing hampered him, the swell flung him back, the only thing in his favor was that the ripples the wind made ran behind him instead of splashing in his face. He swam with a powerful overhand stroke, but he knew that the Cetacea would drift at double his speed unless he could catch her while she was still in shallow water. When he swung up with the swell she was clearly in sight, but he could not judge whether he was gaining. She was still an alarming distance off, and moving away, but he hoped that the cable might check her, as it trailed along the uneven bottom.

But as the moments passed Jimmy began to despair of reaching her. The cold was sapping his vitality, his legs were getting cramped, and his breath was failing; but he turned upon his breast and swam on. He must hold out until his strength was spent; besides, he could not make the beach if he turned back. For a while he could not see the boat: his eyes were full of water, for the swell, which was getting steeper, occasionally broke over his head. Indeed, he hardly cared to look and contemplate the distance still to be covered. At last, however, when he stopped for a moment and raised his head, hope crept into his heart. The Cetacea was much nearer than he had expected. He must make a last, determined effort.

She had swung round, beam to wind, when he feebly clutched her rail amidships. For a few moments he held on; he had now to solve the difficulty of getting on board. As she drifted, his body trailed out away from her, and he could not get his knees against the planking. Even if he were able to do so, he had not the strength to lift himself on deck; and there was no rope hanging over that he could seize.

Then he thought of the wire bobstay that ran down from the end of the bowsprit and was fastened to the stem near the waterline. He must try to reach it and climb on that way. He cautiously moved his hands along the rail; for if they slipped off, he might not be able to get hold again.

Foot by foot he worked forward, and, stopping for some moments, tried to get up by the shrouds. He slipped back with only three fingers on the rail, and the risk he had run of letting go altogether unnerved him. He waited until he recovered, and then dragged himself forward, moving one hand over the other a few inches at a time. This was more difficult now, because as the boat's sheerline rose sharply at the bows he was higher out of the water and there was a greater weight on his arms; but at last he clutched the bowsprit and hung on by it, splashing feebly as he felt for the wire stay with his feet. Now that he was almost in safety, terror seized him. He found the wire, slid his foot along it, and lifting himself to the bowsprit fell forward, limp and inert, on deck. He lay there for a minute, and then with an effort roused himself, realizing that if he remained much longer he would perish of exhaustion and cold.

Staggering aft, he entered the cabin, and pulled off his clothes. There was no liquor on board, but he found some garments which were not very damp, and after trying to rub himself he put them on and munched a ship's biscuit while he did so. Feeling somewhat better after this, he went up on deck, for he must get in the cable and hoist some canvas, in order to gain control of the boat, which was fast driving out to sea. When he seized the chain he realized how greatly the swim had exhausted him. It was a heavy cable, but he had often hauled a long scope of it in when the anchor was holding and he had the boat's resistance to overcome. Now, however, he was beaten when he had laboriously pulled up a fathom or two. Trying again, he raised a few feet, and then had hard work to secure the chain round the bits.

He sat down to rest a minute, and looked about for the dory. He made her out indistinctly, but she seemed a long distance off, and as the breeze was freshening he did not know whether she could over-take the sloop. By setting some canvas he could pick her up, and the foresail would not be hard to hoist; but the Cetacea would not sail to windward with the heavy cable hanging from her bows. Jimmy remembered that there was a good length of it below; indeed, there might be scope enough to allow him to drop several fathoms on the bottom. The weight of this would act as a drag, and might, perhaps, bring her up. It depended on the depth of water.

He let the chain run, and watched it anxiously as it rattled out of the pipe. For a time it showed no sign of stopping, and then he felt a thrill as the harsh clanking slackened. The lower end had found bottom; but the vessel would soon lift a fathom or two, and he could not tell whether she would stop. The links ran slowly forward in a slanting line, and Jimmy saw by the absence of any splashing at the bows that she was still adrift. Then the rattle of the cable recommenced, which showed at least that there was more below, and she slowly stopped. In a few moments he felt her tug and strain, and white ripples broke angrily against the planking. She had either stopped or was drifting very slowly. Standing up on the cabin top, he waved his jacket that his comrades in the dory might see he was on board, and then went below out of the bitter wind. He could do no more.

It was some time later when the dory struck the side, and Moran clambered on board and entered the cabin. Jimmy could not see his face, but his gruff voice had an unusual tone.

"That was a mighty good swim, partner," he said. "I was scared you wouldn't make it."

"So was I," smiled Jimmy. "I was too dead beat to heave the cable when I got on board."

"Of course," Moran agreed sympathetically. "Now you lie off and leave things to us."

Then Bethune came down and let his hand rest for a moment on Jimmy's shoulder.

"Thanks, old man! Neither Hank nor I could have reached her."

They were none of them sentimentalists, and Jimmy felt that enough had been said.

"I'm a bit worried about my thick jacket and sea-boots," he replied. "You see, I'll need them."

"That's so," said Moran. "As soon as we've got sail on her, we'll pull back and look."

Jimmy protested. They were tired and hungry, and it would be a hard row to the beach against the rising breeze, but Moran laughed, and Bethune told him to sit still when he would have gone up to help them. He lighted the stove, and when they called him the reefed mainsail was banging overhead, and Bethune was in the dory, while Moran, kneeling under the jib, freed a coil of chain from the fluke of the anchor.

"I guess that's what made the trouble," he said. "We won't be long, and when you have made two or three tacks you can show a light."

He jumped into the dory, and it disappeared into the dark, while Jimmy drove the sloop ahead, close-hauled, until he dimly made out the boulders on a point. Then he came round and stretched along-shore on the other tack, until he left the helm for a few moments and lighted a lantern. Soon after he had done so he heard a shout and when he hove the boat to there was a splash of oars. Then the dory emerged from the gloom and Moran, seizing the rail, threw a jacket and pair of long boots on deck.

"Got them all right. They were a fathom from the tide; the beach is pretty steep."

"I must have had the sense to throw them well back, though I can't remember it," Jimmy answered with a laugh.

"We're going to have a better supper than I thought we would get not long ago," Bethune remarked as he lifted the dory in; and Jimmy gave the helm to Moran and went below to help in preparing the meal.

CHAPTER XXVIII
A TRUCE

When Jimmy sighted the island where the wreck lay, there was a ghostly white glimmer among the mist that hung heavily along the shore. Most of the land was hidden, but the bank of vapor had a solidity and sharpness of outline that indicated the existence of something behind it. The wind was light, but it freshened as they crept on under easy sail, and the fog rolling back from the water revealed a broad and roughly level streak that glittered in the morning light. Nearer at hand two tall detached masses shone a cold gray-white on a strip of indigo sea. Then the vapor dropped again like a curtain as the breeze died away.

"Ice!" commented Moran. "Guess we've got here too soon."

"It seemed to be banked up north of the point," Bethune remarked. "I imagine we'll be pretty safe in the bight unless some of that thin, cutting stuff is drifting about."

Jimmy hove the boat to and lighted his pipe.

"The matter needs thinking over, and we'll wait a bit for a better view," he said. "It doesn't look as if we could get to work just yet, and if any big floes drove across the banks at high-water, we'd be awkwardly placed in the bight. On the other hand, the ice will probably hang about until a strong breeze breaks it up, and I don't want to keep the sea in wild weather while it's in the neighborhood. The fog comes down thick and the nights are still dark."

The others agreed to this and were afterward moodily silent. Whichever course they took there would be delay. It had been a relief to find that they had reached the island first, but they had no doubt that Clay was not far behind them. All they had gained by an earlier start might be sacrificed unless they could finish their task before he arrived.

The fog held all day and grew thicker when darkness fell; but the red dawn brought a clearer air with signs of a change, and Jimmy steered shoreward, sweeping the beach with his glasses as they approached the channel through the sands. That end of the island was free of ice, and after consulting together they decided to enter the bight. They thought they would be safer there, and they wanted to feel that the voyage was finished and they were ready to get to work. During the afternoon it began to blow strongly off the shore. The sloop lay in smooth water close to the beach, but when night fell the surf was roaring on the sands and they could hear the crash of rending ice. At times the din was awe-striking, but it died away again, and although they kept anchor watch in turns no floe appeared to trouble them. At dawn the greater part of the ice had gone, and they could see white patches shining far out at sea, but it was blowing much too hard for them to think of leaving shelter.

They waited two days, anxiously watching for a trail of smoke, but nothing broke the skyline, and at last the breeze fell. It was a flat calm when they towed the Cetacea out on a gray morning, but the swell ran steep and a thin drizzle obscured the sea. The sloop plunged wildly over the long undulations, jerking back the dory in spite of her crew's toil at the oars, and it was nearly noon when they picked up their cross-bearings and anchored by the wreck. Nobody suggested getting dinner and Jimmy went down as soon as he could put on the diving dress. He found the wreck, which freed him of a keen anxiety, but he had to come up without entering the hold. She had moved a short distance since he last saw her, and now lay almost on her beam-ends with her upper works badly shattered. The gap they had previously crept through was closed by broken beams. Jimmy supposed that heavy ice, floating deep in the water, had ground across her higher part as it drove out to sea.

Moran went down next, and reported on his return that an entrance might be made, with some trouble. Bethune went armed with a crowbar. By nightfall they had wrenched away several obstructing timbers and discovered that there was a good deal of sand to be moved. They ate a hearty supper and went to sleep. The work was the same the next day, but although they began as soon as it was light they realized by noon that the most they could hope for was to clear the way for an entrance on the morrow. All felt the effects of their labors and of breathing the compressed air, and when it was Jimmy's turn to go down toward evening, he leaned on the coaming, reluctant to put on the dress.

"I'll be ready when I've finished this pipe," he said. "You'd better screw up that pump-gland in the meanwhile. I didn't get as much air as I wanted last time."

Moran set about it, and, though time was precious, Jimmy did not try to hurry him, but stood listlessly looking out to sea. A fine rain was falling, there was very little wind, and belts of fog streaked the dim gray water between him and the horizon. He was watching one belt when it seemed to open and a blurred shape crept out. Jimmy dropped his pipe and scrambled to the cabin top. He could distinguish a patch of white hull and a tall mast. As he called to the others a short funnel appeared, and a trail of smoke lay dark along the edge of the fog.

"We don't need the glasses to tell whose boat that is," he said harshly.

They knew her at the first glance and their faces hardened.

"Clay's lost no time," Bethune remarked. "Well, I suppose it means a fight, and we'll gain nothing by running away now, but we may as well stop diving until we find out whether it's worth while to go on."

After securing the pumps and gear they waited, watching the yacht's approach. She came straight on at moderate speed, and stopped three or four hundred yards away. They saw the anchor splash and heard a rattle of chain, but after that there was no sign of activity on board the vessel.

"It's my opinion Clay knows who we are," Moran said.

"You can take that for granted," Bethune replied. "We'll hear from him before long, but he doesn't mean to show any eagerness in sending a boat off. As time's getting on, I think we'll have supper."

As they finished the meal a smart gig, pulled by uniformed seamen, approached the sloop, and when she stopped alongside the helmsman handed Jimmy two notes.

Opening them in the cabin, he showed his companions two sheets of fine paper bearing an embossed flag and the vessel's name. One note stated that Mr. Clay requested their company at supper on board his yacht, and the other, which was longer, was from Aynsley. He said that although he was not sure they had much cause to remember him with gratitude, he would be glad to see them, and hoped they would not refuse his father's invitation.

"Do you think Clay made him write this?" Jimmy asked.

"No," said Bethune. "On the whole, I imagine it was sent without Clay's knowledge. Of course, Aynsley had some reason for writing, but while I can't tell what it is, he's not in the plot."

"Anyway, I'm not going; I've no wish to sit at that man's table."

Bethune grinned as he indicated his pilot jacket, which was shrunk and stained by salt-water, and his old sea-boots.

"Our get-up's hardly smart enough for a yacht's saloon; and I've a notion that it might be wiser to stay where we are. Still, we'll have to see him before long, and you'd better write a civil refusal; though I'm afraid we can't match his decorative stationery."

Jimmy tore a leaf out of his notebook and scribbled a few moments with a pencil. Then he read to his comrades:

"Mr. Farquhar and his friends regret their inability to leave their boat, but would esteem Mr. Clay's company if he cares to visit them."

"Bully!" exclaimed Bethune. "You've sealed it with a thumb-mark, and—well, we haven't an envelope."

When the gig's crew rowed away with the note the three men gathered together in the little cabin.

"Will he come, do you think?" Moran asked.

"Oh, yes; but he'll take his time, and get his supper first comfortably," Bethune replied. "I'm rather anxious about the thing, because if he doesn't come we can look out for trouble."

"If that's what he wants, he'll get it," Moran drawled, from his corner on a locker.

Jimmy sat smoking in thoughtful silence. He had learned that Clay was cunning and unscrupulous; and, if worse came to worse, they were cut off from any outside help by leagues of lonely sea. Their enemy had a strong crew who were, no doubt, well paid and ready to do his bidding; for Jimmy knew that Clay would not have sailed on such an errand with men he could not trust. The sloop's party would be hopelessly outmatched if he used force; and it would be difficult to obtain redress afterward, because they were only three in number, and all interested in the undertaking, while Clay would have many witnesses, who could claim to be independent. The situation needed careful handling, and Jimmy was glad that Bethune was on board. For all that, if things came to the worst, Clay should not find them easy victims.

Presently he went out to look at the weather. The rain had stopped and low mist hung about, but a half-moon was rising in a patch of clear sky. The swell heaved, long and smooth, about the sloop, which swung up and down with a regular motion. Jimmy could see the yacht's anchor light not far away and the yellow blink from her saloon windows, but he could hear nothing that suggested preparations for sending off a boat. As it was cold in the cockpit, he returned to the cabin, where the others had lighted the lamp, and none of them said much for the next hour. They could hear the loose halyards slap the mast and the water splash about beneath the floorings, and the soft lapping of the tide along the planking.

Moran suddenly raised his hand, and, after their long wait in suspense, it was a relief to hear the measured splash of oars.

"That means he's willing to make terms," Bethune said.

Five minutes later the yacht's boat ran alongside and Clay climbed on board.

"You can take a run ashore, boys, and come off when we signal," he said to his crew, and then turned to Jimmy. "I've come for a talk."

"Will you come below," said Jimmy, moving back the scuttle-slide. "Be careful how you get down: there's not much room."

Clay bumped his head before he found a place on a locker, where he sat silent for a moment, looking about. The light of the bulkhead lamp revealed the rough discomfort of the narrow cabin. Condensed moisture glistened on the low roof-beams; the floorings were damp and littered with coils of rope. The end of a torn sail projected from the forecastle door, and damp blankets were loosely spread on the lockers to dry in the warmth of the rusty stove. All this indicated stern, utilitarian economy, and the men's ragged, work-stained clothes were in keeping with it; but Clay noticed that their expression was resolute.

In the meanwhile they were studying him, and it struck them that he looked ill. His face was flabby and there were heavy pouches under his eyes.

"So my invitation didn't bring you off!" he said. "Were you afraid I might carry you out to sea?"

"Not exactly," Bethune replied. "One would not suspect you of so crude a plan. Can't you take it that we were afraid of a change of wind? You see, it's a rather exposed position."

"That's so," Clay agreed; "you have no steam to help you ride out a breeze. But we'll get down to business. I made you an offer of five thousand dollars to give me the first chance of cleaning up this wreck. I'll now go a thousand dollars better."

"Is that your limit?"

"It is; you'll save time by realizing it. I've bid up to the last cent I think worth while."

"Suppose we decline?"

"You would be foolish. You have no claim on the wreck; in a sense, I have, and if we can't come to some understanding I begin work at once. My yacht can hang on through a gale of wind and with our outfit we can get something done in pretty bad weather. You have a small sailing-boat and poor, cheap gear. As soon as a breeze gets up you'll have to quit."

"I imagine you haven't yet mentioned all your advantages over us," Bethune suggested.

Clay looked at him keenly and then smiled. "That's so. I'm trying to be polite."

"In fact, you're keeping your strongest arguments in reserve. Unless we agree to your proposition, there's not much chance of our recovering anything from the wreck?"

"You're pretty near the mark," Clay answered, smiling confidently.

"The odds seem against us. Perhaps I'd better be candid. The truth is, we have already recovered something of importance."

Clay's expression became intent.

"Then you're smarter than I thought and you played your hand well the last time I met you. However, it will probably save us all trouble if we put our cards on the table. What have you got?"

Bethune took out his notebook.

"To begin with, two bags of gold; the weight and marks, so far as we could make the latter out—"

"Shucks!" interrupted Clay. "They don't count. You can keep your share of their salvage. Come to the point."

"One iron-clamped, sealed case. The stencil marks, although partly obliterated, appear to be D.O.C. in a circle; the impress on the seals to attached tracing. Contents"—Bethune paused and looked steadily at Clay—"I dare say you know what these are?"

"Do you?" Clay asked sharply.

"We opened the case."

There was silence for a few moments and all were very still. Clay's voice was not so steady when he spoke again.

"Where is the case?"

"Not here," said Bethune dryly. "If we don't turn up to claim it within a fixed time, or if any attempt is made to obtain possession of it in our absence it will be handed to the underwriters."

"You seem to have taken precautions," Clay remarked.

"We did the best we could," Bethune admitted with a modest air.

"Imagining that you might sell the box to me?"

"No!" Jimmy interposed sternly. "That was not our plan. When my partner first let you make an offer for the wreck—"

Clay stopped him with a gesture.

"It was to lead me on—you needn't explain. Very well; I suggested putting our cards down, and now I'll tell you something you don't suspect. There's a duplicate of that box on board and it contains the gold."

Jimmy started, Moran gazed at Clay with knitted brows, and Bethune looked frankly puzzled. Clay seemed quietly amused at their surprise.

"You don't understand?" he said. "After all, there's no reason why you should do so; but the truth of my statement is easily tested. Now I'll ask you a question to which I want a straight answer. What are you going to do with the gold you get?"

"Deliver it to the underwriters and claim salvage," said Jimmy promptly.

"That's all? You have no other plans?"

"That is all."

"Then I'll exchange the case which holds the gold for the one you have. You can't recover it without my help."

For a time no one spoke. The three partners looked at one another in perplexed indecision, while Clay sat quietly still. There was a mystery behind the matter to which they could find no clue, and Clay would obviously not supply it. They did not know what to think.

"Do you know where to find this case?" Bethune asked.

"I believe so. I suggest that one of you come down to help me; Mr. Farquhar for preference."

"Then you think of going down!" Jimmy exclaimed.

"I am going down the first thing tomorrow, whether you come or not. But what about my offer?"

"We can't answer yet," said Bethune. "It needs some thought."

"Very well," Clay agreed. "For all that, I must make a start in the morning. If you prefer, we can let the matter stand over until we find the case." He paused and smiled at Jimmy. "You don't look a nervous man and you needn't hesitate. I've never put on a diving dress and you have had some experience; and I'm willing to use your boat and let your friends control the pumps."

"I'm not afraid," retorted Jimmy. "The difficulty is that the way into the strong-room is not yet open. It will take at least a day to remove the sand that has banked up against the opening."

"Then I suppose I must wait, but I'll send my diver across to help you at daybreak," said Clay. "When everything is ready you can let me know. Now, if you have no suggestion to make, I think I'll get back."

Moran signaled to the boat's crew, and when Clay had gone they sat down again in the cabin with thoughtful faces.

"I'll admit that things have taken an unexpected turn," Bethune remarked. "It's obvious that we're on the track of a secret of some importance which might explain a cunning fraud, but the matter's complicated by the shipping of the genuine box of gold, and I can't determine yet how far it's our business to investigate it."

"You don't seem so ready at forming theories as usual," Jimmy commented.

"I've made one or two and they look rather plausible until you test them. However, as it might be dangerous to jump to conclusions about the course we ought to take, I think we'd better wait. And now, as we're to start at daybreak, it might be wise to go to sleep."

CHAPTER XXIX

THE HIDDEN GOLD

The breeze was light at daybreak, and while the island still loomed shapeless and shadowy across the leaden water the yacht's gig brought Clay's diver and an excellent set of pumps. As soon as they were rigged the diver and Moran went below and took their turn with the others during the first half of the day, for there was still a good deal to be done before they could clear a passage into the hold. They sent Clay word of their progress and at noon Aynsley was rowed across to the sloop.

"Although you refused last night, I hope you'll come on board to lunch," he said, after greeting them pleasantly.

"We have too much on hand," Jimmy replied. "In fact, we're not going to stop for a meal. It's unusually fine weather and we must get into the strong-room before dark. I expect it will take us three or four hours yet."

"It's a good excuse," returned Aynsley. "In a way, I'm glad you're too busy to come, because I imagine my father is very keen on finishing the job, and I don't want him to get worrying about the delay." He paused, and added frankly: "I'm going to ask a favor. He's not well, and I gather that you and he are to some extent opposed. Now I can't expect you to sacrifice your interest, but you might try to avoid any heated dispute as far as possible. Excitement isn't good for him."

"We can promise that," said Jimmy. "It looks as if you knew nothing about the business."

"I don't. And, more than that, I have no wish to learn anything."

"We're not in a position to tell you much if you pressed us; but it struck us that your father wasn't looking very fit, and it might be better if you stopped him from going down."

"I can't," Aynsley answered with a smile. "I'm afraid I haven't much control over him."

Early in the evening Clay came on board and sat in the cockpit while the men relieved each other below. He asked a question now and then, but for the most part waited quietly, watching the bubbles that rose in milky effervescence.

At last the diver came up, and was followed closely by Bethune, bringing a rope.

"The strong-room's open," he said exultantly. "Heave on that line and see what you get!"

Moran pulled with a will, for there was some resistance to be overcome, and Jimmy leaned down in strong excitement when a wooden case smeared with sand broke the surface. Seizing it he came near to being dragged over the rail, and Bethune had to help him to lift it on board. Clay examined the case coolly, studying the half-washed-out marks.

"You ought to get something handsome for salvage on that, and I won't contest your claim," he said. "Keep it on board if you like; our diver's paid by the day. Now, if you're ready, we'll go down."

They carefully fastened on his dress, but when Bethune gave him a few instructions he said his own man had told him all he needed to know during the voyage. Jimmy put on his helmet and went first down the ladder, waiting at the bottom for Clay. It was, he felt, a strange experience to be walking along the sea-floor with a man who had been his enemy; but he was now master of the situation. Indeed, he had to help his companion when they reached the entrance to the hold and he did not think that Clay could have crept up the dark passage between the shaft tunnel and the hanging weed on the ship's crushed side without his assistance. Their lamps glimmered feebly through the water that sucked in and out, and it was no easy matter to keep signal-lines and air-pipes clear. Clay, however, though awkward and somewhat feeble in his movements, showed no want of nerve.

When they crawled into the strong-room he stood still, moving his lamp. The pale flashes wavered to and fro, searching the rough, iron-bound planks, until they stopped, fixed upon one spot. Clay beckoned Jimmy toward it, and then, losing his balance, lurched and swayed in a ludicrous manner before he could steady himself. Jimmy thought the man must be mistaken, for he had indicated a plank in the deck between two iron plates, although, as the wreck had fallen over, the plank was on one side of them, instead of being overhead. He turned to Clay with a questioning motion of his hands, but the flicker of light was still fixed upon the same spot. Jimmy raised the crowbar he had brought and drove it into a joint nearly level with his head, and Clay indicated that he was doing right.

Jimmy knew that he had no time to lose. Clay was not in good health, and had already been under water as long as was safe for a man unaccustomed to the pressure. If he broke down, it would be difficult to get him out of the hold. For all that, Jimmy was reluctant to abandon the search a moment before it was necessary. It was getting dark, the stream was gaining strength, and it did not seem probable that any one could get down again that night. Jimmy wanted to finish his task.

The beam he attacked was soft, but two bolts ran through it and an iron strap was clamped along its edge. The rotten timber tore away in flakes, but Jimmy could not break out a large piece, and the iron fastenings deflected his bar. He glanced at his companion, who encouraged him by a gesture; and then fell to work again with determined energy. He did not know how long he continued, but he was disturbed by a movement of the water and saw Clay swaying slackly to and fro. It looked as if he were about to fall, but his heavy boots and buoyant dress kept him upright. Still he might go down, and Jimmy knew that it is hard to recover one's balance in a diving dress. Clay must be got out at once. Jimmy seized his arm and made his way toward the opening, thrusting his companion along the side of the shaft tunnel.

It was with keen relief that he dragged him clear of the splintered beams at the entrance to the hold and stepped out on the level bottom of the sea. No light came down through the water, even the shadow of the sloop above was no longer discernible; but Jimmy had his signal-line for guide and followed it with his hand on Clay's shoulder, until he distinguished the ripple of the tide about the ladder.

Pushing his companion toward it, he watched his clumsy ascent and then clambered up. When he got on board Clay was sitting on deck, but he sank back limply against the cabin top as they took his helmet off. It was nearly dark, but they could see that his lips were blue, and that his livid face was mottled by faint purple patches. He gasped once or twice, and then began to fumble awkwardly at the breast of the diving dress.

"I know what he wants!" cried Aynsley. "Get these things off him as quick as you can! Somebody bring me a spoon!"

They hurriedly stripped the canvas covering from the half-conscious man, and, taking a small bottle from his vest pocket, gave him a few drops of the liquid. It took effect, for in a few moments Clay feebly raised himself.

"Better now; not used to diving," he said, and turned to Jimmy as Aynsley and a seaman helped him into the waiting gig. "We'll get the case next time."

The gig pulled away, and the three men watched it disappear into the darkness.

"It's lucky you were able to bring him up," Bethune observed.

"I was scared at first," Jimmy confessed. "Perhaps I should have come up sooner, but he seemed determined to stop."

"What about the case?"

"We hadn't time to get at it. You see, it's not in the strong-room. He made me start cutting out the underside of the deck."

"The deck!" exclaimed Moran. "Then they must have put the stuff in the poop cabin!"

"I don't think so. I expect there's a shallow space between the main beams and the cabin floor."

"And that's where the case is? It strikes me as curious; distinctly curious!"

"I dare say; I didn't think of that. The most important thing is that we ought to reach the case in about an hour."

"It's too risky. The tide's running strong now, and it's going to be very dark. We have kept clear of serious trouble so far, and I see no sign of wind."

Jimmy reluctantly agreed to wait until the morning and Bethune went below to get supper ready.

At daybreak Aynsley pulled across in the yacht's small dinghy, and his face had an anxious look as he entered the Cetacea's cabin, where Jimmy was cleaning some of the pump fittings by lamplight.

"How is Mr. Clay?" Jimmy asked.

"He looks very ill. I left him getting up and sculled across as quietly as I could to have a talk with you. Can you do anything to prevent his going down? I don't think he's fit for it."

"I'm afraid not. You see, we're at variance, in a way, and if we made any objections he'd get suspicious."

"You couldn't play some trick with the diving gear? I'm worried about him; the pressure and exertion might be dangerous."

"We might put our own pump out of action, but we couldn't meddle with yours, and he might insist on going alone."

"That wouldn't do," said Aynsley. "I wouldn't hesitate to smash our outfit, but he'd get so savage about it that the excitement would do more harm than the diving."

"Then you'll have to reason with him."

Aynsley smiled.

"I've been trying it ever since we dropped anchor, and it hasn't been a success; you don't know my father." He gave Jimmy a steady look. "He means you to be his companion, and although I've no claim on you, I want you to promise that you'll take care of him."

Everything considered, it struck Jimmy as curious that he should be the recipient of this request; but he sympathized with Aynsley, and imagined that his anxiety was justified. Clay had treated them harshly, but he was ill and apparently powerless to injure them further.

"Very well," he promised. "I'll do the best I can."

"Thanks!" responded Aynsley in a grateful tone. "I can trust you, and I've a notion that my father feels safe in your hands; though he's not confiding, as a rule."

"If you'll wait a minute we'll give you some coffee," Bethune said hospitably.

"No, thanks!" replied Aynsley. "I must get back before I'm missed. There'd be trouble if my irascible father guessed why I'd come here."

He jumped into the dinghy and sculled her silently into the mist that drifted between the vessels; and half an hour later Clay came off with the diver in the gig. His face had a gray, pinched look, and Jimmy noticed that he breathed rather hard after the slight effort of getting on board the sloop.

"I think you had better let me finish the job, sir," he said. "You'd be more comfortable if you waited quietly on board until we brought up the case."

"I'm going down," Clay answered shortly. "You might not be able to get at it without my help."

"Anyway, you can wait until we break through the deck. It will shorten the time you need stay below."

After some demur, Clay agreed to this; but he suggested that Moran and Bethune should clear the ground instead of sending his own diver, and in a few minutes they were under water. It was some time before they came up, and when they had undressed Clay looked hard at Bethune.

"Have you cut the hole?" he asked.

"Yes," said Bethune; "I think it's big enough."

"You didn't go through?"

"No; we'd been down quite long enough."

"Give me that brandy," Clay said to a steward in the waiting gig, and turned to Jimmy when he had drained a small wineglass. "Now we'll get to work as soon as we can."

Jimmy went down the ladder and Clay followed him steadily across the sand. The tide was low, the stream slack, and the dim green water was filled with strange refractions of the growing light above. The sloop rode overhead, a patch of opaque shadow, and the wreck loomed up, black and shapeless, in front. They reached her without trouble, and Jimmy switched on his lamp and carefully cleared Clay's air-pipe and line before he crawled into the dark gap. The man seemed to move with greater ease and confidence than he had shown on the previous day, and Jimmy felt reassured as he guided him along the side of the shaft tunnel. Glancing at the long streamers of weed that wavered mysteriously through the gloom, he remembered the sense of fear and shrinking he had had to overcome on his first few descents. It looked as if he need not be anxious about his companion.

It was more difficult to get him into the strong-room, but they entered it safely and Jimmy saw that Bethune and Moran had thrown up a bank of sand under the hole between the beams. This would make it easier to reach, but as he was arranging his air-pipe preparatory to entering Clay made an imperative sign. Jimmy felt surprised, because the man obviously meant that he was going first. Though it would not be hard to scramble up after seizing a timber, the feat would require some exertion, and Jimmy tried to make this clear, but Clay disregarded his signaled objections. It was impossible to explain himself properly in pantomime, and, as Clay seemed determined, Jimmy let him go. He might grow suspicious and perhaps combative if force were used to detain him.

Jimmy helped him up, and then felt anxious as Clay's swollen legs and heavy boots disappeared through the hole. The space above must be low, and was probably cumbered with wreckage, but Jimmy saw that Clay's air-pipe and signal-line ran steadily through the gap, which implied that he found no difficulty in moving about. Faint flashes of light, broken up into wavering reflections, came out of the hole and Jimmy switched off his lamp so that he could see them better. Though he meant to keep his promise to Aynsley, he admitted that the tension he felt was not solely on Clay's account. The recovery of the case was of great importance to his party, and if they failed to secure it now a change in the weather might frustrate the next attempt or perhaps place the gold altogether out of reach.

After a while it struck Jimmy that Clay ought to come out. The man was unaccustomed to diving and was in precarious health; moreover, if he could not get at the case, Jimmy meant to try. He pulled the line, and got a signal in answer that gave him no excuse for interfering; so he waited until the pipe and line began to run backward. Then a light flashed sharply as if in warning, and as Jimmy turned on his lamp a dark object fell from the gap. It was large and square and, striking the sand with its edge, darkened the disturbed water.

Thrilled with a sense of triumph, Jimmy turned to help Clay, who was coming out of the hole; but as Clay's legs dangled he lost his grip and fell backward. He did not come down violently, but sank until one foot touched the sand, and then made fantastic contortions. His buoyant dress supported him and he looked a grotesque figure as he lurched about. Jimmy, however, was alarmed, for it dawned on him that this was not the result of inexperienced clumsiness. Clay had lost control of his limbs: he was too weak to keep the balance between his heavy helmet and his weighted boots. Indeed, he was obviously helpless, and it would be a difficult task to get him out of the wreck; but it must be set about at once.

Jimmy dragged him through the opening into the hold and felt keen relief when he saw that both pipes ran clear; then he guided him to the tunnel and, letting him lean on it, pushed him along. Clay was a big, heavy man, but his weight was counteracted by the air in his dress, and he could be moved with a push almost like a floating object. Sometimes he moved too far and fell away from the tunnel. Jimmy long afterward remembered with a shudder the time they spent in reaching the outlet. He could not use his lamp, because he needed both hands; and he was horribly afraid that the pipes and lines might get foul. He believed that he threw Clay down and dragged him out into the open water by his helmet, but he had only a hazy recollection of the matter.

When they reached the level sand, Jimmy signaled urgently with his line, and got a reply. Then the rope he looped round Clay's shoulders tightened and he guided and steadied him as they were drawn toward the ladder. A few moments later Clay was lifted on to the Cetacea's deck, and Jimmy sat down on the cabin top, feeling very limp.

When somebody took off his helmet he saw Clay lying on the deck, with Aynsley bending over him holding a spoon to his mouth. Jimmy thought he could not get him to take the restorative, but he was too dazed and exhausted to notice clearly, and shortly afterward Clay was lifted into the gig. It headed for the yacht, the crew pulling hard, and Jimmy turned to Bethune.

"I was afraid I couldn't get him up," he said weakly. "He seems pretty bad."

"I think he is; but you don't look fit yourself."

"The dizziness is the worst," murmured Jimmy. "I'll go below and lie down. But I'm forgetting; we found the case."

Bethune helped him into the cabin, and made him comfortable on a locker. He had a bad headache and a curious sense of heaviness which grew worse when the pain lessened. In a short time, however, he had fallen into a deep sleep.

And while he slept, Moran went below and brought up the case.

CHAPTER XXX
THE LAST OF THE WRECK

Thick fog lay upon the water when Jimmy wakened. He slipped off the locker and, standing with his bent head among the deckbeams, looked at Bethune with heavy eyes.

"Is it dark?" he asked. "How long have I slept?"

"It is not dark yet. How do you feel?"

"I think I'm all right. Did you get the case?"

"Sure!" smiled Bethune. "It's safe under the floorings and heavy enough to make the salvage worth having. But I came down to bring you this note from Aynsley. One of his men brought it and his gig's waiting alongside."

Jimmy opened the note and read it aloud in the dim light of the cabin.

"I shall consider it a favor if you will come across at once. My father seems very ill and he insists on seeing you."

"I'd better go," Jimmy said. "After all, we couldn't have got the case without his help, and, in a way, I'm sorry for him. He must have known he was running a big risk, but he was very plucky."

"It can't do much harm," Bethune agreed. "Somehow I feel that we have nothing more to fear from him. For all that, I wish I could go with you."

"I suppose that wouldn't do," said Jimmy thoughtfully.

"No; you can't take your lawyer along when you visit a sick man. Still, if he's not quite as bad as Aynsley thinks, you may as well be on your guard."

Jimmy got into the waiting boat and the men plied the oars rhythmically. A bank of clammy fog rested on the slate-green heave that moved in from seaward in slow undulations. The damp condensed on the boat's thwarts and her knees were beaded with moisture. The air felt strangely raw, and the measured beat of the surf rose drearily from the hidden beach. At intervals the tolling of a bell sounded through the noises of the sea; and when the yacht appeared, looming up gray and ghostly, her rigging dripped, her deck was sloppy, and the seamen at the gangway had a limp, bedraggled look. Everything seemed cheerless and depressing; and Aynsley's face was anxious as he hurried toward Jimmy.

"It was good of you to come," he said. "I hope you're none the worse."

"Not much. I'm sorry your father has suffered from the trip, but I really did my best."

"I'm sure of that," Aynsley responded. "But he's waiting to see you."

He led Jimmy into a handsome teak deckhouse between the masts, and opened a door into the owner's cabin, which occupied the full width of the house. Two electric lamps were burning, rich curtains were drawn across the windows to shut out the foggy light, and a fire burned cheerfully in an open-fronted stove, encased in decorated tiles. Its pipe was of polished brass; the walls and the ceiling were enameled a spotless white, with the moldings of the beams picked out in harmonious color; two good marine pictures hung on the cross bulkhead. The place struck Jimmy as being strangely luxurious after the cramped, damp cabin of the sloop; but he soon forgot his surroundings when his eyes rested on the figure lying in the corner-berth.

Clay had thrown off the coverings and was propped up on two large pillows. His silk pajamas showed the massiveness of his short neck and his powerful chest and arms; but his face was pinched and gray except where it was streaked with a faint purple tinge. Jimmy could see that the man was very ill.

"I hear you got the case," Clay began in a strained voice, motioning Jimmy to a seat.

"Yes. The others brought it up; I haven't examined it yet."

"You'll find it all right." Clay smiled weakly. "I suppose you know there's another case and a couple of small packages still in the strong-room?"

"We understood so."

"Get them up; they're in the sand. You can have my diver, and it shouldn't take you long. You're welcome to the salvage; it isn't worth fighting you about. After that, there will be nothing left in her. I give you my word for it, and you can clear out when you like."

"None of us wants to stay; we have had enough. I suppose you have no idea of going down again?"

"No," Clay answered rather grimly; "it doesn't seem probable. I haven't thanked you yet for bringing me up." He turned to Aynsley.

"Mr. Farquhar stuck to me when I was half conscious and helpless. I'd like you to remember that. Now I want a quiet talk with him."

Aynsley left them, and Clay was silent for a moment or two. He lay back on the pillows with his eyes closed, and when he spoke it seemed to be with an effort.

"About the bogus case? What are you going to do with it?"

"We have been too busy to think of that. You spoke of an exchange, but of course we haven't the thing here—"

"No," said Clay. "Your partner's pretty smart and I guess you have got it safely locked up in one of the Island ports. The chances are that you won't be able to give it to me."

Jimmy understood him. Clay seemed to know that he was very ill. He lay quiet again, as if it tired him to talk.

"It has been a straight fight on your side," he resumed after his short rest. "I guess you might give that box to Osborne. You're white men, and, though you might perhaps make trouble about it, the thing's no use to you. You know Osborne?"

"Yes," Jimmy answered rather awkwardly, because he saw what the question implied. Clay had judged him correctly; for Jimmy had no wish to extort a price for keeping a dark secret. He thought he could answer for his comrades, though he would not make a binding promise without their consent.

"I believe you know Ruth Osborne," Clay went on with a searching glance at him.

Jimmy was taken off his guard, and Clay noticed his slight start and change of expression.

"I met Miss Osborne on board the Empress," he replied cautiously. Clay smiled.

"Well," he said, "she's a girl who makes an impression, and my notion is that her character matches her looks." He paused and went on with a thoughtful air: "Anyhow, she wouldn't have Aynsley."

Jimmy colored. Clay's manner was significant, but not hostile. Ill as the man was, Jimmy imagined that he was cleverly playing a game, and, with some object, was trying to turn his recent opponent into an ally. For all that, Jimmy thought his motive was good.

"I mustn't keep you talking too long," Jimmy said. He did not wish to discuss Miss Osborne.

"I soon get tired; but there's something I must mention. You'll clean the wreck out in a few hours, and then you may as well blow her up. My diver will help you, and we have some high-grade powder and a firing outfit."

"It might be wise. If she washed up nearer the bight she would be dangerous. The island's charted, and I dare say vessels now and then run in."

Clay looked at him with a faint twinkle.

"Yes; I think we can take it that she's a danger. I'll tell my man to give you the truck you want and you had better get finished while the weather's fine."

Moving feebly, he held out his hand in sign of dismissal, and Jimmy took it. He had no repugnance to doing so, but he felt that he was making his helpless enemy a promise.

Aynsley was waiting on deck and insisted on Jimmy's staying to dinner. Although well served, it was a melancholy meal, and Jimmy had a sense of loneliness as he sat at the long table. Aynsley was attentive to his comfort and tried to make conversation, but he was obviously depressed.

"What are your plans?" he asked.

"We start to get out the last of the gold at daybreak," Jimmy answered. "If we're fortunate, it should take only three or four hours."

"And then?"

"I agreed with your father that we had better blow up the wreck."

"You should get that done before dark tomorrow."

"I think so, if the water keeps smooth. In fact, I dare say we'll have finished in the afternoon."

"That's a relief," declared Aynsley. "Perhaps I'm not tactful in reminding you that I don't know—and don't want to know—what your business with my father is, but he's seriously ill, and we ought to get away at once in order to put him in a good doctor's hands as soon as possible. The trouble is that he won't hear of our leaving until you have completed the job."

"We'll lose no time," Jimmy assured him. "The glass is dropping, but I don't expect much wind just yet."

"Thanks!" Aynsley responded with deep feeling. "There's another thing—if the wind's light or unfavorable, we'll start under steam and could tow you south as long as it keeps fine. It may save you a few days. And you could stay with us if your friends can spare you. To tell the truth, it would be a kindness to me. I'm worried, and want somebody to talk to."

Jimmy agreed, and was shortly afterward rowed back to the sloop.

By noon the next day they had brought up the last of the gold. After a hasty luncheon, they went down again, but their next task took some time, because the diver insisted on clamping the charges of dynamite firmly to the principal timbers and boring holes in some. Then a series of wires had to be taken below and coupled, and it was nearly supper time when Jimmy came up from his last descent.

A faint breeze flecked the leaden water with ripples too languid to break on the sloop's bows; the island was wrapped in fog, and the swell was gentle. Only a dull murmur rose from the hidden beach. To seaward it was clearer and the yacht rode, a long white shape, lifting her bows with a slow and rhythmic swing, while a gray cloud that spread in a hazy smear rose nearly straight up from her funnel. The sloop's cable was hove short and everything was ready for departure. Her crew sat in the cockpit watching the diver fit the wires to the contact-plug of the firing battery.

The men on the sloop were filled with keen impatience. They had borne many hardships and perils in those lonely waters, and, now that their work was finished, they wanted to get away. There was a mystery connected with the wreck, but they thought they would never unravel it, and, on the whole, they had no wish to try. They were anxious to see the end of her and to leave the fog-wrapped island.

"I guess we're all ready," the diver said at last. "See that you have left nothing loose to fall overboard: she'll shift some water."

He inserted the firing-plug; and a moment afterward the sea opened some distance ahead and rolled back from a gap in the bottom of which shattered timber churned about. Then a foaming wave rose suddenly from the chasm, tossing up black masses of planking and ponderous beams. A few, rearing on end, shot out of the water and fell with a heavy splash among fountains of spray, while a white ridge swept furiously toward the sloop. It broke before it reached her, but she flung her bows high as she plunged over the troubled swell, and the yacht rolled heavily with a yeasty wash along her side.

Jimmy ran forward with a sense of keen satisfaction to break out the anchor. The powerful charge had done its work; the wreck had gone.

While the Cetacea drifted slowly with the stream the yacht's windlass began to clank, and a few minutes later she steamed toward the smaller craft. Her gig brought off a hawser, and a message inviting

Jimmy to come on board. As soon as he reached her deck the gig was run up to the davits and the throb of engines quickened. The sloop, swinging into line astern, followed along the screw-cut wake, and in half an hour the fog-bank about the island faded out of sight.

Jimmy felt more cheerful when he dined with Aynsley in the saloon. The depression that had rested on them all seemed to have been lifted with the disappearance of the wreck. Even Clay appeared to be brighter. He sent a request for Jimmy to come to him as soon as he finished dinner.

When Jimmy entered the cabin, Clay lay in his berth, comfortably raised on pillows. He gave Jimmy a friendly nod.

"She's gone? You made a good job?"

"Yes," Jimmy answered cheerfully. "We didn't spare the dynamite."

Clay beckoned him forward, and, reaching out awkwardly to a small table by his berth, took up a glass of champagne. Another stood near it, ready filled.

"I make a bad host and soon get tired, but Aynsley will do his best for you," he said cordially. He smiled and raised his glass. "Good luck to you; you're a white man!"

Jimmy drained his glass, and took Clay's from his shaking hand. When the elder man thanked him with a gesture, Jimmy saw that he was too ill to talk, and he went out quietly and joined Aynsley on deck.

He spent three days on board the yacht, which steamed steadily south, but late on the fourth night a steward awakened him.

"It's blowing fresh, sir," he said. "The captain thought you'd like to know your boat's towing very wild and he can't hold on to her long."

Jimmy had been prepared for such an emergency, and he was on deck in five minutes, fully dressed with his sea-boots and slickers on; and Aynsley joined him in the lee of the deckhouse with a pilot coat over his pajamas. The engines were turning slowly, and the rolling of the yacht and the showers of spray showed that the sea was getting up.

"They're launching the gig," Aynsley said. "I wish we could keep you, but I suppose your friends need you?"

"Thanks! They couldn't navigate her home."

Jimmy ran toward the bulwarks and shouted to a group of seamen:

"Don't bother with that ladder, boys!"

Somebody lighted a blue flare on the deckhouse top, and the strong light showed the gig lurching on the broken heave on the yacht's lee side. Near by, the Cetacea lay plunging with her staysail up, while a dark figure on her deck flashed a lantern. Jimmy shook hands with Aynsley and sprang up on the rail; then, leaning out, seized a davit-fall and slid swiftly down. A man released the tackle-hook and pushed off the gig; the oars splashed and a sea swept her away from the yacht. In a few minutes Jimmy jumped on board the sloop and helped Moran to cast off the hawser while the gig struggled back. Another flare was burning, and he saw the boat hoisted in. Then the blaze sank down and, with a farewell blast of her whistle, the steamer vanished into the dark.

Spray leaped about the rolling sloop, her low deck was swept by the hurling sea, and a tangle of hard, wet ropes swung about the mast.

"We've double-reefed the mainsail and bent on the storm-jib," Moran said, above the noise of the sea. "She'll carry that lot with the wind on her quarter."

"She ought to," replied Jimmy. "Up with the throat!"

Fumbling in the dark, they hoisted the thrashing sail, and when the Cetacea listed down until her rail was in the foam Jimmy went aft to relieve Bethune at the helm.

"She'll make a short passage if this breeze holds," he said cheerfully. "As I've had three nights' good sleep, I'll take the first watch."

While the sloop was driving wildly south before the following seas, or beating slowly in long tacks when the breeze fell light and drew ahead, the yacht skimmed over the water at her best speed; and one gray morning she steamed up Puget Sound, and a low blast of her whistle rang dolefully as she passed Osborne's house. Clay had made his last voyage; she brought his lifeless body home.

CHAPTER XXXI

A GIFT FROM THE DEAD

Jimmy and his companions sat on the balcony formed by the flat roof of the veranda in front of Jaques' store. It was a fine evening and a light breeze stirred the dust in the streets of the wooden town. Beyond the ugly, square-fronted buildings that straggled down to the wharf, the water lay shining in the evening light, and through a gap the sloop showed up distinctly, riding in the harbor mouth. On the other hand, a blaze of crimson burned above the crest of a hill and the ragged pines stood out harshly sharp against the glow. Work was over for the day, and groups of men lounged in chairs on the sidewalks outside the hotels, while here and there a citizen and his family occupied the stoop of his dwelling.

Jimmy had briefly related their adventures in the North, though nothing had yet been said about the party's future plans. Now, however, Jaques and his wife were waiting to discuss them.

"Clay must have died soon after you left the yacht," the storekeeper said. "As you believe his son is friendly, we have no opposition to fear; and we may as well settle what is to be done."

"Bethune is our business manager," Jimmy said. "Perhaps he will give us his opinion."

Bethune leaned forward with a thoughtful air.

"In the first place, the matter is not so simple as it looks. We don't know the whole story of the wreck, and I'm inclined to think we'll never learn it. On the other hand, there's much to be guessed, and one could form a theory which would be rather hard to contradict. In fact, except for certain prejudices, I believe we could make some money out of it."

"You can call them prejudices, if you like," Mrs. Jaques broke in. "For all that, it would be wiser to act up to them."

"It's possible," Bethune agreed. "Just the same, we're in a rather responsible position."

"I'm a trader," Jaques remarked. "I want a fair profit on the money I lay out; but I stop at that. All the money I take is for value supplied."

Jaques turned to Jimmy.

"Now that we're talking about it, did you see where Clay got that case?"

"I didn't; nor did anybody else. We were too busy to trouble about examining the hole he crawled into. I suppose there must have been a space between the top of the strong-room and the floor of the poop cabin."

"It's a curious place to stow a box of gold. You can understand their putting the sham case in the strong-room if they meant to wreck the boat; but then why didn't they ship the genuine stuff by another vessel?"

"That," said Bethune, smiling, "is the point where my theory breaks down. The only explanation I can think of seems too far-fetched to mention."

"We will let it go," Mrs. Jaques interposed quickly. "What do you suggest doing with the gold you brought home?"

"We'll take it to the underwriters and press for all the salvage we can get. If they're not inclined to be liberal, we'll go to court."

"And the sham box? Will you give them that?" Mrs. Jaques asked.

Jimmy had been expecting the question, and he saw that he must speak. He knew that a fraud had been plotted in connection with the wreck; but it was not his business to investigate the matter. He admitted that this view might be challenged, but he was determined to act upon it. Suspicion rested on Osborne; but Jimmy had made up his mind that, whatever happened, Ruth should not suffer on his account. No sorrow or hint of shame must rest on her. Moreover, he had, in a sense, made Clay a promise; the dying man had trusted him.

"I claim that case," he said quietly. "I told Clay I'd give it to Osborne."

There was silence for a few moments, and then Jaques looked up.

"Well," he said, "I'm not sure that's not the best way out of it. What's your idea, Mr. Bethune?"

"On the whole, I agree with you. Somebody may have meant to wreck the vessel, but we have no proof to offer; and, after all, it's the gold that concerns us, and the underwriters who paid for it when lost will get it back. This ought to satisfy them; and I don't see that it's our part to go any further into the matter." He smiled as he added: "I'll admit it's a course that seems likely to save us a good deal of trouble."

They decided to deposit the gold in the vaults of an express company in Victoria, and that Bethune should then open negotiations with the insurers.

"I guess I could sell the Cetacea for you at a moderate price," Jaques said. "One of the boys here thinks of going into the deep-water fishery."

"I'd be sorry to part with the boat, but we have no use for her," Jimmy replied. "Our idea is that if we can get enough from the insurance people we might make a venture in the towing and transport line. A small wooden, propeller tug wouldn't cost very much; and we might even begin with a big launch or two."

"It ought to pay," declared Jaques. "The coasting trade's pretty good; in fact, I often have to wait some time before I can get my truck brought up."

"It's only beginning," Bethune said. "The coastline of this province is still practically undeveloped, but it's studded with splendid natural harbors, and the extension of the new railroads to the sea will give trade a big impetus. The men who get in first will make their profit. Of course, I'm looking forward a few years to the time when the narrow waters will be covered with steamboats, but in the meanwhile there's a living to be picked up by towing booms for the sawmills and collecting small freight among the northern settlements."

He spoke with enthusiasm, and Jaques looked eager.

"I guess you're right. First of all, you have to see the underwriters; then if you have any use for a few more dollars, let me know. I might help you in several ways."

They talked the project over, though Bethune and Jaques took the leading part, and Jimmy sat by Mrs. Jaques in a state of quiet content. At the cost of much hardship and toil, he had done what he had undertaken, and now a promising future was opening up. He had confidence in Bethune's judgment; the path they were starting on might lead to fortune. The thought of Ruth Osborne beckoned Jimmy forward. He was determined that none of the obstacles they would no doubt meet with should turn him aside. He had not his partner's versatile genius, but he was endowed with a cool courage and a stubborn tenacity which were likely to carry him far.

With a gesture his hostess indicated her husband and Bethune.

"They're getting keen, but I must say that Tom's not often mistaken in business matters. He seems to think your prospects are good."

"We must try to make them good," Jimmy responded. "It was a fortunate thing for us that we met your husband. We were in a very tight place when he helped us."

"I've wondered why you didn't go to sea again before that happened. It would have been the easiest way out of your troubles."

Jimmy grew confidential.

"I had a strong reason for not wishing to leave the province."

"Ah!" exclaimed Mrs. Jaques, and beamed upon him. "I understand. I hope you have made a wise choice. Falling in love is rather a serous thing. I suppose she's pretty?"

"She's beautiful!"

Mrs. Jaques smiled.

"So you stayed in Vancouver on her account! She would naturally wish to keep you."

"I have no reason for believing that," Jimmy answered with a downcast expression.

"You mean—"

Mrs. Jaques gave him a searching look before she finished her sentence:

"—that you don't know whether she is fond of you or not?"

Jimmy hesitated, and the blood crept into his face as he thought of the night he had helped Ruth out of the launch.

"It may be a long time before I find out," he said. "The trouble is that she's a rich man's daughter."

"What is his name? Your confidence is safe."

"Osborne."

Mrs. Jaques showed her surprise, and Jimmy laughed.

"Oh, of course you think I'm mad. Now and then I feel sure of it myself."

She studied him quietly for a moment. He was handsome, and had an honest, good-humored face, but there was a hint of force in it. He looked reliable, a man to trust, and Mrs. Jaques had a warm liking for him.

"No," she said; "I don't think so. Perhaps you're rash; but, after all, daring's better than cautious timidity—it carries one farther. Of course, there will be difficulties; but I wouldn't despair. This a country where a bold man has many chances."

"Thank you," murmured Jimmy. "You have made me hopeful." He looked up abruptly as Bethune addressed him. "Oh, yes," he said hastily. "Quite so."

"Quite so!" exclaimed Bethune. "My impression is that you

haven't heard a word I said."

"I believe that's possible," Mrs. Jaques laughed. "However, he has a good excuse. You can't blame him for talking to me."

The party broke up soon afterward, and the next morning the sloop sailed for Victoria. Jimmy spent several anxious days in the city before he got a telegram from Bethune informing him that he had come to terms with the underwriters. They were more liberal than Jimmy had hoped, and he thought there should be money enough to launch the new venture in a modest way. He gave the express company orders to deliver the gold, and then set off to visit Osborne.

It was evening when he reached the house. He entered it longing to see Ruth and wondering how she would greet him, but disturbed about his meeting with her father. He was shown at once into the library, and Osborne rose to receive him.

"Aynsley Clay told me that you would call, and I am glad you have done so," he said cordially. "I hope you will stay for a few days."

"Thanks, I'm afraid not," Jimmy answered. "Perhaps I had better get my business done. I really came because Clay asked it; he made me promise to bring you something. I left it in the hall."

Osborne rang a bell and a square package neatly sewed up in canvas was brought in. Jimmy placed it on the table as soon as they were alone, and began to cut the stitches.

"I don't know whether you'll be surprised or not," he said, as he uncovered a strong wooden box which showed signs of having long been soaked in water.

"That!" exclaimed Osborne, dropping into the nearest chair. "Who found that box?"

"I did—in the steamer's strong-room."

Beads of perspiration stood on Osborne's forehead, and he was breathing with difficulty.

"Do you know—what it contains?" he gasped.

"Yes," Jimmy answered quietly. "It isn't gold. Some of the stuff is still inside but I took the rest out to save weight."

Osborne leaned back in his chair, limp from the shock.

"When did you find it?" he asked.

"About eight months ago, roughly speaking."

"And Clay knew about it all along?"

"No. We didn't tell him until a week before his death."

"That sounds curious," Osborne said suspiciously. "Since you were silent so long, why did you speak about the thing at last?"

"It looked as if we might have trouble. Clay could have prevented our working, and when he came off to talk matters over we told him about the case. In the end, he lent us his diver and all the assistance he could."

"And was that the only concession he made?"

"Yes," said Jimmy with a flush. "It was all we demanded and all we got. It would simplify things if you took that for granted."

"I suppose you know you were easily satisfied?" Osborne's tone was ironical.

Jimmy made no response.

"Am I to understand that the case is mine absolutely, to do what I like with?" Osborne asked.

"Yes. You may regard it as a gift from Clay."

"Who knows anything about the matter besides yourself?"

"My two partners, and a storekeeper who financed us, and his wife. They're to be trusted. I'll answer for them."

"Well," said Osborne quietly, "you'll allow me to remark that you and your friends seem to have acted in a very honorable manner. That Clay should send me the case was, in a sense, characteristic of him; but I had no claim on you. If you won't resent it, I should like to thank you for the line you have taken."

"I haven't finished my errand yet. You probably know that we salved a quantity of the gold, but you cannot have heard that we recovered and have accounted for every package that was insured."

Osborne looked puzzled. He indicated the box on the table.

"You mean counting this one?"

"No; we found a duplicate, containing gold of rather more than the declared weight, on which the underwriters have paid our salvage claim."

Osborne started, and his face expressed blank astonishment.

"But it sounds impossible! I can't understand—"

"It's puzzling," Jimmy agreed. "There's obviously a mystery; but, after talking the thing over, my partners and I decided that we wouldn't try to unravel it."

"Perhaps you are wise. You are certainly considerate. But, still, I don't see—Did you find the thing in the strong-room?"

"Not in the room. Clay showed me where to cut a hole in the roof. He crawled through and brought out the box. I imagine it was hidden among the deckbeams, but we hadn't time to examine the place."

"Ah!" exclaimed Osborne; for a light dawned on him as he remembered his partner's determined attempt to break through the cabin floor on the night of the wreck. "Perhaps you are right. So the insurance people paid your claim and asked no questions. Did they seem satisfied?"

"Yes. I think the matter's closed."

There was keen relief in Osborne's face, and the slackness of his pose suggested the sudden relaxing of a heavy strain. He sat very still for a few moments and then got up.

"Mr. Farquhar," he said, "you must guess the satisfaction with which I have heard your news. Indeed, I feel that I must think over it quietly. If you will excuse me for a while, Miss Dexter and my daughter will be glad to entertain you."

"But I must get back as soon as possible," Jimmy objected, feeling that to stay, as he longed to do, would be embarrassing both to himself and to his host.

"You can't leave before tomorrow," said Osborne, smiling. "There's no night boat now, the launch is under repairs, and my car's in town. I'm afraid you'll have to put up with our hospitality."

He rang the bell, and when Jimmy left him he sat down with knitted brows. He wondered where Clay had got the gold. Then suddenly his fist clenched tightly and his frown grew deeper: he remembered that somebody had worked out the alluvial mine before they reached it. There was cause for grave suspicion there, particularly as the case had been put on board secretly, without appearing on the ship's papers, which would have brought it to Osborne's knowledge.

The box of gold, however, was not of the first importance. Clay, on his deathbed, perhaps by way of making reparation, had sent him a gift which had banished the apprehensions that had haunted him for years. Whatever Clay had done, Osborne could forgive him now. At last he was a free man: the only evidence against him was in his hands, and he meant to destroy it at once. After all, he had bitterly regretted his one great offense; and his partner's last act had been to save him from its consequences.

CHAPTER XXXII
THE BARRIERS GO DOWN

When Jimmy was shown into the large, cool drawing-room, he stood awkwardly still, with a thrill of keen satisfaction and an effort for self-control. He had so far seen little of Osborne's house, and the beauty of the room had its effect on him. Curtains, rugs, furniture and pictures formed harmonies of soft color and delicate design, which seemed to him a fitting environment for the occupant of the room.

Ruth wore a clinging evening dress, and Jimmy had hitherto seen her only in traveling and outing clothes. He could not have told how the dress was cut, nor have described its shade, but he knew it was exactly what she ought to wear. The way it hung about her hinted at the graceful lines of her figure; it matched the purity of her coloring and showed up the gloss of her hair. But although the effect was admirable, it was daunting, in a sense. She was wonderfully beautiful and in her proper place; he felt himself rough and awkward, and was conscious of his disadvantages.

Then, as she came toward him, his heart began beating hard. He thought of their last meeting with embarrassment. He had expected to find some change of manner in her that would, so to speak, keep him at a distance. There was, however, no hint of this. It looked as if she had not forgotten how he had helped her from the launch, but had somehow recognized it and its consequences. He was not a clever reader of other people's minds, but he knew that they were nearer than they had ever been before.

As she gave him her hand Ruth smiled up at him, but she spoke in a very matter-of-fact voice.

"I am glad you have come at last. It is pleasant to know that you have got back safely." She pouted prettily. "No doubt you had some business with my father, which explains the visit."

"It gave me an excuse for doing what I wished."

"Did you need an excuse? We gave you an open invitation."

"I felt that I did," Jimmy answered slowly; and Ruth understood. He was diffident but proud, and shrank from entering her circle by favor. She preferred that he should regard her, however, not as the daughter of a rich man but as an attractive woman.

"You are too retiring," she rebuked him smilingly. "But I shall not begin by finding fault. I want you to tell me some of your exciting adventures. Aynsley Clay was here, but he could not tell us much about you—and he was, of course, in trouble."

"Yes," said Jimmy softly. "I'm sorry for him. He's a man you soon feel a strong liking for; and there was a good deal to admire in his father. In fact, we were on very friendly terms during the last few days we spent at the wreck."

Ruth was silent for a moment. Then:

"Tell me about the wreck," she requested.

"It's rather a long story, and you may find it tiresome."

"I've asked you to tell it."

Jimmy was glad of the opportunity, because he was determined that she should have no cause to doubt her father. There was much still unexplained, but she must not suspect this, for it was unthinkable that she should bear any trouble from which he could save her. Still, he saw that he must be careful, for there were points which needed delicate handling.

While he began the narrative Ruth studied him carefully. He looked very virile and handsome with his bronzed skin, his steady eyes, and his figure fined down by privation and toil. Indeed, he had somehow an air of distinction; but he had changed and developed since she first met him. This was a different man from the pleasant, easy-going steamship officer. He had grown alert and determined, but he had lost nothing of his sincerity. He could be trusted without reserve, and she felt that she liked him even better than before.

His story of their adventures in the North was deeply interesting to the girl; and she prompted him with leading questions now and then, for she was keenly anxious to learn the truth about the wreck. For the last few months she had been troubled by dark suspicions.

"But, in spite of everything, you reached the gold!" she exclaimed at last.

"Yes," said Jimmy, seizing the opening he had waited for. "We got it all."

"All!" For a moment Ruth was thrown off her guard by a shock of relief that was poignant in its intensity.

"I believe so," Jimmy answered. "Anyway, we got every case that was insured. The underwriters seemed perfectly satisfied."

A wave of color flushed Ruth's face. She had, it seemed, tormented herself without a cause. Her father, whom she had suspected, was innocent. There was no dark secret attached to the wreck, as she had unjustly thought. Jimmy had banished her fears. The hardships he had borne had bought her release from a haunting dread.

She realized that he might wonder at her agitation, but, after all, this did not count. She was carried away by gratitude to him.

"Thank you for telling me," she said, feeling the inadequacy of the words. "It makes a thrilling tale."

"If it has pleased you, I'm content."

"Pleased me! Well, I can assure you that it has done so."

"Then I'm rewarded," said Jimmy boldly, losing his head as he saw the gratitude in her eyes. "That's all I wanted; finding the gold is less important."

Ruth saw what was happening; his restraint was breaking down, and she meant to give it the last blow.

"And yet you must have been determined to get the gold, since all you had to face didn't daunt you."

"Yes," said Jimmy with a steady look, "I wanted it badly, for a purpose."

"Didn't you want it for itself? That would have been a very natural thing." Ruth hesitated. "But you haven't mentioned your real reason."

He gathered courage from the glance she gave him, though the next moment she turned her head.

"I'm half afraid, but it must be told. I was a steamboat mate without a ship, a laborer about the wharves and mills, and all the time I had a mad ambition locked up in my heart. Then my partner, Bethune, showed me a chance of realizing it, and I took that chance."

"It must have been a strong ambition that sent you up to fight with the gales and ice."

"It was. In fact, it was stronger than my judgment. I knew it was a forlorn hope, but I couldn't give it up. You see, I had fallen in love with a girl."

"Ah! I wonder when that happened? Was it one night when you met the Sound steamer with your launch?"

"Oh, no; long before that. It began one afternoon at Yokohama, when a girl in a dust-veil and the prettiest dress I'd ever seen came up the Empress's gangway."

"Then it must have been very sudden," Ruth answered with a blush and a smile. "The veil was rather thick, and she didn't speak to you."

"That didn't matter. She smiled her thanks, when I drew away a rope, and I'd never got so sweet and gracious a look. After that there were calm evenings when the Empress swung gently over the smooth heave and the girl left her friends and walked up and down the deck with me. I knew I was a presumptuous fool, but as soon as my watch was over I used to wait with an anxious heart, hoping that she might come."

"And sometimes she didn't."

"Those were black nights," said Jimmy. "While I waited I tried to think it would be better if I saw no more of her. But I knew all the time that I couldn't take that prudent course." He paused with an appealing gesture. "Ruth, haven't I said enough?"

"Not quite. Did you think, when you went to find the wreck, that your success would make me think of you with more favor?"

"If the wreck had been full of gold, it would not have made me your equal; but I knew what your friends would think. It would have been insufferable that you should have had to apologize to them for me."

Ruth gave him a smile that sent a thrill through him.

"Dear," he said suddenly, "I want you—that's all in the world that matters."

She yielded shyly when he gathered her to him; and the little gilt clock on the mantel, with its poised Cupid, seemed to tick exultantly in the silence that followed.

A half-hour had passed when they heard footsteps in the hall, and Osborne came in. He glanced at them sharply, and Jimmy's triumphant air and Ruth's blush confirmed his suspicions.

"Ah!" he said. "I imagine you have something to tell me?"

"That is true," said Jimmy; and Ruth smiled at her father.

"There is no reason why you should object, and you needn't pretend to be vexed!" she pouted.

"I think Mr. Farquhar and I must have a talk," Osborne answered quietly.

He made Jimmy sit down when Ruth had left them.

"Now," he began, "I'll confess to some surprise, and though, from what I've seen and heard of you, I can find no fault of a personal nature, there are some drawbacks."

"Nobody realizes that better than myself," Jimmy answered

ruefully. "In fact, I can honestly say that they seemed serious enough to prevent my hopes from ever being realized until half an hour ago. The only excuse I can make is that I love your daughter."

"It's a good one, but, unfortunately, it doesn't quite cover all the ground. May I ask about your plans for the future?"

"I'm afraid they're not very ambitious, but they may lead to something. My partners and I intend to start a small towing and transport business with the salvage money."

Osborne asked for an outline of the scheme, and listened with interest while Jimmy supplied it. The venture had obviously been well thought out, and he believed it would succeed. Farquhar and his friends had carried out their salvage operations in spite of Clay's opposition, which spoke well for their resourcefulness and determination. Knowing something of his late partner's methods, he could imagine the difficulties they had had to meet.

"I think you have chosen a suitable time, because it looks as if we were about to see a big extension of the coasting trade," he said. "There is, however, the disadvantage that you'll have to start in a small way. Now it's possible that I might find you some more capital."

"No, thanks!" said Jimmy firmly. "We have made up our minds not to borrow."

Osborne gave him a dry smile.

"I suppose that means that you don't see your way to taking any help from me?"

Jimmy felt embarrassed. As a matter of fact, he still suspected Osborne of complicity in some scheme to make an unlawful profit out of the wreck; and in that sense his offer might be regarded as a bribe.

"We feel that it would be better if we stood, so to speak, on our own feet," he said.

"Perhaps you're right. However, I don't think you need object if I'm able to put any business in your way; but this is not what I meant to talk about. I cannot consent to an engagement just now, but after you have been twelve months in business you may come to me again, and we'll see what progress you are making."

"And in the meanwhile?" Jimmy asked anxiously.

"You are both free; I make no other stipulation. If Miss Dexter approves, my house is open to you."

A few minutes afterward Jimmy found Ruth in the hall.

"Well?" she asked. "Was he very formidable?"

"I believe I got off better than I deserved." Jimmy told her what Osborne had insisted on.

"So you are free for another year! I wonder whether you're fickle."

"I'm bound hand and foot forever! What's more, I'll hug my chains. But your father hinted that if I wished to see you, I'd have to win your aunt's approval."

"That won't be hard," Ruth laughed. "If you have no confidence in your own merits, you can leave it to me. Now, perhaps, you had better come and see her."

Miss Dexter spent some time talking to Jimmy, and he found her blunt questions embarrassing; but she afterward remarked to her niece: "I like your sailor. He looks honest, and that is the great thing. Still, for some reasons, I'm sorry you didn't take Aynsley, whom I'm fond of. It's curious how little that young man resembles his father."

"Clay had his good points," Ruth said warmly. "He was very generous, and, although I don't quite understand the matter, I think he really lost his life because he wanted to clear himself of all suspicion for his son's sake."

"It's possible; there was something very curious about the wreck. He was a brigand, my dear; perhaps a rather gallant and magnanimous one, but a brigand, for all that."

Osborne had come in quietly while she was talking.

"I owe Clay a good deal, and feel that he deserved more sympathy than he got," he said. "He had his detractors, but the people who found most fault with him were not above suspicion themselves."

"You are all brigands at heart," Miss Dexter declared.

"I'm afraid there's some truth in that," Osborne admitted with a smile.

Jimmy left the house the next morning, and soon after he opened his modest office in Vancouver Aynsley called on him.

"I've come to congratulate you, first of all," he said. "No doubt, you know you are an exceptionally lucky man."

"I'm convinced of it," Jimmy answered. "But in a sense, you're premature; I'm only on probation yet."

He was conscious of some embarrassment, because he had learned from Clay about Aynsley's affection for Ruth.

"Well, there's another matter. We raft a good deal of lumber down to the sea for shipment, and now and then buy logs of special quality on the coast. I don't see why you shouldn't do our towing for us. I suppose you're open for business?"

"We surely are." Jimmy gave him a steady look. "You're very generous in offering me a lift up."

There was silence for a few moments, and then Aynsley smiled.

"I'll admit that if I'd ever had a chance before you entered the field, I might have felt very bitter, but I know I hadn't one from the first. As Ruth has taken you, I'm trying sincerely to wish you both happiness; and, if you don't mind my putting it so, I've a feeling that she might have chosen worse."

"Thank you!"

"Well, we'll let that go. I suspect my father had some reason for being grateful to you; he gave me the impression that you had taken a load off his mind. I'm in your debt on that score, but quite apart from this, it might be advantageous to both of us if you did our towing. Suppose we see what we can make of it as a business proposition?"

They had arrived at a satisfactory arrangement when Aynsley left the office, and during the next few weeks more work was offered the new firm than they could comfortably attend to. In a few months they decided to buy a large and powerful tug, which was somewhat out of repair, and after refitting her they found that they were able to keep her busy. Then they were fortunate in towing one or two exceptionally large booms of logs safely down the coast in bad weather, and it soon became known that they could be relied on. When the work was difficult Jimmy took charge of it in person with Moran's help, while Bethune attended to the office and secured the good opinion of their customers.

It was, however, not until early in the next year that they really made their mark. A big American collier had stranded and been damaged when approaching the Wellington mines, and Jimmy assisted the salvors in getting her off. Then the owners, deciding that it would be cheaper to send her home for repairs, asked for tenders for towing her to Portland. Getting a hint from the captain, Jimmy hurried back and held a consultation with his partners.

"We must get this contract, even if we make nothing out of it," Bethune declared. "It's our first big job and will give us a chance of showing what we can do. I suppose you feel confident about taking her down the coast?"

"It won't be easy. She has lost her propeller and carried her stern-frame away. The jury rudder they have rigged won't steer her well, and I don't think the plates they've bolted on to her torn bilge will keep out much water if she gets straining hard. However, I'll try it if you can find me another tug. She's too big for one boat to hold."

"There's the old Guillemot. We ought to get her cheap on a short charter."

Jimmy told him to see what he could do, and the next day Bethune sent off a formal offer. On receiving it, the managing owner of the collier crossed the boundary to consult with the captain.

"I'd like to give the San Francisco people the contract," he said. "They're accustomed to this kind of thing, and their boats are the best on the Pacific. They ask a big sum, but I feel we can rely on them."

"You can rely on Farquhar. The salvage gang wouldn't have got her off if it hadn't been for him."

"I understand his firm's a small one. His bid's low, but he says he can tow her down."

"Then you had better let him," advised the captain. "What that man undertakes he'll do. I've seen him at work."

He said more to the same purpose, with the result that Bethune secured the contract, and Jimmy left Vancouver with two tugs immediately afterward. They passed Victoria with the broken-down vessel in fine weather, but that night it began to blow, and the gale that followed lasted a fortnight. What was worse, it blew for the most part straight in from the Pacific, piling a furious surf on shore. Three days after Jimmy left the Strait, the chartered tug put back with engines disabled, badly battered by the gale. Her skipper stated that he had left Jimmy with a broken hawser, hanging on to the collier, which was dragging him to leeward, nearer the dangerous coast. After that an incoming steamer reported having passed a disabled vessel with a tug standing by in the middle of a furious gale, but although in a dangerous position, she showed no signals and the weather prevented a close approach. Then there was no news for some time.

When offers to reinsure the collier were asked for, Bethune was summoned to Osborne's house. He found it difficult to express a hopeful view, and Ruth's anxious look haunted him long after he left. Then, as public interest was excited in the fate of the missing vessel, paragraphs about her began to appear in the newspapers. It was suggested that she and the tug had foundered in deep water, since no wreckage had been found along the coast.

At last, when hope had almost gone, she reeled in across the smoking Columbia bar one wild morning with her tug ahead, and Jimmy found himself famous when he brought her safe into harbor. Escaping from the reporters, he went off in search of coal, and put to sea as soon as he could; but the grateful captain talked, and the papers made a sensational story of the tow. It appeared that Jimmy had smashed two boats in replacing broken hawsers in a dangerous sea, and had held on to the disabled vessel while she drove up to the edge of the breakers that hammered a rocky coast. Then a sudden shift of wind saved them, but the next night the collier broke adrift, and he spent two days stubbornly searching for her in the haze and spray. She was in serious peril when he found her, but again he towed her clear, and afterward fought a long, stern fight that seemed bound to be a losing one against the fury of the sea.

Jimmy arrived in Vancouver early one morning, and that afternoon he reached Osborne's house, looking gaunt and worn. Osborne met him in the hall and gave him his hand in a very friendly manner.

"I must congratulate you," he said. "You have lifted your firm into first rank by one bold stroke. If you allow your friends to help you, there's an opportunity for a big development of your business."

"That isn't what concerns me most," Jimmy replied meaningly.

"Well," smiled Osborne, "I think I'm safe in trusting Ruth to you. Though the year's not up yet, you have made good."

As Ruth came forward Osborne moved away, and the girl looked at Jimmy with glowing eyes before she yielded herself to his arms.

"I've been hearing wonderful things about you, dear, but, after all, I knew what you could do, and now I only want to realize that I've got you safely back," she said.

THE END

www.ingramcontent.com/pod-product-compliance
Lightning Source LLC
Chambersburg PA
CBHW030410020726
47493CB00003B/1018